ZIGGY'S VOICE

THE WILDE MEN
BOOK 2

SAXON JAMES

BLURB

KENNEDY

I've always been the relationship guy.

I love big, hard and fast … but unfortunately for me, that's the quickest way to make a new romance crash and burn.

Moving to Wilde's End, our not-so-abandoned town, is exactly the fresh start I need. What's better than a town in the middle of nowhere and long days of hard work to swear off relationships? At least that's what I think, until I meet Ziggy.

He's the town electrician who has a weird habit of making sparks fly whenever I'm around him. He's cute, snarky, and his piercings are hot as hell.

Too bad I don't trust myself not to make the same mistakes I always do.

ZIGGY

I've always been the weird loner. The strange kid who doesn't talk.

So when Kennedy shows up in my life, with his big energy

and sunny personality, I don't know how to take him. I'm used to being the invisible shadow that goes unnoticed in the Wilde.

Kennedy makes me feel seen.

He doesn't expect me to talk when the voices in my head get too loud, he doesn't expect me to be funny or witty or anything that I'm not. He's happy just to be around me, and that's not something I've experienced before.

He's sworn off dating. And I've never so much as been kissed.

But with the sunshine he brings to my life, it's impossible to feel like a shadow anymore. I'm determined to win him over, no matter what it takes.

THANK YOU

I want to spare a second to thank everyone who picked up Ziggy's Voice. These two are the sweethearts of the series and I hope you fall for them as much as I did!

If you're someone who needs a visual for the characters, you can check out my Pinterest board here:
https://pin.it/31U7wClAM

If music is more your vibe, you can find the Ziggy's Voice playlist here:
https://open.spotify.com/playlist/6Kqhx8b82DeNX6zb1f73MK? si=bbc020aac8eb442f

(While every effort has been made during the editing process, if you're someone who likes to spot and report ninja typos, you can send them to: admin@saxonjamesauthor.com)

*To the losers in love. There's a reason Kenny's the strong brother.
Love hard.*

TRIGGER WARNINGS

One of the main characters has extreme social anxiety due to the bullying and abuse he lived through as a child. Past events are not shown on page.

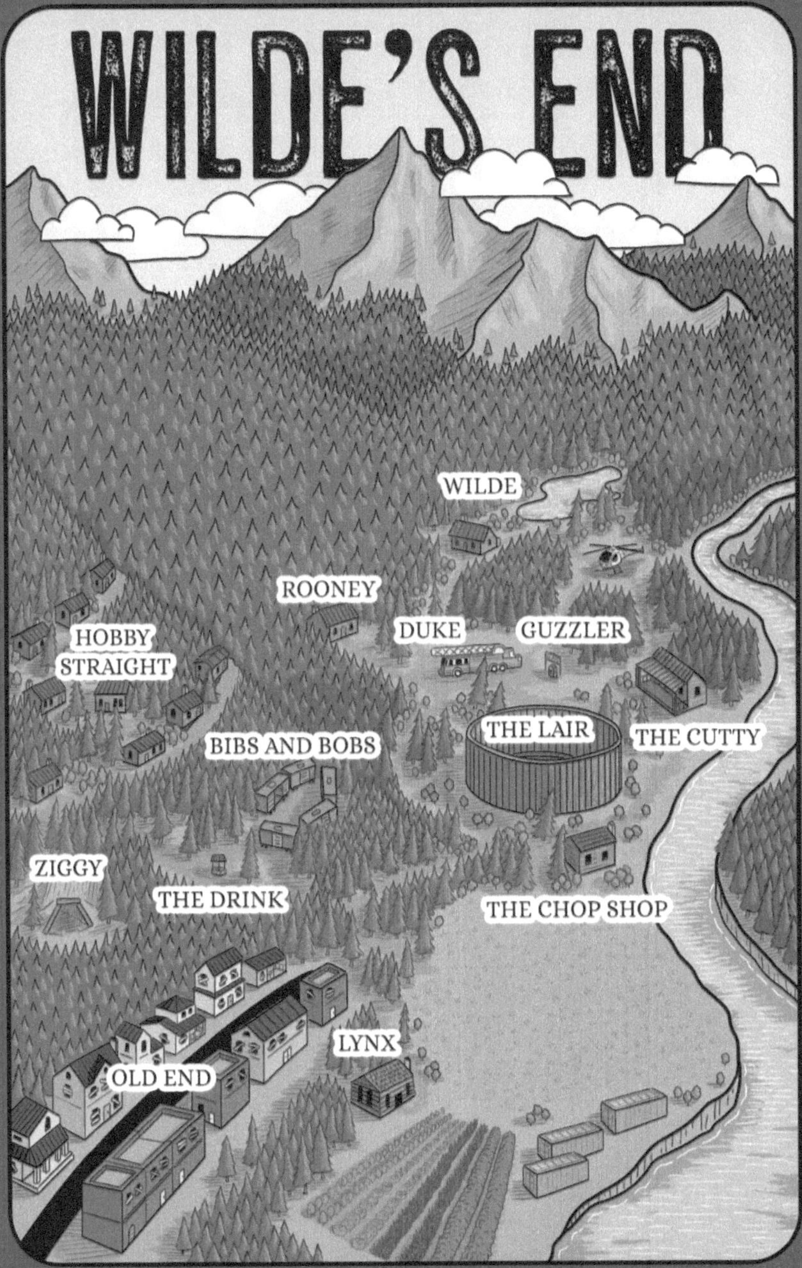

WILDE'S END
WILDE
ROONEY
DUKE
GUZZLER
HOBBY STRAIGHT
THE LAIR
THE CUTTY
BIBS AND BOBS
ZIGGY
THE DRINK
THE CHOP SHOP
LYNX
OLD END

CHAPTER
ONE

ZIGGY

Wilde's End is a lot of things to me.

It's a place to lose myself.

It's a new beginning.

It's shelter and hopelessness and beauty and untamed wilderness.

It's my home.

And it's also where I met Kennedy Bellamy.

He's got music playing through his phone, large body moving to the unfamiliar sounds, and whenever I'm around him, things feel loud. Ever since I first saw him singing and dancing along to "My, My, My," one of the few songs I recognize, it created this connection between us that is completely one-sided but I can't seem to let drop. Kennedy has a constant hum of life orbiting him, and I want to step into the pull and be swept up in the chaos.

I won't though. Because that kind of life-altering jump isn't for people like me.

Kennedy is a hurricane.

I'm a leaf starting its slow descent to the forest floor, far, far away.

He pulls off a step-slide thing, and damn, he looks hot doing it. Even wearing a full white jumpsuit with hood, face mask, and goggles for protection. The insulation he's cutting and fitting in the wall cavity has caught on everything in tiny, fluffy clumps.

I've done all the electrical work I can for today, so I plant my ass on my toolbox and watch him, at war with myself. I have two distinct sides of my personality, and it's anyone's guess who'll win on any given day. There's the scared side that refuses to let go of everything that's happened to me, and then there's the spark of a person trapped. The side of me that wants to break out and be a normal goddamn person.

That side gets stronger with Kennedy around.

While I love living in this town, and I love that people mind their own business, we're mostly loners out this way, and it works for me. Until now, maybe it doesn't.

I didn't know people like Kennedy could exist.

Always singing, whistling, talking, *moving*.

He's just so … happy.

I wish I could tell him what a good quality that is, but I can never find my moment. Whenever the words get trapped in my throat, the stress of letting them out almost chokes me. It takes me a really long time to get my thoughts in order, and then I have to run the words through my mind over and over until I feel ready to open my mouth. Usually by the time I get there, the moment has moved on, and if I let out the words I've been building, conversation pulls to a jerky halt with a noise in my head like the obnoxious crunch of dying brakes.

Kennedy yanks me from my thoughts as his exhale huffs from him. He pushes back his hood, flicks up his face mask, and sets his goggles on top of his messy blond hair, sweat damp at his hairline.

"This job's a pain in the ass," he says. He crosses the half-demolished house with long strides and throws himself down on the floor beside me. "It's always when it comes to the insulation that Hart and Hudson are nowhere to be found."

Even though his brothers have abandoned him to this, his voice is full of affection for them. Personally, I don't think either of them deserves someone as amazing as Kennedy, and if I could goddamn talk around people, I'd tell them that myself.

I try for a sympathetic smile.

"Ah, it's okay." He pats my knee with one of his large, gloved hands, and the spot burns long after he stops. "I like hard work. It makes me feel like I have purpose."

I know exactly what he means. It's taken us years to get the solar farm up and operational in Wilde's End, then connected to all the properties spread out across the land, and I loved having a reason to get up in the morning. Now that the brothers are doing up the abandoned mining town that we've dubbed Old End, I have a new project.

Getting electricity to this town that will be able to support whatever the end goal is.

It's a really big fucking job.

I've craved this kind of purpose again.

"I don't know what I'll do after this," he murmurs.

The contemplative tone catches my attention, even though these musings are common for him. It's more *what* he's contemplating that I'm interested in.

He plows on like he's picked up on my curiosity. "Yeah ... I mean, don't get me wrong, I know that we'll be here for a while." He sounds like he's thinking out loud, and I appreciate that he never expects me to fill in the gaps in conversation, just carries it himself. "The plan, as far as my brothers are concerned, is that we leave as soon as we're done here. Let's be real, there's no way Hudson and Wilde are going to last beyond that." He throws me a grin like I should be in on the joke, but I only arch my eyebrow his way. He might not know Wilde, but I do, and

I've never seen him as restlessly not himself as he's been since meeting Hudson. The thought of them ending isn't something I can picture.

Kennedy studies my face. "You think they'll last?"

I shrug a little, and then after a moment, I nod. Why shouldn't I expect them to last? Wilde willingly left the End and went to a place with people to bring Hudson back here. Other than his occasional trips into Wayward, he never leaves Wilde's End, especially not to go to a town as big as the one they came from. Towns like that scare him. Busy places, mild traffic, being social.

It was … sweet.

Having someone want me so much that they'd face their fears to keep me? I'll never know what that's like, because while I might be exploding with feelings for Kennedy, those feelings will only ever go one way.

Because how can you fall for someone who refuses to talk?

"Huh …" Kennedy mutters, expression torn between disbelief and awe. "You know … my brothers like to joke that I'm the romantic one. So you'd expect that if one of us was going to find his person in the middle of nowhere, it would be me." His sigh is long and heavy, like he loses himself for a moment. Thankfully, he's back to his happy self in no time at all. "Whatever is meant to be, will be, am I right?"

I don't answer him because I'm not so sure I believe in fate. If fate were real, would it have beaten me down as completely as it has? Would it have left me without a voice while it filled my soul with words?

"Besides," he continues, like he didn't ask a question at all. "We have more than enough work to keep us busy here. We can't afford for two brothers to be distracted by sex."

A flush rushes through me at him even saying the word. Just like that. Just so casually.

He lifts his hand and waves his fingers between us. "Me and my hand are doing okay together."

The imagery of Kennedy unzipping that suit and reaching his hand inside, taking hold of his dick …

Holy fuck.

I stand quickly, hands shaking as I attempt to pick up my toolbox and get the hell out of here. I jerk off all the time; I know exactly how good it feels, but I have no idea how good it would feel to do it to *him*. And I really, really want to.

To see Kennedy's eyes flutter back as his large body ripples with tension.

"Whoa, hey." He sets his hand on my toolbox. "I know leaving mid-conversation is your thing, but do you *really* have to go?"

I don't answer him because of course I don't. I have nowhere else to be, and that longing ache in my gut wants to stay right here. The ache between my legs has other plans though.

With Kennedy holding down my things, I'm tempted to leave them there and bail, but his voice keeps me rooted in place.

"Come on … this stupid job isn't half as annoying with you keeping me company."

His warm, hopeful voice always melts me.

Like the first person to actually give a shit about me has all the wires in my brain short-circuiting. I know he only wants company, any company, and without his brothers here, I'll do. That reminder is enough to make my boner flag, and after a long inhale, I can look at him again.

At those sweet, speckled green eyes, his kind face, the way his lips are tugging up in a smile, like they're trying to show mine how to do the same.

Slowly, I sit back on my toolbox.

"I know you're taking pity on me," he says, "but *thank you*. I'd go out of my mind having to do this alone. One of the things I love about this place is how peaceful it is, but I also don't do well by myself."

I know what he means. Having him around helps distract from how loud it gets in my head. The roaring thoughts that are never given life make it hard to sleep at night, and the days I go without seeing anyone make me question if this is even existing.

At least if I moved to a city, I'd not be existing around other people, and the noise might help distract from those depressing thoughts.

On a whim, I reach over and give Kennedy's sleeve a tug. Then, when I have his attention, I gesture to myself.

His eyes narrow a little, like he's trying to read me, so I do the motion again.

"You … want one of these?"

It's a relief that he gets it easily.

"I think Hartwell's should fit you."

I nod again, faster, and understanding dawns across his face.

"You're going to help me."

I pin him with a look that I hope conveys my *what the fuck else would I do with the suit*, and it must come close because he laughs and raises his gloved hands.

"Okay, okay, put the sass away. I'll go grab it."

The few minutes he's gone force me to face my decision and come to the conclusion that yes, I am offering to help with the worst job in existence because he has me completely under his thumb.

Without even trying.

I'm a real goddamn sucker.

He gets back faster than I'm expecting and hands over the white coveralls for me to step into. I pull my arms into the sleeves, but before I can reach for the zipper, Kennedy is there.

He's standing close, radiating sunshine, and pulls the zipper from my waist all the way up to my throat. His hand lingers there.

"This is going to be horrible," he promises. "Just warning you now."

Even if I wanted to talk, there's no way I'd be able to. I'm struggling to breathe with how close he is.

I'm slightly taller than he is, but because of his size, he feels bigger than this goddamn room. Especially when he has no issues holding my eye contact, and as much as I wish I could find some sort of interest there, all I'm picking up is friendly vibes.

I've never had much practice with reading people, but Kennedy isn't a hard guy to read. Unlike everyone here who keeps their secrets under lock and key, I don't believe he's ever had a secret in his life.

I can't imagine what it's like to live that way.

He lifts a pair of gloves and some goggles.

"They should fit," he says, proving that the tension I'm feeling is only on my end. "You're smaller than Hart, but your fingers are longer."

I frown and direct my gaze to my hands. I've never given much thought to anything about me, but as I inspect my hand, Kennedy lifts his beside mine. His is broader, and his fingers are thick and rough.

"See?" He takes my wrist with his other hand and presses our palms together. The heat from his hand warms me all the way to my shoulder. The simple touch, his gentle expression, there's something about this moment that reaches into the dusty, forgotten parts of me and tries to tempt them back to life. "Your hands are as delicate as the rest of you."

Delicate?

I'm a shadow, a void, a figment of people's imaginations. People don't think about me, and they definitely do not think about words like delicate when it comes to me.

Useless.

Pussy.

Waste of space.

I pull out of his hold and force a smile before I pull on the gloves. Then I point to the insulation, and like that, the moment is gone.

Destined to live in my memories forever.

CHAPTER
TWO

The waitress slides Hart's plate in front of him before turning to me. Caroline holds eye contact for a beat too long, then blushes and sets down my order.

"There you go, Kenny," she says, smile curling prettily, and my gut does that little *whoosh* thing.

My lips tug upward in return, which pulls a cute giggle from her, and a long, loud sigh from my brother.

She walks away, and I turn to him.

"What?"

Hart takes his time dipping a fry into the pile of ketchup on his plate before answering in a bored voice, "Just wondering how long it will be before you declare her my new sister-in-law."

"Don't be dramatic."

"Dramatic? This might be the longest relationship you've ever had."

I know he's exaggerating for effect, but I can't deny that he has a point. We've been coming to this same diner in Wayward a few times a week since we got to Wilde's End, and *Caroline* has worked most of those days. When I'm interested in someone, I normally ask them out right away, and by the second date …

No. Nope. Can't do it. I'm not going there again. Every time I think I've found someone amazing, I come on too strong and scare them off. Wilde's End is in the middle of nowhere, and we have a big job ahead of us, even with how much we've done already.

Surely being out here is the one time I can escape dating and love and instead focus on accomplishing something.

When I return home, then I can think about relationships again.

I level my twin with the most serious look I can manage. "No relationship. I'm off dating, remember?"

The mocking expression he wears as he continues to eat his fries shows how much he believes me.

"I'm serious this time."

"The fact you need to say *this time* gives me a pass for not believing you."

I can't argue with him. I want to, but I can't. "You'll see."

"Maybe." He stabs at the side salad that's mostly lettuce and some tomato. "I'm still waiting for you and Hudson to get bored of this place and move home, and it hasn't happened yet."

Not that Hudson didn't try. Last week, when it looked like the wild man he'd been sleeping with wanted to end their arrangement, he'd taken off. They've worked things out now, but damn, that had been a long two days between when he left and when he came back. Our older brother has always been terrible with making decisions, and it wasn't my place to interfere, but asking someone to treat your sibling right shouldn't be that much of an issue.

I love Hudson and want the best for him.

Hartwell too.

Sometimes it feels like out of the three of us, I'm the only one who actually wants to be happy.

Wilde and Hudson are … dating now? If you can call fucking like rabbits and grunting at each other dating, and while I don't believe it's serious or going to last, I've already said my piece and need to leave it at that.

Sometimes I feel *so much* that when I'm upset, it's world-ending. It's why my brothers are over all of the breakups. But the heightened emotion isn't only for me; it's for everyone in my life. When I love someone—romantic or platonic—I want to do every-thing in my power to make sure they're living their happiest life, and if they're not … sometimes it's like I can't breathe under the weight of it all. Like I've failed at the one thing I'm good at.

"Oh no …" Hart monotones around the food in his mouth. "I'm ninety percent sure she's bringing you her number."

My body is at war with itself as I perk up at the same time as regret floods me. Under any other circumstances, I'd be interested, but I've promised myself, dammit.

"Hey," Caroline says, warm brown stare focused on the tile floor. "I wanted to give you this. Use it, don't use it, I … yeah." She drops the paper on the table and hurries away like she's ready for the floor to swallow her whole.

My respect for her is through the roof because how brave is she? Clearly nervous but came over anyway. I pick up the paper, and Hart was right: her number is scrawled under her name, dotted with a heart.

"You called it," I tell him.

The handwriting taunts my vision until Hart groans and pulls my attention back to him.

"Can you go anywhere without someone wanting to sleep with you?"

I shrug and stuff the number into my pocket. "We're good-looking guys."

"I look nothing like you."

"We're identical twins. You know what identical means." Though there is something to his comment. I did heavy weights before moving here, and between eating enough to keep my energy up and how heavy I was lifting, I'm a solid motherfucker. I'm thick, where Hart is our natural, wiry build. He also refuses to grow facial hair, and my mustache is one of my favorite things because of how positively my partners react to it.

We ignore each other and eat in silence. It hasn't always been like this. Growing up, we had each other's backs, even though we're so different, and we shared an apartment together before we moved here. But over the years, it's like Hart has gotten more bitter, and I've gotten more hopeful, and that common ground we used to meet on is now on a separate continent.

I miss the days when my brothers and I were fiercely on each other's side. When it was the three of us against the world.

Some days, I wonder if that's why I'm so quick to latch onto people. That I'm looking for that partnership I've lost and desperately crave.

It's why, as much as I'd like to call Caroline, I won't. It's time to focus on myself for a bit.

"I'm going to go talk to her," I tell Hart, and at his *of course you are* eye roll, I add, "So she knows why I won't call. I don't want her waiting and thinking she did anything wrong."

"You have no obligation just because she gave you her number."

"I know that." It isn't about obligation; it's about making sure she doesn't get her feelings hurt. "But I want to anyway."

"Ten bucks says you've named all your future children before you've gotten back to the table."

I don't give him the benefit of an answer as I leave my empty plate behind and approach where Caroline is behind the counter. She's restocking the display, and the second she notices me, her face lights up.

"Hey," she says. "Do you need anything?"

"Yeah, uh, do you have a second?" I tilt my head toward a quieter corner.

"Of course." She hurries to meet me on the customer side, and I lead her away from the other people here, guilt gnawing away at my insides.

"I wanted to tell you that I'm not going to call you." The second her face falls, I quickly clarify. "Not that I don't want to! You're very pretty and sweet, and I think it's so cool that you gave me your number."

Her disappointment turns to confusion. "I don't understand."

"I'm …" I scrunch up my face, already knowing how this is going to sound before I even say it. "Working on myself. That's not some bullshit excuse either. My brothers and I bought that small town—Wilde's End?"

She nods that she knows it.

"It's a lot of work, and it's far away. We don't get much reception up there either, and I have a bad habit of dating someone and getting too attached too soon, so I decided that while we're here, the town is my only focus. No relationships. No dating. No numbers." I pull the paper out and hold it up between us. "I wanted you to know that it wasn't anything you did."

"Right …" She takes the paper from me. "This isn't just you, like, letting me down easy?"

"No, really. Back home, you're exactly the kind of girl I'd go for."

Her sweet smile is back. "In that case, I'm going to take it as a not right now."

You know what? I don't hate it. "Do whatever you need to as long as you know that I'm not promising you anything, and I have absolutely no idea how long this build is going to take us."

"I get the feeling you're the kind of guy worth waiting on."

Well, if that doesn't make me feel like a giant inflatable, I don't know what will.

I'm grinning as I leave her behind and rejoin Hart.

"Let me guess," he drags out in a flat voice. "She's pregnant?"

I shake my head and throw some money on the table. "One

day, you'll be happy, and I can't wait to tease you endlessly about it."

"One day, I'll be dead. You gonna tease me about that too?"

He's looking for a bite, and I refuse. I'm not Hudson, who'd latch onto that and say something equally as fucked-up back.

I'm the mediator.

And I'm tired.

All I want is for everyone to be happy.

Is that so much to ask?

CHAPTER
THREE

ZIGGY

Shit.

The metal slices through my finger, and a bubble of blood springs out, then slips from the cut. *Stupid.* How hard is it for me to pay attention? I suck my finger into my mouth, pressing my tongue piercing to the sting as I inspect my handiwork.

I've raided our supplies barn for everything I need to make a little wire bird, and while it's slowly building into something recognizable, it's taking longer than I thought it would.

Slow, talentless, thoughtless.

I set the little statue down and walk back inside to drown out the words. My home is built into the hillside and was used as a mine shaft back when Wilde's End was built. Something caused it to cave in and kill a bunch of people, so since then, the town has all but been forgotten about. Until us Wenders took over.

I love my home. It's cozy. And most importantly, *echoey.*

The small box TV is turned up loud, and voices from whichever show it is are filling the cave-like space, bouncing them back to me in a way that makes no sense but keeps my head so full my thoughts can't run away with themselves.

Between the TV, the road that passes overhead through Hobby Straight, and the birds that wake me every morning, I've landed in the best spot I could have hoped for.

Especially now that the brothers are here.

Unlike Wilde, our leader out here, I'm not scared of what the brothers are planning. Do I want to be pushed out of my home? Of course not. But I packed it up once and moved out here, so I know that if I need to do that again, I'll manage. We're squatting on this land, so it was only a matter of time before all this good came to an end.

I'm not here to make an enemy of anyone ... especially not Kennedy.

The way I get all floaty—and sick—thinking about him isn't something I've ever experienced before. Sure, I had crushes when I was younger, and thought Wilde was hot when I first moved here, but that died quickly.

Wilde is ... closed off. I don't do well with people who bottle everything up inside, because I have enough of my own stuff bottled.

Kennedy doesn't even seem to know where the bottles are stored.

And more importantly, he talks. Even when I don't. There's rarely a moment of silence when I'm with him, and the way it fills that deep, frightened gap in my soul isn't something I'll ever be able to put into words.

And I'm full of them.

Words, I mean. They're on an ever-present rotation in my head, loud and needy and sometimes too much. All the words I'm scared to let out build and build, until it's this constant buzz of words and letters and shapes that don't make sense but weigh me down.

I reach my sink and open the side drawers as I rinse my still-bleeding finger under the water. The second one has most of my first aid shit in it, and I snag a Band-Aid before drying off my hands and wrapping it around the cut. It's not deep enough to worry about, but the damn thing stings, and I don't need to catch an infection out here. That will lead me to Booker, which is a visit I always avoid.

And *still* I don't have a gift for Kennedy.

I look around my place for the millionth time to see if I have anything that works, but other than the necessities, my place is barren. Gifts and trinkets aren't something I've ever worried about before. Beyond washing his bike *again* or checking his car's oil *again*, there isn't a lot else I can offer him. Like me, he doesn't have a lot of things, at least not here, so there's only so many acts of service I can shower him with.

Even if he never knows the way I feel about him, it doesn't matter. I'm a realist. I know I don't have a chance with someone as sunshiny as him, but that doesn't mean I won't do everything in my power to make him smile.

A birdlike whistle from outside makes my ears perk up because there's only one person who gets my attention that way.

I reach the entrance to my place as Lynx appears from the tree line, Bob, his adoptive bobcat, trailing close behind.

"Got a nice, fat rabbit this week," he says, holding up the large pot, forearms and biceps more distinct under the weight. "Should do you for a couple of days."

That means stew, and Lynx's stews are some of the greatest things I've ever tasted. He passes me to walk inside and tuck the pot away in my fridge.

"Heat it up whenever you're hungry."

I tap my chest twice in thanks, but he pretends not to see me. Lynx drops by twice a week with food since he knows I don't cook, then normally leaves right away, but this time, instead of disappearing, he rocks back on his heels.

"So." His deep voice comes out cold as a snake. "I heard you're working with those outsiders?"

News sure travels fast. The way I see it, the brothers need an electrician, and I am one. Well, I was in my life before here. If I can help them, there's no reason why I shouldn't, considering they'll find someone else for the job anyway.

And this way, I get to spend time with Kennedy, doing something that will make his life easier.

Not that I can or will tell Lynx any of those things. It's not like I *can't* talk. My voice works. Apparently. Sometimes the anxiety of letting out words is barely present, but most of the time, it's like the words are strangling me. Like my whole body is braced against them, at war with myself over setting them free. Because once the words are out there, I can't get them back, and people have a real skill for using those words against you.

"Why don't you ever talk? What, you think you're too good for us?"

I shake the memories away.

It's easier to let things happen around me rather than to me. The soundless, inoffensive shadow that goes unnoticed and forgotten.

Because Lynx is still waiting on an answer, I nod.

"They're using you," he says in a low, deadly voice. "They're mining our resources and disrupting our homes, and you're helping them do it."

Again, I say nothing, only blink at him, waiting for him to get bored of this and leave.

"Don't let them walk all over you."

While I agree that Hudson and Hartwell are more than capable of using people and spitting them out, there's no way Kennedy could. He's not cruel. It's one of the many reasons I gravitate toward him.

Lynx can sense my disinterest in the conversation, so he changes topics. "Wilde is fucking one of them. The oldest one." He paces closer to the entrance of the mine and looks warily up at the sky. "First twins. Then Wilde falling under their spell, and now you. Something bad is coming. The forest feels dark."

Since meeting Kennedy, the forest feels like pure sunshine. I wait until Lynx looks at me and give him my most skeptical expression.

"You don't believe me? Bob feels it too, don't you, Bob?"

Like it can understand him, the huge thing stands and lets out a creepy demon sound.

Whether that was supposed to be confirmation or not, I'm not about to take an animal's word for it, especially when the animal willingly chose Lynx to bond with. It doesn't strike me as having sound judgment.

I slap my thigh loudly, pulling Lynx's attention back my way. "What?"

I do it again, then make a slashing motion over it before pointing to Bob, then my throat. If he wants to talk about *bad*, I'll remind him how that's already happened, thanks to him and his animal attacking Wilde.

Lynx's hand flexes toward the machete strapped to his leg. "Wilde touched me. Of course Bob was going to attack. The leg was an accident, thanks to his pretty boy toy. Trust an outsider to not know what happens when you push a man with a knife." He spits on the ground. "Could have killed me. No one cares about that though, do they?" He turns his hazel eyes on me and gives me a narrow, searching stare. "Who would make your rabbit stew then?"

I make sure he's holding my eyes when I tap my heart again, forcing him to see it this time.

His gaze darkens, and he looks away. "Right. Enjoy. Don't forget to heat it over one seventy." I'm sure I'm not supposed to hear his mutters as he walks away, but I do. "Don't want you getting sick."

The thing about Lynx is that he never tries to be liked, but sometimes he does things that make me like him anyway. Even though he's as much of an animal as Bob is.

They leave, and I'm once again alone with the TV voices and my thoughts.

Thoughts that follow Lynx instead of focusing on the stabbing voices inside. Follow him down the hill, through the forest, and stray back into Old End.

I turn back to the twisted metal and grab the blowtorch to keep working, anything to help distract my mind. By the time this thing is done, I'm going to have so many scratches and burns that it'll be easier to remove my fingers than deal with them.

But it will be worth it.

To see Kennedy smile.

CHAPTER
FOUR

KENNEDY

need … something. Work isn't doing its usual job of distracting me this morning, and even with Hudson and Hart here, I'm jittery. Part of me wants to drive back into Wayward and make sure Caroline is okay, while the other part of me knows that I'm being dramatic. She's a near stranger, and as of right now, I have nothing to offer her.

That reminder doesn't help shake the fact that I feel personally responsible for her feelings.

Fuck, I hate the way I cling to people.

Maybe Hudson's right and I am a loser? How many other grown-ass men obsess the way I do?

"You okay?" Hart asks, words flat and drawn out like he's doing it under duress.

"Fine."

"You're not singing. Normally, I have to put my earplugs in by now."

"I'm thinking."

"About?"

I'm honest, even though I know they'll tease me, because I'm still hoping there's a chance we'll bond and get as close as we used to be. "Caroline."

Hart's echoed laugh catches Hudson's attention. "You wish you didn't give back her number, don't you?"

"Wait," Hudson says, drifting closer. "Caroline, as in the waitress?"

Here we go. "Yep."

He spreads his hands like he's confused. "Why didn't you call her?"

"Really?"

"She's pretty. Objectively."

I'm staring at him, trying to figure out if he's teasing me. "You told me I need to give dating a break."

"I fell for a man who hates me, so what do I know about relationships?"

"Umm …" Hart and I share a worried glance. *Fell for?*

Hudson waves our concern away. "Maybe. Probably. We'll see."

We'll see?

Right.

I'm suddenly thinking Ziggy might have been right about their relationship. Hudson has never been great at picking men because they all end up treating him like trash. But I've never been great at picking men *or* women because the second I show interest, they ghost me, so maybe Hudson's had the right idea all along. His partners might be repulsive, but at least they're never repulsed *by* him.

Based on my past experiences, his interest should turn Wilde off, but considering the man drove four hours out of his way to drag Hudson back here, I'm getting the creeping suspicion that isn't happening.

That Hudson and Wilde are … an actual couple.

The only thing I can hope for is that Wilde took our talk to heart and is actually treating my brother right.

Meanwhile, there's a small, bitter seed in my chest that I wasn't the one who came out here and miraculously found a mountain man to love me. Surely there's an attention-starved recluse who'd find my brand of love sweet rather than suffocating.

I groan at the pathetic thoughts.

"Is Ziggy coming today?" Hudson asks, getting us back on track with work. "We really need this wiring done before we can do anything else to house two."

"Dunno." Then, I jokingly add, "Didn't say."

"Funny," Hart says dryly. "I wonder why he's like that."

"You? Actually interested in something?" Hudson throws back.

"I never said I was interested, but it's normal to question why. The guy can talk. He just … won't."

"That's his business," I remind them before they can get mean. I'd like to think the conversation wouldn't lead to that, but you never can tell. Hudson can be a real asshole when he's feeling hurt, and Hart mostly says shit for shock value and reactions, like he has zero attachment to the words coming out of his mouth.

Whether this is natural curiosity or them mocking him, I want to end it before it can get started.

Ziggy is willingly helping us out, and we owe him big-time for that.

"Of course it's his business," Hartwell says like it's obvious. "But it's not normal."

"Hey—"

"Shut up, I don't mean that in a bad way. I'm pointing out that there has to be a reason why he doesn't speak."

I grunt, not comfortable talking about him when he's not here. "Why would he talk when you're proof that most of what people say is fucked-up?"

"Why are you so protective of him?" Hudson asks through a laugh. "You have been since the day he showed up here."

"It's called being nice. I realize you need that pointed out to you." Which really isn't *nice* of me to say, but I want them to let it drop before the teasing starts.

"Maybe you're in luuuurve."

And there it is. It's ridiculous that I can't even be friends with someone without them resorting to this, but considering my history with people, I can't blame them either. "No. I'm not."

"Sure about that?"

Considering Ziggy is maybe the first and only person I've met where I didn't immediately check them out and test for interest, I'm sure. Ever since we met, this deep need to protect him has taken over me. "I barely know anything about him."

"And how much did you know about Ryan after one date and a night of sex, when you texted us to clear our schedules so we could meet him?"

"Maybe if you'd cleared your schedules, we would have worked out."

"Or maybe you *still* would have gone over the next day to find him screwing someone else."

It's hard to be angry about that anymore. After a week of heartache and working myself to exhaustion, then a weekend of drinking with them both, I was able to set aside some of the hurt.

For me, dating means giving things a real go and focusing on the one person you're seeing. If you have split focus, how can you ever know if you're meant to be?

Unfortunately, the other ninety-nine percent of the population aren't clingy men with the yearning for a rom-com of their own.

It amuses me to imagine telling someone that. To sit down on a date and confess that I'd love nothing more than to be swept off my feet. For us to be exclusive from the get-go. Things don't work like that anymore. And after my constant strikeouts, and Hudson settling for being treated like dirt, and Hartwell never talking about any relationships he may or may not have, it's getting really hard to keep believing in love.

I don't *want* to be a bitter person.

I *like* being a romantic.

But little by little, that part of me is shrinking.

"You don't have to worry about me anymore," I tell them. "I'm not dating for the whole time we're here. I'm taking a break from all of that so that once we're home, I'll know exactly what I'm after."

The problem is that I really, really like it here. Staying in Wilde's End is where my head is currently at, but I won't find my person here.

Could I really spend the rest of my life alone? If it came to that, if I actually decided to stay, would I be able to live by myself … forever? No romance. No partner. No one to share all my thoughts and feelings with.

As much as I'd like to dream that someone who buys one of our houses would fall in love with the town and me, I know that realistically, it's likely to be a wealthy couple.

Who will shove their happy love in my face.

So as much as I love it here, I can't stay. I need to know what it feels like to be loved.

There's a soft knock on the door, and I glance around Hudson to see Ziggy lingering there. I have no idea when he showed up since the man drifts in like a ghost, but a smile splits my face at the sight of him.

No matter what Hart and Hudson say about him, I enjoy his company. He's the kind of calm I've never had in my life, and something about that is really goddamn appealing. I can be myself with him in a way I can't with anyone else.

Not even my brothers.

I feel the shift almost immediately though. Ziggy's guard is up with Hudson here, and my brothers still aren't sure they trust anyone in this town. Even with Hudson dating Wilde, I have no clue what they really think about each other.

Hudson isn't a talk-about-your-feelings guy.

It only takes one glance between the three of them before I make up my mind.

"I'm taking the rest of the day off."

Ziggy's eyes widen with alarm, and Hudson's expression morphs into concern.

"What's wrong?"

"Nothing's wrong."

"But …" He glances at Hart, who ignores us both. "You never take the day off."

"All the more reason to do it today."

"I'm not arguing with you, just surprised."

I pat his shoulder on the way past. "We'll be fine."

"We?"

"Yeah, I'm taking Ziggy with me."

That gets Hart involved. "But we need him."

"And you'll still need him tomorrow." I turn to Ziggy. "Wanna play hooky with me?"

His warm, brown gaze slowly moves from me to my brothers and back again. Then he turns on his heel and walks away.

"I guess that's a yes."

I hurry to catch up, but Ziggy doesn't slow until he reaches the road out the front. It's the only paved road in and out of Wilde's End and leads to a dirt one that runs through the trees to … who the fuck knows where. I've been so busy working that I haven't explored anywhere outside of the one-street town, even though our land extends for miles. Land that Ziggy, Wilde, and who the hell else live on.

"Can you show me around?" I call after him.

He tilts his head, chunks of longish black hair slipping from his headband to fall over his sweet face. He's pale, with big eyes and the prettiest pink lips I've ever seen. Underneath the bottom one, he has snakebite piercings, which are two of the six facial piercings he has. I've counted them a few times just to make sure I'm remembering correctly, and I know why Hart's curious about him.

Because Ziggy makes me so, so curious as well.

I wish I could break him open and sift through everything about him, but I have to trust that if he ever wants to share with me, he will.

For an oversharer like me, patience makes me want to scratch off my skin.

Ziggy leaves me to walk along the side of the house, and when he's back a moment later, he's no longer carrying his toolbox. He motions for me to follow him.

"This is cool," I say, adding extra excitement into my voice so he knows I mean it. "I love exploring, and I've wanted to do this for a while now, but I had no idea where to start. At least if I'm with you, I won't get lost."

He gives me a sly smile from the corner of his eye.

"Ooh, that looked evil. Don't you dare run off and leave me."

His shrug doesn't fill me with confidence.

"I'm serious!"

He actually laughs, and the sound sweeps over me and strikes me dumb. Just like every time I hear his voice, it's like I've witnessed something special.

And I use every moment I have to try and make it happen again.

CHAPTER
FIVE

Leave him out here? That would require me not being obsessively addicted to his company. He might as well tell me to stop breathing.

Luckily for Kennedy, Wilde's End isn't a hard place to get around, once you know where everything is. We stick to the dirt road as we walk, and while I'm listening to him excitedly point out birds or trees, or whatever else he's rambling about, I keep sneaking glances his way.

So Kennedy is giving up dating, is he?

Figures that the second my interest in love rattles to consciousness, the person giving it a jump start takes himself off the market indefinitely. It's one thing to think you don't have a chance with someone; it's another to have it confirmed.

I desperately want to ask why. To find out how the man Wilde told me is a romantic has gone from all things hearts and rainbows to swearing off relationships. Only while he's here, of course. It's like the universe is really slamming home the reminder that I have no chance with him.

Which brings me to the only conclusion I can draw from that: the universe is an asshole.

I don't have experience with men, have never been with one, but Kennedy makes me want to try. I'm inhumanly attracted to him, and it's hard to determine whether it's his physical features, who he is inside, or a combination of both.

Maybe … just maybe … if I can convince him that I'm worth breaking his no-dating rule for, then—

Sure. And maybe aliens will show up and take me away.

Proving that I'm worth him starts with *actually* being worthy of him.

"So where are you taking me?" he asks suddenly. And for someone so in tune with my moods and the way I don't like to talk, the question surprises me. Until he adds, "To see your freaky doctor?"

It's the usual yes/no question most people stick to around me. It helps because I don't have to think about talking, but it occurs to me that it means I never really get the chance.

But Kennedy jumping to the assumption I'm taking him to *Booker*? Way off base. I shiver and shake my head.

"Hmm …" He rubs his scratchy jaw. "Who's that other guy I've seen? He was wearing a ball cap and had his hair in a ponytail."

That sounds like Rooney. I tap my lips three times, and he watches me, that look taking over his expression like he's puzzling me out.

Kennedy copies tapping his lips. "Does this mean … whatever his name is?"

The answer to his question pops up in my mind, and it's an easy one. One word. That's it.

Rooney. Just say Rooney. *Rooney. Rooney. Roooooney.* It's lodged in my throat, growing and growing, but even when I open my mouth, when I form the word with my lips, the sound won't come. The harder I fight it, the longer it takes, the more my stress skyrockets, and then the stupider I feel for not being able to get the fucking thing out. I can't stop the sickening nerves or the lockjaw tension that builds whenever I imagine hearing my voice between us.

Pussy.

Wimp.

Ungrateful.

"Hey, it's okay," Kennedy says, the warm weight of his hand on my shoulder as he squeezes it.

But it's not okay. Pressure builds in my chest, and I want to scream at how useless I am. How frustratingly *pathetic*.

But Kennedy squeezes harder this time and angles his face until he's in my line of sight.

"Ziggy." He makes a slashing motion over his mouth. "That's Ziggy. Right?"

I study him, waiting for a sneer or fake pity to take over his face. I brace for him to shove me or for his lips to form one of a million insults I've had hurled my way.

Instead, he makes the slashing motion again. Then the corners of his lips twitch upward. "Do you have one for me?"

For … him? Slowly, I pull my focus away from myself and the ringing in my head to the man standing in front of me. The man who's not shouting or pushing or mocking me.

I study him for a moment, everything from his golden hair to his golden smile, and I'm filled with the same warmth he's always funneled into me.

It's where my name for him came from. But as he watches me and waits, it gets too hard to lift my hands. I never learned sign language because when I was younger, I had no problems with talking. It was only as I got older and started learning how evil the world is that my voice shrank and shriveled inside of me.

Telling Kennedy the name I have for him would be easy, and I want to, but self-preservation wins out. There's a chance it would give away how I feel about him, and when I can't even have a goddamn conversation with the guy, that feels like skipping a lot of steps.

I shake my head instead. Normally, I'm not a liar, but there isn't a whole lot that I won't do to protect myself.

"Ah, damn. You'll have to tell me when you think of one." He resumes walking and chuckles to himself. "What about this?" he asks, holding a finger beneath his nose like he's sniffing it.

I pull a disgusted face, and his chuckle turns into a laugh. "I'll take that as a no."

If I didn't already have something, it would work, but Kennedy deserves to be known for more than his mustache.

I take a right off the path and follow a long, narrow one deeper into the forest. It's the way to Lynx's place. He lives beside the crop fields and the battery containers, and maybe if Kennedy sees that, he can get an understanding of what I want to achieve in Old End. Given they're planning to market the houses there as high-end luxury weekenders or whatever, our batteries won't have enough energy to supply those too, but I can work out a similar arrangement up there.

It takes ten minutes of walking and Kennedy telling me about where he used to live before we pass the tree line into the clearing. It's as large as a football field, with Lynx's small house right on the edge, rows and rows of crops, protected by his intricate fencing, and then the shipping containers on the other side.

"Oh, wow," he mutters, following me. "Is this where you live? It's like a fairy-tale cottage."

I almost laugh at that. Me? Grow food when I can barely cook it? I'm not sure exactly what I contribute to the town other than being an eagle-eyed lookout, but feeding people would never come close to being on the list.

I lift my hand and use my fore and little fingers to make horns above my head.

"That's who lives here?"

I nod and, throat feeling tight, manage a whisper before I'm too in my head. "Lynx."

Kennedy's whole body jolts with tension, and I recoil. It's on instinct, and I hate that it's my instinct, but thankfully, Kennedy doesn't notice because he's back staring at the house. "Jesus fucking Christ, do you want me to get killed?"

He looks like he's about to bolt, so I grab him before he can. I know why he's spooked, and I don't blame him. Lynx showed up where they were working a month ago and scared the shit out of them. Wilde got in the way, protecting Hudson, and it all went downhill from there. Lynx ended up slashing up Wilde with his knife, Bob attacked Wilde for threatening Lynx ... and Kennedy was there to witness the whole thing.

I give him my best pleading eyes.

"Ziggy ..."

I yank on his arm more aggressively this time.

"I want to trust you, but that's a big ask after what that psycho did."

He's making an excellent point that I unfortunately can't argue with without words. Why do I have to be so damn at war with myself? I hang my head back toward the sky, keeping a firm grip on his arm, and give him a small, needy tug. Take pity on me, *please*.

Some of the tension drains from him. "Don't get me killed."

I quickly catch his eye, trying to pour all the promises I can into our eye contact. Get him killed? I would never. I'm no fighter, but I'd take on Lynx for him if I had to. Thankfully, I won't have to since even Lynx isn't reckless enough to attack again.

"I trust you," he says.

And that makes me hopeful in a way I've never been before. All I want is to lean in and kiss him on the cheek in thanks, but my pounding heart refuses.

So I step back and gesture at him to follow me, then lead the way to the containers.

There are only two keys to get into the batteries, and they belong to me and Wilde. He has a basic understanding of how it all works, but it's my baby. I put it together and am constantly tinkering and updating when I can. It's expensive, but Wilde never has issues getting me what I need.

When I click open the padlock and pull aside the heavy door, Kennedy's suitably impressed.

"What the hell is this?"

I point to the closest solar battery as Kennedy passes me and walks inside.

"Hudson mentioned you guys had electricity, but this is …" His head is shaking as he looks around at it all. "Wait a minute … did *you* do all this?"

I confirm it, and his jaw drops further.

"This is incredible. I don't understand most of it, but to put this together doesn't look easy."

It's not, and I sort of like that he knows that.

"How long did it take you? Weeks?"

I shake my head.

"Months?"

Not even close. When I wrinkle my nose, his awe fills his face.

"Years? Fuck me, Ziggy, you are one clever guy."

Unfortunately, my mind is stuck on the *fuck me, Ziggy* part of what he said instead of the compliment. It takes me a moment to work out that he's still talking.

"Do you think we could set up something like this? To get electricity on at the town?"

That's the entire plan.

He bounces closer and grabs my face in both hands. "You're a genius." He gives me a little shake in his excitement. Then, before I know it, his arm is around my shoulders, and he's got me pulled in close to his side.

I choke on air.

It's so fucking warm here. He's been working today, and his scent is a mix of sweat and something really, really appealing. I want to lean in closer and breathe it in, but even I know that's crossing boundaries.

I might live out in the wild, but that doesn't mean I don't have manners.

Mostly.

Even if it is really hard to remember that with him so damn close.

"We'll have to figure out a way to hide the containers so that they don't ruin the luxury angle we're going for. And if we can get some electricity hardwired in, at least as a backup, that would be good too. I doubt there's much out this way, but I'll find out whatever I can for you. Oh! Maybe you could come into town with me one day this week? I don't really know what I'm looking for, so I'd probably need you to help me with the search. Then we can make a plan? Yeah?"

He looks over at me, almost nose to nose, and I'm trying to keep my expression as anything other than terrified. Terrified that I'm dangerously close to licking him, yes, but also terrified by everything he said. He wants me to … go into town. With him. Where the people are.

Lots and lots of people.

It's been so long. The most I encounter these days are the Wilde's End residents at the Cutty—our town bar—and even then, outside of holidays, there's only a handful of people there at any one time. Plus, I know everyone out here.

Going to Wayward. Away from my protective bubble. It's … unimaginable.

But then I think of the long drive and being huddled up next to Kennedy while we look at his computer. And all those worries? All those stressors and triggers and every reason not to just …

leave my head. All I can concentrate on is dancing, green eyes under the excited tilt to his eyebrows.

I'm nodding before I'm aware I'm nodding.

Kennedy's smiling before he's probably aware he's smiling.

Then the one voice I'm hoping we won't hear today comes from behind us both.

"Well, this looks cozy."

CHAPTER
SIX

KENNEDY

almost swallow my damn tongue. Warning alarms go off in my head, telling me not to turn around, because if I go on pretending I can't hear him, he'll go away.

And definitely not stab me in the back. Literally.

Considering he had no issue with stabbing Wilde in the *front*, I have no clue why I'd assume that plan would work.

Ziggy pulls away from me before I can test out my theory, and it's hard not to be frustrated when it felt like I was getting through to him. This little thread of connection was building between us, and as soon as Lynx spoke, it snapped. I want to kick him for ruining it.

Though it's hard to be pissed when I'm worried about my life.

"Why did you bring him here?" Lynx asks, and I hurry to turn around too.

Ziggy stares him down, and instinct makes me angle myself in front of him.

Lynx is blocking our way out of the container, and his stupid bobcat is sitting behind him.

"He was showing me something," I say, trying to keep my tone light, even as my pulse picks up at the sight of them. "It's okay though. We aren't hanging around. I think I've seen everything I need to."

Lynx's glare turns on me. "I wasn't talking to you."

"I was just explain—"

Beside me, Ziggy huffs and elbows me out of the way.

Lynx actually laughs. "Ziggy can speak for himself."

"He can?" I glance at Ziggy and the withering look he's directing my way. I quickly throw up my hands in surrender. "Of course you can."

I'm almost dumbstruck as he steps into Lynx's path, that urge to push him behind me only getting stronger.

"It wasn't a smart move to bring him here," Lynx warns.

Ziggy plants his hands on his hips.

For some reason, that makes Lynx's jaw tick. "I'm happy to ignore the little boys existing, but you really need to make it easier on me. Bringing him here? On my territory?" Lynx lifts his machete between us. "You're lucky I don't send him to visit Booker."

"Are you threatening me?" I'm asking because I genuinely don't know, but from memory, Booker is their doctor, so that's the only conclusion I can come up with.

Ziggy's expression clearly says *shut up.*

So I shut up.

He turns to Lynx and slashes at his throat, and I watch on as Lynx gets more menacing and Ziggy inches closer to him. I'm twitching to pull Ziggy away, because I don't care what either of them says, the urge to protect Ziggy is strong. I might have muscles, but I've never had an urge to fight, and even now, the only reason I want to pull him back is so that we can run away.

But if Lynx tried to hurt the guy I'm slowly becoming friends with, I doubt my pacifist side would hold up.

In fact, I'm almost positive I'd bury my fist in his face.

Lynx scoffs loudly, pulling my attention back to him as his cat stands up in warning. "Wilde could try. Hell, maybe he'd even kill me. But the only way I stop protecting this place is if I'm dead."

Ziggy gestures sharply at me, getting frustrated.

"I'm not going to get to know them." Lynx's sharp eyes connect with mine, and I'm thrown that he understands Ziggy, even without words. "You're ruining our home. Some of the others might be weak when it comes to standing up for what's right, but that will never be me. Stay hiding behind Ziggy, or Wilde, it doesn't matter. The second one of you wanders off alone, no one will hear from you again."

"Now I know you're threatening me." As much as I want to get angry like Hudson does, that didn't work out so well for us last time. My palms are clammy, and I'm getting nervous like I always do before a confrontation, but dammit if that will stop me. "Ziggy's right." I'm assuming. "Get to know us. Give me a chance to prove that we're not bad guys."

"You going to sell off those houses?"

"Well, yes—"

"That's all I need to know." He taps his big knife against the container with a metallic *chink chink*. "Enjoy your day, gentlemen. I'll be watching."

He leaves, and the second he's out of sight, a full-body shiver runs through me.

It pulls Ziggy's attention, and he tilts his head, watching me like he's confused.

"What?" I ask defensively. "He's scary as hell."

Ziggy … *rolls his eyes*?

"Nuh-uh," I say, stepping closer. "You don't get to brush this off. He threatened to kill me and my brothers."

Ziggy waves my concern away as he leads me from the container.

"You don't think he'd do it. But he just said—" I almost barge right into Ziggy when he turns suddenly so he's facing me.

There's sympathy in his brown eyes, but he leans in, hand finding my face, and those long, smooth fingers feel cool against my skin. I completely forget what I was about to say.

His eyes lock on mine, and he slowly, purposefully shakes his head. I watch him, replaying the movement, wanting to puzzle him out and read him as easily as Lynx did. He's ... not scary? He ... won't do it? But how can Ziggy be sure?

The more he stares at me, the more it feels like he's trying to say something important. Something convincing.

Like he wants me to believe Lynx won't hurt me, all because he says so.

Fuck me. I did say I trust him.

I cover Ziggy's hand with mine and give it a squeeze. "Okay. I'll stop worrying about being murdered. Or gutted. Or skinned alive. But if you're wrong, I *will* haunt you forever."

That earns me his sly grin, and he pulls away too soon, then waits for me to leave before locking up the container again.

"Right. Where to next? I can't wait to meet more people who hate my guts."

We end up following the river to an impressive-looking timber building. It's large, with a front deck that overlooks the water, and when we head inside, all I can do is look around in shock for a minute. It's a bar. Huge gleaming counter, racks of alcohol behind it, chairs and tables all along the left, and down the end are pool tables and a jukebox.

I turn to Ziggy like I might be hallucinating. "Is that actually real?"

His eyes crease with amusement as he takes my sleeve and leads me toward the bar. Then he steps around to the other side.

"What are you doing?"

He waves his hand over the bottles behind him before pointing to a lower fridge.

"Get out from behind there before you get into trouble."

He lets out a laugh that I have a second to bask in before it's joined by another. A man with a ball cap and ponytail comes out from the back, cradling an armful of Coke bottles.

"No one's getting into trouble," he says. "We serve ourselves. Now, can you tell him what you want so he can get out of my way?"

"A … a Coke. Is fine."

The man hands over a bottle before Ziggy shifts so he can get to the lower fridges.

"Didn't think I'd see another brother here," the guy says.

"Ziggy was showing me around. I'm guessing Hudson's been here too?"

"A few times with Wilde." He and Ziggy share an amused look. "Never thought I'd see the day he was swooning over some guy."

"Wilde? Scary dude with a beard? *Swooning*?"

"Oh yeah. I've never seen that man so giddy in my life."

Considering every time I see him, he's all scowly and grunting, I'm going to call bullshit on that one. "I don't see it."

"You don't know him." The man finishes putting the bottles away and then straightens and offers me his hand. "I'm Rooney, the only mildly sociable one around here."

That pulls a smile from me. "Kennedy."

"Ah, yes. The nice brother."

"Is that what I'm known as?"

Rooney plants his elbows on the bar top and props his chin in his hands. "Is it a lie?"

"Not … a lie. Exactly." When it comes to my brothers, I'm a saint in comparison, but nice is such a bland description. "What do you know Hudson and Hartwell as?"

"The Romeo and the ghost."

"Ghost?"

"Sure. No one ever sees him."

"And … Hudson's *Romeo*?" Well, that would be a first. Goddammit, *I* should be Romeo.

"He did bring our savage leader to his knees."

I don't get it. All they did was gripe at each other the whole time they were sleeping together, and that somehow led them to being the Romeo and Juliet of this place? Maybe Wilde's End is more backward than I thought.

Seriously, is there *anywhere* on this goddamn Earth where being sweet and considerate is appreciated? I know I'm not supposed to be focused on relationships, but it's starting to hurt.

Did I miss my chance at happiness when I turned down Caroline? Maybe that was the universe finally giving me my person.

"Or was it your brother who got on his knees?" Rooney muses out loud. "Either way, they got their happy ending."

"Now I'm worried about which happy ending you're referring to."

"Only the fun kind."

"I think both ways are the fun kind."

He looks like a guy used to smiling as he checks me out. "Are you straight? Or do you take after your brother?"

"Bi." Or … wait. Maybe my forever person is Rooney? I don't feel any type of way toward him, but who can say? "Why do you ask?"

"Because you're hot. Duh."

"Oh, uh, thanks." My face is heating. "That's really—"

Ziggy slams his hand down on the bar between us with an echoing *thwack*.

My rambling cuts off, and when I glance over, his face is twisted in anger. Even under his loose bangs, I can make out the way his pierced eyebrows are pulled down sharply.

"Shit, Ziggy, were we leaving you out?" Rooney asks lightly, reaching over to pat him on the back.

Ziggy slaps his hand away, but guilt is sinking through me. We *were* leaving him out. Fuck. I didn't even notice I was doing it. I'm so used to being around my brothers or our friends, people who'll talk over the top of each other and never shy away from having themselves heard.

Ziggy isn't like that.

"I'm sorry," I tell him as convincingly as I can. "That was really rude."

He still looks mad—along with something else—but when his gaze drops toward the floor, some of the tension leaves his features.

"It's my fault," Rooney says, eyeing Ziggy curiously. "I get excited meeting new people."

"Me too," I admit.

Ziggy passes him and joins me around the other side of the bar, then grabs my Coke and pulls me toward a table by the window. He sets my drink down and points to the chair behind it, and I'm so confused about whether he forgives me or if he's putting me in the naughty corner. I sit slowly, trying to read his face, and it's not until he takes the seat beside me and lets the annoyance slide from his features that I relax again.

Ziggy sighs, turning back to Rooney, and points at the chair across the table from us.

"Be right over," Rooney calls, not sounding at all like he's going to curl over from the guilt. Me, on the other hand? I feel bad for squishing bugs, so upsetting Ziggy is going to sit with me.

I drop my voice so only he can hear me. "I really am sorry."

It takes him a moment before he looks at me, his searching gaze wary, and slowly, the irritation is replaced by something else. His lips pull out into a sad, flat smile. Is that supposed to be forgiveness? Or resignation?

"Nope, don't do that." Surprise lights up his eyes, and he cocks his head to the side. Is he challenging me? Or ... asking me to keep talking? "Don't pretend you're okay. I feel bad, and I should." Taking a chance, I reach out and run my fingers along his arm, wanting to build that connection we had earlier but scared I'll spook him. "I want to know you better, and that includes the things that annoy you."

He's watching me, unresponsive, and slowly, it feels like I'm getting through to him. That he's hearing the truth behind the words I'm speaking.

The guardedness seeps away.

It shouldn't feel so good to see him relax again, but I wasn't lying when I said that I felt bad. In the short time since meeting him, the moments we spend together only leave me eager to know more.

Know everything.

Now, I've catalogued one more thing about him.

Ziggy really, really hates to be ignored.

So I guess I'll have to smother him in attention instead.

CHAPTER
SEVEN

ZIGGY

Apparently, when it comes to Kennedy, I'm a jealous guy. Who knew?

The way Rooney was looking at him, how the two of them were leaning closer, their conversation so fast and excited, I never had a chance to get a word in … I hated it. It made me feel as invisible as I always think I am, and it's the first time that's happened around Kennedy.

I'd wanted to smash my glass bottle between them, but luckily, I reined in that urge.

I'm sure Kennedy already thinks I'm weird, and I don't need to do anything to encourage that image.

My TV is on a low hum, giving me background noise, but not enough to echo off the walls. I take another deep breath, nails digging into my palms, and say, "Kennedy."

The word almost dies on my lips, and as soon as it's out, I resist the urge to flinch around and check behind me.

It's okay. I'm okay.

This is fine and normal and fine.

You'd think that eight years later, it would be easier. That I'd stop instinctively waiting for the pulse-spiking scream. Growing up, my parents were … angry. They worked a lot and slept all the time in between, so if I woke them between shifts, the screaming would start. The shouting and anger and names. Being dragged back to my room. Locked in there all day or night until they were up and would let me out again with an exhausted, dead-eyed sneer and warnings about showing respect.

Between keeping as silent as possible at home and the way my anxiety would ramp up every time I tried to talk at school, it's no wonder dread smothers my words so often.

Friends used to ask me why I was so quiet. People I didn't know would call me weird. Then, when I did talk, it was met with mock surprise or snide comments until I stopped talking altogether.

Is that what your voice sounds like? I wouldn't talk either if I sounded like that.

I cup my mouth in a silent scream before blowing air out through my fingers. They're not here anymore. They can't hurt me again. I'm okay.

I'm a work in progress, but the important part is that I *am* making progress. I'm slowly getting more comfortable with the people in town, and while it's easier not to talk, I can manage conversations when I need to. With Kennedy? Someone so new and shiny? Who gets me all twisted up inside? It's near fucking impossible.

I steel myself, nails digging harder this time, and try again. "Kennedy."

His name comes out weak but is getting familiar the more I do it. I'm determined that one day, we'll be able to have a real conversation. To laugh and joke and have him as mesmerized as Rooney did. I'm *determined*.

I'm about to try again when a new noise breaks through the quiet murmur of the TV. A distant *thud* that I've heard a few times before and can place instantly now.

A car has gone off Hobby Straight.

The road winds through the hill above me, but with the tight turns and narrow lanes, it's not unusual for someone to take a bend too wide.

I switch off the TV, grab the keys to the truck I never drive, and hightail it down to Wilde's. He's always the first point of call before we pick up the doctor and head out, looking for the accident. Usually, the driver is uninjured and only needs help to tow their car back onto the road, but it never hurts to have Booker on hand, just in case.

I pull up out front of Wilde's house, and he reaches his door before I can knock on it. I point to his truck.

"Hobby Straight?" he checks.

At my answering nod, he grabs his keys and meets me outside. I climb in with him since he refuses to ride passenger, and then we drive over to the chop shop. When Booker climbs in beside me, he's rubbing his hands together.

"Wonder what we'll have today," he says. "Nothing as fun as what Hudson brought me, I'd guess, but it's not unreasonable to hope for a broken bone."

Wilde throws his truck in drive and tosses a concerned look across me. "Let's *hope* for nothing so we can pull them out of there and get them on their way."

Booker tsks. "You're never any fun."

"Sorry that I don't like wishing harm on people."

"It's not serious harm. A mild compound fracture is easily managed."

"And probably hurts like a bitch."

I swear I hear Booker mutter beside me, "Even better."

And people think *I'm* weird.

Someone needs to teach Booker what an inside thought is.

"What about you?" he asks, patting my thigh. "Ready for me to take a look at those vocal cords yet?"

"Ziggy's voice works fine," Wilde answers before I can.

As much as I appreciate not *having* to talk, it would also be nice to have the option to. To practice and be given the time I need to get the words flowing. I know Wilde thinks he's helping, and out here, we don't ask, but maybe, *maybe* if someone *had* asked, I wouldn't be as bad as I am now.

So I sit here, feeling more detached than at peace, like I normally would.

We make it up the hill to Hobby Straight, and it takes a few minutes of searching before we spot the car. There are a handful of problem areas, and the one this driver has gone off is a tight bend with low visibility.

Wilde parks, and we climb out of the truck for a closer look. There's a sheer fifteen-foot drop before the tree line, and while the car has hit the trees, it doesn't look badly damaged. At least from here. Along the back windshield, a line of colorful plushies stares blankly up at me, and I really hope there's no kid in there.

I climb into the back of Wilde's truck, next to his winch, and hand him the end that he clips over his belt. We've done this enough times that it's second nature, and I control the winch as he goes over the side.

When Wilde gets to the car, Booker holds up his hand for me to stop.

"How does it look?" he calls.

There's no answer right away, and I assume he's searching. "It's empty."

Empty? I lean forward, unsure if I heard him right, but when Booker throws me a *what the fuck* look, it confirms my hearing isn't the problem.

Whoever it was left their car.

That's a first.

I help Wilde back up onto the road, and he unclips the makeshift harness.

"How many people do you think were in there?" Booker asks.

"My guess is one. Maybe two."

"Kids?"

"With all the luggage on the back seat, unlikely."

Booker glances back down at the car. "Interesting."

"No point moving the car if there's no one to drive it away," he says. "We'll send Rooney back up to tow it to his place."

I wave my hand across the trees.

"Yeah," he agrees. "They've probably wandered off."

I agree that it's not a smart thing to do, but someone who's been in an accident isn't focused on being clever. Survival instincts make us do weird shit.

My gaze roams the blanket of trees below, trying to figure out which way they would have gone. Would they have followed the road? Ventured toward town, which you can't even see from here, or gone deeper into the wilderness?

Too many options, and if they're lost and injured, they're not going to get far.

Wilde sets the winch back in the truck, but before he can turn for the cab, I grab his arm. I give him my best pleading look, and the longer we make eye contact, the warier his gaze gets.

"There's no guarantee we'd even find them."

The alternative is definitely not finding them, and I'm not okay with a person or people dying because we didn't try.

My throat feels tight as I push out one word. "*Please.*"

Wilde isn't thrilled that I'm making this our problem, but we know this forest better than anyone. An unspoken rule in this town is that we help people who need it, and whoever this is *definitely* needs it.

"Fine," he finally relents. "I'll talk to Lynx. If anyone is going to be able to hunt down a stray, it's him."

The doubt I'm feeling must come through on my face.

"I know, I know. He doesn't like to play nice, but if it means getting rid of strangers, he'll be on it. His whole job is to keep the pests away."

Considering he hasn't been able to accomplish that with the brothers is part of the reason he hates them so much.

"That's a good idea," Booker agrees, and it's not until he keeps speaking that I follow why he's so supportive. "And don't stress. If Lynx takes things too far, you know I'm here to put the stranger back together."

"So generous of you," Wilde deadpans.

"I'm always happy to help."

It wouldn't surprise me at all if he caused problems so he could fix them again. It's half of the reason Peril got so popular so quickly. Sure, it brings in good money, but Booker isn't short on patients to play with after each match. The thing about Booker is that he's a hard guy to read.

He has a sweet, innocent face, and his tone always feels so happy and warm. He's friendly and enthusiastic about every-thing, but sometimes my subconscious picks up on a vibe that's not quite right, even if I can't name exactly why.

I have another one of those moments when we climb back into the truck, me in the middle, and Booker turns his focus on me. His smile is genuine, and he scratches my head like someone would scratch a cat. "You're something special," he says, and everything about it is sincere and warm—but my suspicion kicks in anyway. "What I wouldn't give to see inside your brain."

There it is. Because I get the feeling when Booker says that, he doesn't mean figuratively, like he wants to know what makes me tick.

He's talking literally.

He wants to cut open my brain and see how it compares.

I bat his hand away and give him a grossed-out expression that makes him laugh.

"It's purely professional curiosity, my dear."

"It better be," Wilde says in his growly voice.

"You two are so serious." The sigh he lets out manages to sound disgruntled. "Since the exciting morning came to nothing, should we do something together? Drive down to Wayward for lunch? Help Lynx on his manhunt?" There's a brief pause. "Visit those delicious brothers?"

"You're not going near them."

"But Hudson and I are such good friends. I've seen his insides, after all."

His *what*?

Wilde grunts and throws Booker an unimpressed look. "It was a burn. Hardly his insides."

Booker's chubby cheeks stretch in an innocent smile. "We're close, is all. But he's yours. It's the other two I'm interested in getting to know because I have a feeling they'd be fun. The happy one sounds boring, but I've heard the other one is … my type of man."

My ears ring over the thought of him finding Kennedy boring. "He's not." It doesn't come out as loud as I want it to.

Booker turns curious eyes on me. "He's not my type?"

Of course he's going to make me talk. "Boring."

"Huh." His muddy brown gaze slides over me. "Good to know."

Before I can get the courage to say anything else, Wilde cuts in.

"And that's all you'll ever know. I've told you to stay away, and I mean it."

"I'm never allowed to have any fun."

"Bullshit. You have too much fun."

We turn back into the trees, headed for Lynx's place, and I keep my eye out for any unfamiliar faces. Booker and Wilde bicker between themselves, and for maybe the first time ever, I wish I could join them.

I'm sick of living on the outskirts.

Of that constant feeling of being here, but not here.

My confidence is too temporary, and even though I just spoke, I can't bring myself to do it again. Their conversation is fast and natural, and anything I say will drag it to a close.

I fucking hate this.

And I'm scared I'll always feel this way.

CHAPTER
EIGHT

One thing I hadn't realized until this very moment: I have no idea where Ziggy lives. I mean, I *knew that*, but it wasn't something I ever worried about knowing.

Except now it's been three days since I've seen him, so I'm worrying about it a lot. The next time we play hooky, I'm making him take me there so that I don't always have to wait for him to come to me.

"Do you know where Ziggy lives?"

Hudson's sitting on the floor not far from me, and he looks up from the plans he's checking over. "No. How would I know that?"

"Because Wilde showed you around. I thought you might have seen it."

"Why would he show me Ziggy's place?"

"I dunno. I've seen where that psycho Lynx lives."

Hudson tosses the plans aside and slides closer. "You have? Is it in a cave?"

"Nah, it's a little fairy-tale cabin type of thing."

My brother hums as he thinks. "Like Wilde's. Maybe we should burn it down?"

"Or maybe we don't anger the monster any more than we already have." There's a burning intensity inside Lynx that I don't want to see explode. Maybe I'm a wimp, or maybe I'm exercising basic self-preservation, but I have no interest in discovering the answer.

"You could take him," Hudson says like I was contemplating that in the first place.

"Not a theory I want to test out."

"So …" He turns his attention to balancing a nail on its head. "Why did you want to know about Ziggy?"

"He hasn't been around. I wanted to make sure he's okay."

He's quiet while he plays with the nail. The tiny *chicks* of it hitting the floor over and over swell between us. "You're a really good person, you know."

The comment catches me off guard. "I try to be. Don't always manage it though."

"You do more than you think."

"A good person wouldn't have messed up your relationship." I'm half holding my breath as I say that because I've wanted to bring it up properly ever since he got back, but there hasn't been a good time to do it without him getting mad again. The thing about Hudson is that getting mad is his way of covering all the other emotions lurking under the surface that he doesn't want to face. But I guess we're doing this now, and I just hope I've picked my moment right.

"Nah, I … You were right." He shrugs aggressively, like he's expecting me to rub it in. "We weren't talking. We didn't really know each other, and the fight fucking sucked, but it made him open up to me, so …"

I'm still not confident in their relationship, but what would I know? To me, romance is all about grand gestures and public affection, wanting to spend all of your time with the other person. That's never been Hudson, and I can't understand that way of loving. I probably never will.

"I'm glad things are going well."

He lets out an aggressive exhale. "I should never have called you a loser."

Something inside of me relaxes. It's as good an apology as I'll get from him, and the fact that he's bringing it up now proves that it's been on his mind since it happened. Did I like hearing that from my big brother? Not really. But I didn't let it get to me because I'm not in elementary school, and I know he only went there because he was hurting.

Hudson doesn't know how to hurt.

Just explode.

Whereas I've held hurt in my heart since my first girlfriend dumped me. It was a prickly lesson to learn that even when you think someone is more beautiful than the sky, they don't have to feel the same way back.

So I can handle being called a loser.

"You shouldn't have," I confirm. "We're good though. I've been called worse." Needy, clingy, suffocating, Mommy issues. It would be a lot easier to deny those things if they weren't partially true.

"No one should be calling you worse." He scowls, looking ready to fight all my past demons.

I give him a teasing shove. "I don't like when people are assholes to my brothers either. Now will you believe me when I say you deserve better?"

He glowers and turns back to the nail. "I already do."

"What?"

"Know that," he grumbles. "It's why I left when I did."

"I thought you left because Wilde broke up with you?"

"No, I left because he couldn't open up to me, and everything you kept telling me got into my head, and I realized that if Wilde couldn't even say he wanted me, then we were doomed already."

"Wait. *You* ended it?"

"Kind of."

I'm so happy, I could hug him. All of his past relationships have been horrible, and knowing that he's finally put his foot down fills me with more relief than I'm expecting it to. "You chose yourself."

"I guess." He dusts his hands off and pushes to his feet. "And so did Wilde. So it all worked out okay."

I know I should quit while I'm ahead, but I can't. "And if it didn't? If Wilde didn't step up, would you have come back? Would you have forgiven me?"

A small smile sneaks through his defenses. "I was never mad at you. Unfortunately, you're my safety, and Wilde wasn't here to yell at, so you caught it all. I shouldn't have done that. And I'm working on it."

"I've noticed."

"You have?" His messy eyebrows lift toward his hairline.

"I don't think I've heard you yell at anyone all week."

"It's a start."

"And we all start somewhere."

"You need to make motivational posters." He leaves, passing Hart in the doorway, who's back from his drive.

"What are you doing?" Hart asks, letting go of his tape measure with an aggressive *ziiiip* as he eyes where I'm sitting on the floor.

"Motivational posters, apparently."

"I think I'd be great at that," he deadpans. "Like … hang in there."

"That one's already taken."

"Yeah, but instead of having a cat, mine would have a picture of a noose."

I should have picked that he was going somewhere like that. "Sounds more demotivating to me."

"Art is up for interpretation." He points to the back frame of the house. "I think we went too short. I'm about to measure it, but we might need to bump out that back wall."

Of course we do. Nothing about this build is going to plan, and hoping that something as simple as a measurement would go smoothly feels like too much to ask for at this point.

"I'm not doing that today," I grumble.

"Did I say you had to?"

"I'm getting in before you do."

He ignores me. "Grab the end of this and stand there."

I grab the end of the tape measure and do as I'm told as Hart pulls it the length of the room.

He's quiet for a few moments.

"Is it too short?"

"Yes. But I think it's close enough that we can get away with it."

"Are you sure?"

He gives me a flat look. "What part of *I think* tells you I'm sure?"

I let the snark go. Having lived with Hart for my entire life, he doesn't get to me. Just like with Hudson, I know they have their own demons, and I love them no matter what. That's family. "I'm assuming you can find out?"

"Yes. I'll head into town tomorrow and call my guy."

I let go of the tape, and it zips loudly back into the holder.

"Or …" I'm pushing because he's gone more than he's here. "You could stay here and try to call. The reception picks up best on the road."

"*Or* I can drive to a slightly bigger shithole town and waste most of my day rather than spending it here. That sounds like the better option."

"What do you have against this place?"

"There are only so many times I can list how much I hate it."

"Then maybe you should give loving it a try."

His expression fills with disgust. "Should I love the smell? Or the constant work? Or our draining finances? Or the way someone out there wants to kill us? There's so many options, it makes it hard to pick."

"When you're determined to only see the bad, of course it's hard."

He lifts his hands either side of himself and looks around. "My bad. There's a lot of *timber* here too."

At least one of my brothers is heading in a good direction. And I'm working on myself too. Hart has always been the one of us who doesn't have ambition or drive or … passion, maybe? Whatever that flicker of something is that most people have pushing them along. It's absent with him.

Sometimes I want to know what's happening in his head, and other times I assume it would only scare me. I'm not going to give up on him, but Wilde's End might not be the answer like it was for Hudson, and I'm hoping it will be for me.

"And if you look outside," I say, matching his tone, "you'll see some trees. And the sky. And maybe even hear birds calling."

"Think the birds will still be calling after we flatten their home, or …"

"You're not going to put a dent in my good mood."

He plays with the tape measure, pulling it out and letting it snap back, over and over. "Never do. Wouldn't want you to end up like me anyway."

"Nothing wrong with being like you."

"Uh-huh," he monotones. "Say it again and I might believe you." There's a short pause. "Ziggy's out the front, by the way."

My gut flips suddenly. "Why didn't he come in?"

"I'm assuming it's hard to clean the car while it's out there and he's in here."

That isn't at all what I meant, but there's no point in arguing with Hart about it. Ziggy's been gone for days, and then he suddenly shows up to wash our car? It's not the first time he's done it, and no matter how many times I tell him not to, he ignores me. I'm really starting to see that Ziggy has a mind of his own. I like it.

I hurry for the front door, something inside me lighting up that he's back. I brush the dirt on my hands off onto my shorts, and I spot him the second I step outside. He looks exactly the same as he always does. He's in baggy jeans and a loose T-shirt, and his wild black hair is pulled back into that wire headband he always wears.

"Ziggy-zag!" I call on my way over, and his head snaps in my direction.

His whole face softens whenever he sees me, and I hope it's because he's comfortable with me around. Whatever the reason, I like that I get that reaction from him.

"I've told you that you don't have to wash our shit."

He rolls his eyes at me and turns to dip the sponge into the bucket. Talking or not talking, no one can call Ziggy a pushover.

I hate washing the car, but I'm not about to let him do it alone, so I grab a cloth floating in the soapy water and take the place beside him. His curious gaze runs over the side of my face, but I pretend not to notice.

Finally, I'm treated to the sound of his voice. Soft as the breeze and craggy like it crawled out of the depths to reach me. "What are you doing?"

"Helping." I shoot him a little wink and acknowledge the curiosity staring back at me this time. "I figure the sooner this is done, the sooner you can take me somewhere."

He tilts his head for me to go on.

"Maybe you can show me your favorite place. That would be cool, right?"

He goes back to washing the car without a response, and I have to trust that he's thinking about it. I want to ask him where he's been and what he's been doing, but those kinds of questions are the type that would overwhelm him and make him disappear on me. So I keep them inside, and instead of expecting him to tell me about it all, I stay silent.

Painfully, patiently silent.

Ziggy will show me when he's ready.

CHAPTER
NINE

ZIGGY

My favorite place in Wilde's End? My immediate thought is home. My mine. Where everything feels right, and I don't have to think about the outside world or force myself to act a certain way.

But I'm not taking Kennedy there.

Part of the reason is because it feels private, but the other part couldn't handle it if he saw my home and didn't like it. Kennedy's opinion means more to me than it should, and since my home is the only place where I've ever felt safe, I can't let anything disrupt that.

We finish cleaning the car, and even after polishing the tires, I still haven't come to a decision. There're only so many times I can check the window wipers are in good condition.

"So what are we doing?" Kennedy asks, dropping his rag back into the bucket with a splat. He's filthy from a day's work, hair a wild mess, but he's smiling because he's always smiling.

Without an answer for him, I want to turn and walk away, but that would mean not spending time with him, and after three days, I need this.

His presence pulls at me in a way no one else's does.

There are so many places in Wilde's End we could go; miles and miles of wilderness hide so many amazing things. The trails through the trees, the swimming hole, the jagged rocky outcrop by Hobby Straight that I like to watch the sunset from sometimes. Natural beauty is everywhere out here, but I want to hold Kennedy's interest in the same way Rooney did, and unless I'm going to suddenly fuck off my anxiety and start talking, I need something else.

Something fun.

The tire swing down on a quiet stretch of river flitters through my memories, and excitement tickles me at the thought of showing it to him. It's a hot day, and at least it should keep us entertained for a while.

I tap my temple and give his sleeve a tug. Whether he gets that I've had an idea or not, I have no clue, but he waves his hand ahead.

"Lead the way. After following you directly toward Lynx, I think I've proved that I'll follow you anywhere."

I muffle my laugh as I dig my elbow into his ribs, and Kennedy playfully grabs both my shoulders to shake me. We leave the road and walk past the old shops as we jostle and shove each other, and I'm almost able to get lost in the moment of being with a friend.

"Where are you taking me this time, huh? A cliff face to push me off? A sinkhole where no one will ever find my body." His fingers squirm against my stomach, and a giggle slips out as I slap his hand away. "You're so feisty. You're going to kill me with your bare hands, aren't you?"

If he doesn't stop tickling me, I might. I hate being tickled, but for him to do it, he has to get close enough, touch me, and I can't say I hate being touched. Still, I glare at him to show how stupid I think that comment is. He's completely unaffected.

Just like he said though, he doesn't question following me once. I lead him through narrow paths with sheer drops on one side, then through stretches of forest where there is no path, only knee-high, scratchy grass and speckled patches of sun that have to fight past the thick tree coverage.

We're on a narrow, single-person track, and Kennedy's close behind me, his whistle filling in the still day and bringing it alive.

I wish I knew how to be so perfectly content in every moment, but that will never be me.

We reach the stretch of river that I found by accident and like to come to when it's hot as hell. Like today. There's a large, flat rock overhanging the water that heats up in the sun and is perfect for lying on while I dry off. The huge oak on the other side has a tire swing that I've never used, and we're sheltered in a small part of the river that dips inward, creating a secluded natural cove.

"This is pretty," Kennedy says, stepping past me. "Wish I'd brought my swim shorts."

Swim shorts. Fuck.

It isn't something I thought of because I normally come here alone, so getting naked isn't an issue. Getting naked in front of Kennedy? I might die. I run my tongue piercing behind my teeth, trying to convince myself that this is nothing. We're friends. He won't glance at me twice. It's not like I have to get all the way naked either, but even contemplating it feels like a lot.

With nerves threatening to make me feel sick, I strip off my T-shirt and reach for my jeans. The denim is too hot anyway, but I like being covered. I like hiding in my clothes, and the way my heart is heavily thumping only reminds me of how exposed I'm about to be.

But even with how tense I am ... I don't *want* to hide from him.

When I'm down to my briefs, I pull my gaze away from the water and over to him, just in time to see his eyes drop to my chest and slowly run downward. My skin prickles under his attention.

As soon as he notices me watching, his eyes snap back to mine, and he grins. "Good idea."

Then Kennedy strips off before I'm ready for it.

Lots and lots of golden skin, big shoulders, a soft belly, and strong legs. His briefs are tight, and I refuse to look at that area, or my face might actually catch fire.

A loud exhale leaves him. "I didn't realize how hot today was."

He means the weather, obviously. There's no way his body is overheating the way mine is. I need a distraction, and fast, because if I stand here too much longer, my cock will definitely give me away.

Instead of tugging him like I normally would, I point toward the swing.

"Think it will take my weight?" he asks as we approach.

I squint up at the weathered rope, but it still looks thick and strong. I take hold of one side of the tire, and like he can read my mind, he grabs the other side. We both pull down hard against it, but the rope doesn't give, so I take that as a good sign.

"Only way to know is to test it, I guess," he says.

That's true. I set a foot on the tire, prepared to go up, when Kennedy's face drops.

"I don't mean *you*."

I *tsk* at the worry in his voice. Of course it's going to be me. I'm lighter than he is; it's the basic process of elimination.

"What if you get hurt?"

Then it will save him from being hurt. While I appreciate him looking out for me, I get this a lot. This ... *suffocating* kind of protection. There might be some wires crossed between my brain and my mouth, and I might be scrawnier than him or Wilde, but it doesn't mean I'm helpless. I like people looking out for me; I don't like being babied.

I stare Kennedy down until he lets go of the tire with a laugh. "Okay, okay. But if it breaks on you, I'm going to feel really bad."

I can guarantee I'll feel worse in that scenario.

I climb up onto the tire and then gesture for him to give me a push. I've never done this before, but I assume once he gives me a solid shove, all I have to do is let go once I'm over the water. I already know it's deep enough.

"Ready?" he asks, pulling me back, but before Kennedy lets me go, he chokes out, "*Goddamn*, Ziggy."

I glance down and find my ass in line with his face, but before I can ask—before I can even *think* to ask—anything else, he lets go.

My gut performs a painful somersault as I fly forward, and I'm still so focused on the moment I left behind that I almost forget to let go. My hands loosen on the rope, and I'm suspended for a freeing moment before I drop.

I plunge beneath the surface, cool water wrapping around me, and I fight the buoyancy to dive deeper, loving the coolness on my overheated skin. Under here, there's no Kennedy, there's no awkwardness, just murky water in every direction.

Until the muffled sound of another body breaking water comes, and a few seconds later, Kennedy appears. He swims toward me, hair a fluffy cloud around his head, and doesn't stop until he's a foot or two away. We blink at each other, and down here, we feel equal. A world without words, just every emotion playing across our faces.

Kennedy drifts closer. Closer. At first, I assume it's the current, but then his face is leaning in, his eyes close, and he … it kind of … I think he's going to *kiss* me.

Nerves explode in my gut, and I know there's no way it will happen, no way he'd want to, but he's inches away and still moving into my space and—

He blows all his air out in a burst, bubbles exploding in my face, and I almost react before I remember I'm holding my breath.

I kick to the surface and suck in so much oxygen my vision goes wobbly for a second. Somehow, Kennedy made me forget I need oxygen to exist, and when he appears right after me, it's easy to see why.

Kennedy is normally attractive.

With wet hair and the water reflecting off those eyes, he's stunning.

"Your hair is everywhere," he says, affection heavy in his tone. He moves closer, and before I know what he's doing, he pulls out my headband and runs a hand back over my hair. The usual strands in my vision disappear before he tucks the rest behind my ears. His hands linger, his eyes soft, and I wait for him to look his fill, hating the way I'm searching his eyes for approval.

Something in his gaze lights up. "I almost forgot there was a face under there."

I cup my hands and send a barrage of water his way, putting distance between us as his laugh rings out through the cove.

"Let's do that again!"

I take the headband back and wave him ahead, still reeling from how I thought he might kiss me and how desperately I wanted him to. It was a ridiculous thing to assume, *stupid, useless, inconsiderate*, so the disappointment kicking in shouldn't be this intense.

I leave the water behind and lie back on my sunning rock, watching Kennedy take turn after turn on the swing. His enthusiasm for everything makes me smile, makes me *happy*, and I know I'll never be larger than life in the way he is, but I don't want to be.

Seeing him enjoy himself is enough.

It takes way too long for him to get over it, and once my briefs are dry, I grab my shirt and pull it back on to avoid being burned.

"I needed that," he says, flopping back on the rock like a seal, droplets of water flinging everywhere. "We should do this again."

I nod so he knows that I'd like that.

"I really love Wilde's End," he continues. "This place is the perfect example. It's like a hidden paradise, and I bet there are so many other great spots like this one."

Wilde's End is as familiar to me as a city. The trails are the streets, the trees are direction markers, and everywhere I go has a destination I'm traveling to. I can understand why it's all so fascinating and mysterious to Kennedy, but I doubt he'll feel the same once the newness wears off. I'm about to get up the courage to ask him when he continues.

"Maybe I'll bring Hartwell here. He's so determined to be negative about everything, but this place has to change his mind. He used to have fun—maybe this will remind him what that was like."

What kind of fun? It's a perfectly normal, average question that will keep the conversation going. Something easy to start with. Something that will keep Kennedy interested in talking. I repeat the line in my head, get familiar with it and how to make it sound. I'm about to push the words out when he chuckles to himself.

"I bet there'd be something wrong with … I don't know, the color of the water or … the sun being too hot."

Like that, my chance to ask is gone. Frustration flickers in my chest. I *want* to be part of the conversation. Normally, I love that Kennedy can carry it by himself. It's helped me get comfortable with him, taken the pressure out of spending time with him, but moments like this, where I want to be involved, it hurts to not get the chance.

I want it to make a difference that I'm here.

"Damn, the sun's *so* warm," he moans happily, stretching out. Before I can agree, he continues. "I'm probably getting burned, and I don't even care." Another short pause. "You know, the sky is my favorite thing in maybe the whole wide world." Words are clawing at my throat. "It's so big, you know? Just covers everything. Goes so far." There's another short gap, and as he opens his lips to continue, I lean over and cover his mouth with my hand.

His eyes fly wide in surprise, and I squeeze mine closed so I don't get intimidated by his expression. I don't want to see curiosity or worry or surprise or any of it.

I want to be *involved*.

I have so many questions stockpiled for Kennedy that I don't even know which to start with. My hands are shaking, and somewhere deep in my soul, the wrong kinds of words echo, like scars that will never fade. *Weird, loser, talk like a girl …*

My deep inhale burns in my lungs, and I hold it for a moment before breathing out again.

I'm at the river. I'm with Kennedy.

He wouldn't know the first thing about being mean.

Instead of asking a question about him, different words come. Ones that offer up a small piece of myself to him.

"I like … spending time … with you."

CHAPTER
TEN

KENNEDY

Ziggy's eyes are squashed closed, but those whispered words pull at something in my gut. I'm smiling hard behind his hand, and I have so many things I want to say back, but I've sort of blinked offline.

His eyes peek open as he slowly releases my mouth.

"If you like hanging out with me so much," I start, throat strangled with something I can't place, "why the hell did you disappear for three whole days?"

I'm expecting him to shrug me off, but he doesn't. He doesn't answer either. I sit up to see him closer, and I'm about to rephrase the question into a yes or no one for him, when his hand slaps over my mouth again.

He's breathing deeply, eyes locked on the rock under us this time, and I study him, trying to figure out what's going on.

"I was busy," he murmurs, lips barely moving, like he's scared to open his mouth too much.

Wait … like he's *scared?*

It suddenly clicks what's happening here. Keeping me quiet,

the steady breathing, the slight tremor in his arm … he's working really hard at this.

"You don't need to talk if it's too much for you," I reassure him. "I like spending time with you too. Whether you talk or not, it's fun." Because as much as I want to push him to talk *more*, I don't want him to be uncomfortable.

It's the wrong thing to say, though, because Ziggy scowls at me.

"I'm sorry," I quickly add, shifting closer. "Don't get grumpy with me. I don't know what I'm supposed to say." But after that reaction, and the way he got cranky with me for not letting him try the swing first, plus how he acted when I spoke for him with Lynx …

"Should try being me." His lips twitch, and it takes me a second.

"Wait. That was a joke."

He stares at me.

"You just made a *joke*."

Ziggy's trying to look annoyed with me, but there's amusement in his big, brown eyes. His hair has dried the way I fixed it, and I'm able to make out all of his features for once. The little nose, his expressive eyes, those deep red lips that hold so many secrets. His piercings somehow enhance all of his best features as well. The piercings at the end of each eyebrow, with a bar through the top of his nose, draw my attention to his eyes. The two under his bottom lip and the septum piercing all frame out his lips. I've always known Ziggy was cute, but after seeing that long, lean body, his perky butt, and the way he's watching me now … attraction kicks up in my gut.

Attraction that I absolutely will not be acting on.

"Do you want to keep talking?" I ask, voice lower than normal.

He's about to nod when he catches himself. "Yes."

Happiness floods me. He doesn't give me more than that, and

I figure I'll have to be the one to lead the conversation, but I don't have an issue with that.

"How old are you?" I ask, starting easy. If this is my chance to get to know him, I'm going to get as many of the important, quick things out of the way as I can. When he doesn't answer, I'm about to fill in the silence on impulse, but then I remember him covering my mouth, like he was asking for time. So I swallow the words and give it to him.

"Twenty-eight."

I probably could have guessed that, now that I can actually see his face. "I'm thirty. I think I look way older than you though."

He studies me for a second. "You have happy lines." Every word sounds like it's costing him energy, and the way he pauses after he speaks to check my reaction has curiosity at what he's looking for gnawing at me. He reaches for me, and his thumb brushes softly beside my eye. "Here."

Goose bumps chase each other over my skin, spreading outward from his touch. "Did you call me wrinkly? How *dare* you."

He snatches his hand back, like he thinks I'm being serious.

"I'm joking, Ziggy."

The tension leaves his shoulders, and I get a small smile. "Asshole."

It's an insult, I know that, but my body reacts to the word in a completely different way. To distract myself, I ask, "How long have you been here?"

"Eight years."

"Then … you were twenty. Where did you live before here?"

"Lincoln. Near Sacramento."

"I'm from Lancaster. Grew up near LA, but the three of us got out of there as soon as we could. Too busy. Too many bad memories."

"Like?"

"Our parents were mostly absent. Hudson had issues. It was a lot, but we got through it. Can I ask … about the talking? It's like you're scared of it. Did something happen?"

He pulls his bottom lip between his teeth, and when he releases it, it's puffier than usual. I pull my gaze away as Ziggy shakes his head roughly.

Okay, new topic.

Something lighter.

"How do you date out here? I'm assuming you don't have a girlfriend … boyfriend?" I'm fishing, and I'm not subtle about it. "Considering you spend a lot of time with me."

He turns his attention to his fingers. "I don't."

"You don't date? What a tragedy to keep yourself away from all those girls … boys?"

He flicks me with the back of his hand, and his smile tells me he's picked up on what I'm asking. "I'm … umm … gay."

Ooof, hello, nerves. They swim happily in my gut, and I shift closer again. "But no boyfriend?"

His smile widens until it lights up his eyes. "No. Never."

"*Never*? Lies!"

He almost laughs, and I'm just gaping, wondering how the hell all the queer men ever let him get away from Lincoln.

Then he whispers, "I'm not easy to get to know."

I can't argue about that, but I do know that every minute of the last month or so that I've known him has been worth it to get to this point. It's not coming easily to him, but he doesn't feel like he's fighting every word now either.

"Anyone who doesn't take the time is missing out." My words don't give him the boost I'm hoping for though.

"Sweet, but … doesn't help … the loneliness."

Loneliness? Ziggy's *lonely*? While I know he's quiet and doesn't leave Wilde's End much, I never would have guessed. I assumed everyone who lives out here likes their solitude.

Was that his real reason for helping us? He wanted to be around people?

Thankfully, I'm already dry, and I sling an arm around Ziggy's shoulders. "No more being lonely. You have me. Which is lucky because I *really* need you. I love my brothers, but they're such pains in the ass, and I need you to keep me sane out here."

"Sane?"

"Yes. Because I am also not dating anyone. I've been banned."

"Banned?"

I tilt my head side to side. "Well, *I've* banned myself. Dating only gets you into trouble, and I have a lot of issues with being clingy, so I've sworn off it. We'll be two best bachelors, living the bachelor life together and keeping each other company. Doesn't that sound awesome?" Because while I don't want Ziggy to feel lonely, I also don't want to feel that way either. I like being around people, and I really, really like being around him.

He slowly shifts around so my arm falls away, and I lie back, smooth rock hot against my back. "You should date."

"Why?" I ask, but it's rhetorical. "So that I can smother my date with affection, make them hate me, and then walk away brokenhearted? Been there, done that too many times."

"Smother?"

I wave a hand like I don't care, but I *do* care. I want to be able to show someone how much I love them without having to hold back. "I come on strong. Nothing creepy, but I like to show people what they mean to me, and apparently, buying lots of gifts or showing up for a spontaneous weekend away or calling to make sure they got home from the date safely is *too much, Kenny.*" I put on a joking tone that matches how much of a joke some people think I am. Normally, it doesn't get to me, but talking to Ziggy is easy. He's never given the impression he's judging me, and I've never met someone who feels like they're hanging off my every word.

"That … actually sounds nice," he says.

"What? Being too much?"

He dips his head, and for a second, I worry that's all I'm going to get. "Having someone care like that."

I meet his gaze, and this heavy moment of understanding passes between us. It's a lingering thing, like every fresh hurt we've ever experienced is laid out between us, and Ziggy makes a whole lot more sense to me. He craves connection as deeply as I do.

"You know what … I've got you."

He studies me like he's trying to pull the meaning from my face. And maybe he doesn't have words for what he wants to ask, or maybe I talk too soon, but I want to make sure he's following.

"We're friends. Bachelor bros. I get lonely too. Even with my brothers around, sometimes it makes it worse. I want someone who understands me, you know."

His lips clamp together before he turns away. Ziggy's small nod is his only answer, and I vow, silently and to myself, that I am going to make sure he knows how much his friendship means to me. I'm going to care about him so damn hard he won't know what's hit him.

But he's closed himself off to the conversation, so it's time to move on. Take advantage of his words while I have them.

"Hey, what about *this* action for me?" I ask, wrapping my arms tightly around myself. "Because I'm clingy. Get it?"

He immediately rejects the idea.

"I didn't realize you were so picky about these names."

"I'm not."

"Well, you can't tell me that doesn't work. It's like a clingy koala. That's me. I'm the koala."

The dry look I get back reminds me so much of Hart.

"Fine, but we're going to find something. I want a name. I feel left out."

Something brightens his face, but he keeps it to himself.

"You going to share whatever made you happy just now?"

His expression turns sly, and he still doesn't say anything.

"Fine. Keep your secrets." I tuck my hands behind my head and close my eyes against the sun. Our conversation might be over, but his soft voice still consumes me. Our conversation has given my whole self a boost, and I'm in one of those rare moods where I can't stress or worry about anything when I'm this happy.

I turn his way, but when I open my eyes, he's not looking at me.

Well, he's not looking at *my face*.

Ziggy's gaze is running over my body, and either he's gotten sunburned really quickly, or his face is red from something else. Something else that is slowly making my blood warm as well.

I quickly close my eyes before he realizes he's been caught because I think I want him to keep looking. I want to give him the freedom to check me out and appreciate me, the same way I was subtly doing to him earlier.

We're just two men, appreciating the view that Mother Nature has gifted us with.

And I've thankfully sworn off dating at the right time.

Making a move on Ziggy would only end in disaster, like every person I've tried to date before him, and I have a suspicion that losing my new friend would be worse than any heartbreak I've had so far.

We'll both have to stay content with looking. Friends picture each other naked all the time.

Absolutely nothing wrong with it.

CHAPTER
ELEVEN

ZIGGY

"I can't remember the last time I went fishing," Kennedy says. He's sitting to my left, holding a fishing rod with one hand and a can of Coke in the other. Every time he reels something in, his elbow skims my elbow, and air keeps getting caught in my throat.

I'm haunted by the image from yesterday of a near naked Kennedy, wet briefs hugging his cock, lazed out on the warm rock like a lizard in the sun. He was soaking up every ray of happiness, like I do when I'm around him.

Like I'm doing right now.

All up and down my body, little sparks and zaps are distracting me from fishing and making me hyperaware of the man beside me.

"Do you do this often?"

Kennedy's watching me, giving me the chance to answer without words. I really, really don't want to do that, but his proximity is taking up too much of my focus to add speaking on top.

I nod. Fishing isn't something I do constantly, but it's relaxing in the summer to sit by the water and see what I can catch. I eat fish, even if I don't love the taste that much, but I know some of the others really like it, and I'm always happy to share around whatever I walk away with.

Especially with Lynx.

"Can you bring me with you next time?" he asks. "I like it."

I duck my head to try and hide my thoughts, but I can still feel his eyes on me. The lingering, searching gaze is heated against my skin, and when I finally give in and meet it, he's closer than I remember.

My gut is a twisted pot of nerves as I force myself to keep looking. "S-sure."

"Thanks." His answering smile is everything. So swift and effortless, like the sun breaking free of heavy storm clouds and reminding you of how bright the world is.

"Do you ever do this with anyone else?"

No.

Wilde has come a couple of times, and Rooney joins me occasionally, but those are all sporadic moments. Most of the time, it's me and the sky and the river stretching off in both directions.

Alone.

"I think I've got another one!" Kennedy excitedly starts reeling the fish in, his arm rubbing torturously against mine. Bare skin on skin.

He pulls the fish free, and it's a good-sized one. I immediately open the cooler while he removes the hook, and then we stash it away with the others.

I bring my line back in and stand.

"Wait, that's it?"

As much as I'd love to stay out here for longer and fish the river dry, we have what we need. I pick up the cooler to show him we're done, and Kennedy immediately takes my fishing rod from me and rests them over his shoulder.

We start back down the forest path, Kennedy a few steps behind me.

"We could go swimming again?" he suggests.

After seeing him naked yesterday and nearly giving myself away in front of him? No way. I shake my head.

"What about … exploring some more? You could show me around?"

It's getting late, and we've already had a long day of work. I *want* to show him around, but I'm always worried about spending too much time with him. The more I do, the deeper I fall for his voice and his energy and his big heart. And the deeper I fall, the less I trust myself not to act on those feelings.

"What about getting a drink at the Cutty? Or … your place! I still haven't seen it."

Before he can push that thought any more, I turn to face him. Kennedy pauses, rocking back on his heels, free hand tucked into one of his pockets as his gaze sweeps over me.

"That could be fun … right?"

"No." I couldn't think of anything less fun than Kennedy seeing my home.

"Okay, umm … I'm open to ideas. We can do anything."

Anything … His eyes are hesitant as they meet mine, and a smile trembles his mustache.

"If you wanna hang out, that is." He pokes me in the shoulder. "Unless you're sick of me already."

I bat his finger away and tap the cooler. "Dinner."

He lights up, and I tell my excitement to ignore it. "Yeah? You'll stay for dinner? That's awesome. Hudson and Hart will be nice, I promise. And I can cook, but …" He squints at the cooler. "I don't know how to prep the fish."

"Wilde does."

"Oh. So we'll invite Wilde, then. I guess."

He needs to get over this grudge he has because I don't get the impression that Hudson and Wilde are coming to an end anytime soon. Kennedy might not think they're serious, but Wilde's never been involved with someone before, and the fact that he is now says all I need it to.

I tilt my head the way we were walking, suggesting we keep moving.

"Yeah. Let's go. Now you've mentioned it, I'm starving."

Kennedy leads the way, and I know how he feels.

But as my attention drifts down to his ass, I'm hungry for something different. My need for him is getting out of control, and I'm worried it will take the smallest thing for me to slip.

At least at dinner, with people around, there will be fewer chances for that to happen.

This is all going to be okay.

CHAPTER
TWELVE

KENNEDY

Working side by side with Wilde as he wordlessly walks me through how to descale and prepare the fish for cooking is awkward as fuck. He grunts at me, I try not to glare at him, and the entire time, I'm overly aware of Ziggy sitting silently a few feet away while Hart and Hudson bicker between themselves like he's not even there.

The least they could do is pretend to include him in the conversation.

All the way through cooking dinner, I'm on edge. It's not the fun, relaxing dinner I thought it would be. I'm torn between assessing every interaction between Hudson and Wilde, and Ziggy.

And honestly, it's mostly Ziggy. I should be more worried about my brother than I am, but I can't get my eyes to focus anywhere but on my friend. He's so … he's just so …

I drop the cooking utensils so many times I worry if I've overdone it today, and when dinner is finally plated up, it's a relief to finally sit down. Ziggy's in my usual camping chair, with Hart across from him and Wilde and Hudson testing the structural integrity of the third, so I grab the cooler, set it next to Ziggy, and sit on that instead.

His big eyes meet mine, and he pats the arm of the chair he's on.

"I'm good," I promise him. Considering I'm already thinking ahead for ways to have him stick around after dinner, there's no way I'm letting him out of that chair. Besides, making sure he's comfortable is more important to me than getting a numb ass.

"Does it taste okay?" I ask almost as soon as he's put the first piece of fish into his mouth. "Do you like it?"

He chews for a second and swallows, and then a quizzical look crosses his face.

"The fish, is it …" I'm leaning forward, and it occurs a second too late that maybe I'm being *too* eager. "Good?" I finish, wishing I could swallow my words again.

His nod is small.

"I could grab some salt or pepper … we also have ketchup, if that's your thing?"

Ziggy sets his hand on my thigh, which I didn't even notice was bouncing anxiously, and his touch sends a bolt of want right to my cock. Jesus. I swallow tightly.

"It's good," he whispers.

Right. Space. Give him that so he can talk. Even though I know that's how it works for him, it's hard to remember when I've been so on edge all day. Ziggy is bringing out all these soft, protective feelings I really like, and it's been a while since I had someone I enjoy spending time with.

"Sorry," I say back, matching his volume. "Just wanted to make sure."

"You made sure."

It's like my whole body swells at the sound of his voice. After yesterday, I'd hoped we'd turned a corner with communicating, but today, he's barely said more than a few words. "Are you snarking me?"

He tries to hide his smile by having another bite. But I wait him out. "You deserved to be snarked at."

"Oh, really."

"You're fussing over me."

His words still don't have much confidence behind them, but they seem to be coming easier. "Sorry that I care."

"I like it … that you care." His smile turns sly. "But I'm a grown-ass adult who will tell you if your fish is shit."

I bark out a loud laugh before I can stop myself. It's less from amusement and more because Ziggy caught me completely off guard.

"You choking?" Hart asks.

"I'm good. I'm good."

"Great. But if you do start choking, do it silently. Some of us are trying to enjoy our dinner."

I flip him off, and when I turn my dopey grin back on Ziggy, he's glaring Hart's way.

"He's joking," I assure him.

Ziggy doesn't answer, just glares deeper.

"Hey …" This time, I tap his thigh to pull his attention back to me. "If I can't fuss over you, you can't be all stabby over me." I'm saying it because I'm supposed to, but I can't say I hate the way Ziggy is offended on my behalf. It gives the impression he cares, and I'd almost forgotten what that's like.

I'd almost forgotten about, well, all of this. Feeling that closeness to someone. That addictive want to be around them. Knowing that he makes me happy just by being here.

"You've barely spoken all day," I point out. "Is it something that comes and goes?"

He nods.

"And it's gone now?"

His laugh is quick and soft. "N-no. I … it's harder. For me."

"Do I make it hard?"

He shakes his head hard, eyes meeting mine. "You make it easy."

Those four words, barely louder than a breath, bring my heart alive. All I've ever wanted was to make things easier for the people I care about, and when it comes to Ziggy, I haven't even actively *tried*. I've only been myself.

Something that's never been enough for anyone before.

He doesn't know all the annoying, messed-up sides to me yet, so I know that will change eventually, but for now … well, for now, it feels really fucking amazing.

Ziggy sees me. And I hope he knows I need him to.

I've never had this kind of bone-deep friendship before, and I want to cling to it and refuse to let go.

But I won't. Because that's not a normal thing that friends do.

That reminder doesn't stop me from pushing my luck though. "Want to make that trip into Wayward tomorrow? Look up solar things?" I'm holding my breath, waiting for an answer. The way I want him to say yes is gripping me, but I refuse to show it outwardly.

If Ziggy wants to spend time with me, he will.

If he doesn't, well, I'll just hole up in bed for the next week and cry about what a failure of a human I am.

His pretty lips pull up in the corners, and it's impossible not to watch them. "Okay."

I exhale. "Okay."

CHAPTER
THIRTEEN

ZIGGY

Leaving Wilde's End isn't something I enjoy. Out there, past the trees and the safety of the familiar, people are unpredictable and mean. I'm safe here.

I leave, but only when I need to. Getting solar power hooked up to the town was a lot of trial and error. Solar isn't something I'd ever learned about, so when I started the project, I needed more help than playing with parts could get me. Rooney found people who knew what they were doing, and they helped me learn everything I could.

And then I came right back home again.

I remind myself, yet again, that it's only for the day. Just a few hours to go with Kennedy, look up whatever we need to, and then come back here. He'll be with me the entire time, and he might have been the one to say that he'll follow me anywhere, but that goes both ways.

When it comes to getting to spend time with him, I don't think there's anything I wouldn't do.

Kennedy is waiting for me, leaning against the hood of his car, wearing denim jeans that hug his thick thighs and a button-down that looks fancier than anything I've seen him wear before.

Wish I'd gotten the memo that we're dressing up. Though it's not like that would have mattered when I own exactly three outfits. Well, *two*, considering I couldn't find my favorite shirt this morning.

And even in my oversized T-shirt and jeans, Kennedy's face splits into a grin when he spots me.

"I was starting to get scared you'd changed your mind."

From spending time with him? Impossible.

I round the car to climb into the passenger seat, and it takes me a second to realize that he was watching me expectantly. We make eye contact through the window, and then he shrugs and joins me in the cab.

"I'll figure you out yet," he says, starting the car. "After yester-day, I assumed that you needed time to answer, and since *I* talk so much, I thought you didn't bother around me because I never shut up. But that's not it, is it?"

I could say the word *no*, but it's not worth the effort when I can shake my head instead.

"Interesting …"

There's nothing about me that's interesting. Kennedy's impression of me has grown to the point that I'm scared that if I do get comfortable enough around him to talk beyond a couple of forced and rehearsed sentences, I'm going to shock him with the reality. There's nothing interesting. Or delicate. Or fun. I'm a useless, pathetic waste of space, and I hate that he's going to figure it out one day.

The constant battle I have with myself over wanting us to get closer and not wanting him to discover all my broken pieces is endless.

"We'll head to the diner today," he says, cutting through my nosediving thoughts. "They have free Wi-Fi, and I can buy you lunch."

I'm about to decline his offer, but Kennedy turns away from me quickly. "What's that? Thank you, Kenny? Oh, you're welcome, Ziggy. It's the least I can do since you're working with us and not letting us pay you."

I glare at the side of his face, and while he doesn't acknowledge the evil eye, I know he can feel it.

"Ziggy, stop," he whines in that same over-the-top voice. "I know I'm amazing and so generous, but you don't have to keep thanking me. You're embarrassing me now."

I throw up my hands because there's no arguing with him. Kennedy risks a quick look over from the corner of his eyes, and even though I give him my sternest expression, his smile doesn't waver.

"You look like an evil kitten."

A kitten? What the hell?

"*Yes*, a kitten." His teasing is as irritatingly attractive as always. "You're so cute and little."

I'm taller than he is!

"Yeah, yeah. We're close to the same height, but that doesn't mean anything. You've got a sweet little face, and I bet if you could talk right now, you'd be telling me to fuck off." He looks over again. "I'm right, aren't I?"

If he wants a response, I'll give him one. In the form of my middle finger.

Kennedy barks out a laugh and grabs my finger, giving it a gentle squeeze. "See? I'm learning. I told you that I'd figure you out, and I meant it."

Why he'd want to waste his time is beyond me. Still, a tiny trickle of warmth streams into my stomach that he's actually making the effort. He'll end up disappointed, but that's on him. The problem is that I'm going to end up disappointed as well because no matter how much I try to live up to his opinion of me, I'll never come close.

Goddammit.

Despite what the voices in my head say, I *know* I'm not a bad person. Why shouldn't I deserve someone like Kennedy? All those past relationships of his didn't know how to treat him right, and if I had his attention, if he smothered me in it, made me the center of his universe, I'd worship the hell out of him every goddamn day.

I'd treat Kennedy the way he deserves.

So if he's going to try to get to know me, I'm going to try and let him in.

Feeling like I've been possessed, breath bottled in my lungs, I reach over and dip my fingers into the hair at the base of his skull. It's slightly dry and fluffy, long enough to twist through my grip.

"Ziggy?" he asks, surprised, but doesn't pull away.

I focus on two words. Just two. It's important to me to get them out so he knows that I don't take him for granted. That I appreciate the way he's here, just to be here, and doesn't expect more than what I can give him.

It's what makes me want to give him everything I can.

And when I finally let the words go, it's relief. "Thank you."

The diner is louder than I was expecting. I like it. Mostly because people leave us alone to get on with our work, and sitting in this booth, pressed tighter to Kennedy's side than I strictly need to be to see the screen, it feels like we're in our own little bubble.

Am I deluding myself?

Of course. This isn't real, and it never will be, but he's letting me sit this close and get away with it, so I plan to take full advantage. I spent the first little while being fascinated by how much technology has changed since I've been off the grid, but slowly, that fascination strayed from the screen to his fingers.

For hands that look like they're made to be hauling timber and tearing apart insulation, his fingers move surprisingly nimbly over the keys. He talks through everything he's doing, and I'm smart enough to follow along while being completely fucking enamored by him.

My heart hasn't stopped all the little, sudden hiccups since we sat down. The smallest things bring it on, from him asking my opinion on site layout, to him having me point out what I want from the menu so he could order for me, to him chuckling over my amazement at his phone.

I dunno, Kennedy's just a considerate guy. Growing up, my parents were more focused on working themselves into the ground to survive than anything else. In Wilde's End, we're a community, and we work together, but we're still very much loners.

I've never had real friends, so I don't know if this is how it normally is, but I don't care. All I want is to focus on Kennedy. Maybe it's some aspect of him being a shiny new toy or me becoming legitimately obsessed with what a perfect person he is, but I can't stop thinking about him. Craving him. Wanting to be around him and nowhere else.

"Hey, Kenny."

The cute voice makes me look up suddenly, and my gut lurches at the sight of a gorgeous woman in the diner uniform. Her curls are pulled back messily, and she has big lips and even bigger eyes. Eyes that are currently focused on the man beside me.

"Hey, Caroline. Late start today?"

"Had to take Mom for a doctor's visit. Glad I got here in time to see you though." Her gaze dips to his shirt. "You're looking smart today."

All the warmth and happiness from today disappears, like her flirty tone is the poison to my happiness. Kennedy doesn't immediately answer her, but when I look over at him, he's wearing the same smile he normally directs at me. Is *she* why we came here?

Why he dressed up? Work was a convenient excuse for him to get to see this … this …

I look her over, and my lips pull back in a sneer.

"This is Ziggy," Kennedy says suddenly. "Ziggy, this is Caroline. She makes the best latte I've ever tasted."

Caroline pulls her eyes to me. "Nice to meet you, Ziggy. Is that a nickname?"

I stare at her until the friendly expression fades.

"He's shy," Kennedy tells her, giving my shoulder a squeeze. I don't know if it's supposed to be a warning to play nice with his girlfriend or a gesture of support, but I don't care. They're both lucky my voice is stuck, or I'd be telling her to go and thirst after some other guy.

"Aww, you're so cute," she offers, not picking up on my *go away* vibes. "You know what? I'm going to sneak you both a slice of cake."

"You don't have to—" Kennedy tries, attempting to be polite as always.

"Hush, you." She bats her notepad toward Kennedy. "Anything for my favorite customer and his cute friend."

She leaves us, and there's no doubt in my mind that her friendliness has nothing to do with wanting a good tip.

I'm completely caught off guard by the sick feeling growing thick and fast in my gut. There's a nasty little voice reminding me that this woman is exactly the type of person Kennedy should be with. Sweet, pretty, easy to talk to. But the thought of him being with anyone but me is excruciating. Especially when I notice that he watched her walk away.

"You like her." My voice is so weak, I'm not sure he's heard me, but then he turns his attention my way.

"Caroline?"

I nod, bracing myself for his response.

Kennedy sighs, and my chest twists painfully when he doesn't immediately deny it. "She gave me her number last time I was here."

There it is. My teeth clench so hard I hear them crunch together.

"I gave it back to her." His tone takes on a hint of something softer. "I like her enough as a person to know that I don't want to lead her on. I've fallen in love too many times, and the next time I do it, I want to be sure. I want it to be for the last time." His speckled green eyes meet mine suddenly. "I want to fall in love with someone who'll appreciate it, Ziggy. Because there has to be *someone*."

Me. I'll appreciate it. I'd savor every goddamn minute of it. The problem though?

I have no idea what love is.

I've never been given it. I've never felt it. I've never been able to get familiar with the look and shape and texture of something too many people take for granted.

Caroline drops off the cake, interrupting our moment, and the hopeful smile she gives Kennedy isn't returned. For one brief, unwanted second, I understand what she's feeling.

Then I go back to hating her.

We eat the cake, and Kennedy switches back to work, and while he's not watching, I swipe his phone off the table. He told me his passcode earlier, so I unlock it and open the browser. Using a phone similar to this is a vague memory that doesn't feel real.

Then I type into the search box.

What is love?

I scour entry after entry while he works.

When I'm done, I'm more confused than ever.

CHAPTER
FOURTEEN

KENNEDY

t's darker than I'm expecting when we leave the diner, thanks to the heavy clouds pressing overhead. I'm guessing we're about to be in for one of those freak afternoon storms that hit suddenly and disappear just as quickly.

"Maybe we should wait out the rain," I suggest.

Ziggy tips his head up to the sky, and since he knows this place better than I do, I'm going to take his opinion on it. With his head back, all that dark hair falls away from his face, and I get another rare glimpse of his relaxed features. Like with swimming at the river, it feels like being let in on a secret, and the strong tug I get behind my ribs is a warning.

I do this. Fixate on people. Pick out all the incredible, wonderful things about them and ignore the glaring red flags. But taking in Ziggy's big eyes and sweet features reminds me that he has no red flags. He's a quiet man who likes a quiet life.

His gaze falls on me. It takes a few seconds of looking at each other for me to realize I'm staring.

Maybe *I'm* the red flag. Staring creepily at new friends is a fast way to turn them off. Even after a day so close to him I could hardly breathe, and whenever I did breathe, my nostrils filled with his lemony scent.

"There's a bar down the street. Want to grab a drink while we wait?" It occurs to me that I have no clue what he actually does drink. "Alcoholic or nonalcoholic. Whichever."

Ziggy gives me his snarky smile and tugs my sleeve, the way I'm starting to pick up he does whenever I'm being too fussy over him. I don't want to handle Ziggy with kid gloves because he's more than capable of a lot of things, but without that chance to know him better, I'm constantly on the back foot.

I don't know what he likes. I don't know what offends him. I'm left to guess at everything, and thankfully, he doesn't mind when I fuck up—or at least, like the other day with Rooney, he doesn't hold it against me—but I am determined to figure out the person he keeps locked inside.

We enter the Wayward Traveler, and since it's late afternoon, there are a few people in here, but it's not overly busy.

"You know how to play pool?" I ask, pointing toward the tables in the back.

Ziggy shakes his head.

"Awesome. I'll teach you." I lead the way to the bar and hover for a second, debating whether I should bring up the drinking thing again or suggest a Coke. Ziggy preempts me, like he's plucking the thoughts from my mind, and reaches over to tap the top of one of the beer logos.

That makes it easy. I pay for our order, and he follows me toward the back, where two of the pool tables sit empty.

Ziggy sips his drink while I rack up, then chalk two sticks and hand him one.

"The whole point of the game is to get your balls into the holes."

His eyes flick to me, and I just make out the way he pumps his eyebrows under the thick hair hanging over his face.

"Who knew you had such a dirty mind?" I step closer and untangle the metal headband from his hair. Then I slide it back in, making sure to catch all the hair I'm able to. "I *do* know you like to hide, but being able to see is important in this game."

In the dim lighting, his brown eyes look bottomless, and it's hard to tell if he's blushing again or if it's the lighting in the bar. Either way, I'm definitely doing the staring thing again and have to bite down on my cheek and make myself step away. I told myself that checking out friends was a totally normal thing to do, except now that I've started, I'm finding it hard to stop.

Ziggy is … mesmerizing. There's no other way to put it. His face is so expressive, and I have a hard time not watching it because the smallest twitches give away what he's thinking, and I don't want to miss a thing.

It also doesn't help that having his ass so close to my face at the river literally rearranged brain cells. With how baggy his clothes are, I never would have guessed at the mouthwatering body he's hiding.

He tilts his head, clearly asking me what I'm doing, and I switch to joking mode so he doesn't know what's going through my mind.

"Hey, if you want to give me the advantage, that's cool too. But I'm basically a professional at this, so you need all the advantages you can get."

He laughs, but it's silent, and I wish I could bring out the one that bursts from him when he's not thinking about it.

Pool. *Focus.*

"The full-color balls are called solids, and the ones with white on them are stripes. I'll break, and whichever I sink is the one I am. You're the opposite. To get the balls in the holes—" I pause to share a smirk with him this time. "—you have to hit the white ball into them."

I set up and take the first shot, showing him what I mean. The triangle flies apart, and at least two balls drop into the pockets.

"I'm stripes."

He's assessing the table, sizing up the layout, and then he takes a long drink of his beer. Ziggy walks over and tries to mimic the way I was standing, but it's way off. He's standing too tall, his arms too straight.

A stray thought to help him flitters through my mind, and my pulse kicks up a notch. How would Ziggy react to that? To standing close and taking his hand, guiding him through his first shot.

I shouldn't.

Maybe if I weren't aching to touch him, it wouldn't be an issue, but the thought of curling over his body is almost too hard to resist. I'd like to think it's because I'm a helpful guy, but there's nothing altruistic about my thoughts.

He takes a shot while I'm still debating with myself, and it's so bad I can't *not* help him.

It would be cruel to let him suffer.

"Like this," I say, vowing to behave as I lean down toward the table and show Ziggy how to stand. He eyes me, then moves into position. It's better, but still not great. "Lower so you can aim properly."

He tries again, and it's like he *wants* me to touch him with how awkward he looks. The universe is killing me.

I swallow roughly and move closer. "Can I?"

Confusion fills his expression.

"I can help if you're okay with me touching you."

The way his pale cheeks go red this time leaves no doubts whatsoever that he's blushing, prettily staining the soft skin under his dark eyes. It does something deep, deep in my gut, and when Ziggy nods, it's a relief to stop looking at his face.

I move beside him and press my hand between his shoulder blades, guiding him forward. Slutty, slutty images fill my brain, and I have to remind myself to be good and *not* look at his ass as I reach around him to fix his grip on the cue.

"Like this," I murmur by his ear. We're side by side, my right hand closed over his on the stick, and his left hand hovering over mine on the table. I've never been this close to him before, his hair tickling my cheek, his soft fingers brushing the backs of mine, the lemony scent of soap filling my nose in a way that's warming me to a fruit I've always hated.

"Then you pull back," I rasp, guiding his hand. "And because the one we're aiming for is close to the pocket, you don't want to use too much force. Like this." We give the white ball a smooth tap, and his red one drops into the side.

Ziggy's smile stretches wide, and we break apart as we straighten, the connection gone but still haunting me.

I drain my glass, then take my shot as he finishes his own drink. "I'll get us another beer."

I don't wait for his reply because I'm worried that if I stay, I'll help him again, and there's no way I can go through that twice. I'm tempted to polish off my second drink at the bar and buy a third, but I still need to drive us back tonight, and three drinks is pushing things.

Like Mother Nature can hear me, there's a loud rumble outside, and droplets start to hit the windows.

Who knows how quickly this will pass.

Double fisting the beers, I head back through to the pool tables and find Ziggy hovering awkwardly by ours as a group of people set up next to us. I guess there goes our private little bubble, which is a good thing. Definitely a good thing.

"How did you do?" I ask, handing over his glass.

Ziggy reaches into the pocket closest to him and pulls out his blue ball.

"You got it?" The excitement on his face boosts my mood. "How do I know you didn't cheat?"

He rolls his eyes, but his smile doesn't drop. Ziggy returns the ball to the hole he sunk it in.

"Okay, guess I need to step it up." And by stepping it up, I mean sinking three balls one after the other. Sure, I *could* take it easy on Ziggy, but I have a healthy competitive streak—and I say healthy because it's nothing like Hudson's—plus, I have the feeling Ziggy wouldn't like me letting him win. He has a stubborn independent streak that I like.

"I think you've been hustled," one of the guys beside us leans over to say.

Ziggy doesn't answer him, just studies the man like he's spoken another language.

I laugh to distract from the awkwardness. "It's his first game. I'm teaching him how to play."

"Teaching? Looks more to me like you're wiping the floor with him."

From an outsider's point of view, I can understand why. "The harder he has to work for it, the better he'll get."

"That's the truth. My dad never let me win anything, God rest his soul."

I wish my dad had focused on us kids long enough to not let us win. "You've gotta be taught resilience." I'm pretty sure that's the thing Hudson, Hart, and I all lost out on. Hudson, because he hates being told no. Me, because every relationship ending feels like a personal failure of mine. And Hart, because he's stopped trying when it comes to anything.

"Haven't seen you around here before," the man says. "You new?"

"From Wilde's End. It's a few hours away."

"Never heard of it."

That's not surprising. "It's an abandoned town. My brothers and I bought it."

He points back Ziggy's way. "That your brother?"

"Nah, he's a friend."

"He ever talk for himself?"

I glance back at Ziggy to see if he wants to take this one, but he's got his back to us, so I go with the same excuse as last time. "He's shy."

"Shy?" The guy laughs. "Not hard to say hello though, is it?"

How am I supposed to know what's easy and what's hard? I'm not in Ziggy's head. From what I've seen though, saying hello *is* hard for him, and this guy is talking about something he doesn't know anything about. "Apparently, it is."

"Good thing you're easy to talk to." The guy steps up to me with a cocky smile. "Maybe we should go a round. More level playing field, if you know what I mean." He lets the words stretch between us, and I pick up on the suggestion in his tone, while one of his friends snickers behind him. "At … pool. Of course."

"Of course." It's tempting. To take him *at pool*. While he's attractive in a blue-collar way, I'm not exactly thrilled with the way he dismissed Ziggy so easily. I'm sure I could hand this guy his ass since I rarely miss a shot. My jaw is tight as I continue, intending to turn and fill Ziggy in on my plan. "Let me finish up here first."

But almost as soon as I say that, the loud *clack* of a pool cue hitting the table comes from behind me. I turn in time to see Ziggy storming through the bar.

"What's his problem?" someone asks, but I don't stick around to answer.

Watching him disappear has dread seeping through me. I go after him.

Was I doing it again? Was I ignoring him?

Fuck, fuck, *fuck*.

I'm knocked off center as a thousand excuses fly through my head. Ziggy's made it clear before how he feels to be left out, and instead of listening, I did it again. The worst part is that I didn't do it consciously. I got so caught up in the moment, and it's not like I wasn't thinking of him—I was, that's part of the problem— but he had no way to know that. He had no way to know that I was only agreeing to play against that guy for some misplaced sense of Ziggy's honor.

For all he knew, I was agreeing to ditch him.

I'm the worst friend in history.

And still, I know that this gripping panic at upsetting him isn't exactly normal friend behavior.

I burst out of the bar and stagger toward the parking lot, rain coming down over my head. It's getting heavier, but as I blink through it, I can't spot Ziggy, and the longer I go without seeing him, the higher my guilt creeps up my throat.

A hand closes over my shoulder, and I'm hauled backward under an awning. At first, I think it's the guy dragging me back for more pool, but when my brain catches up with me, I turn and find Ziggy. He's all narrowed eyes and pouty lips, the darkness creeping over his features. He's still dry, despite the rain coming down only inches away from us.

"I'm sorry," explodes out. "I know I've said that a million times before, and I'm sorry I have to keep saying sorry. I didn't mean to ignore you in there, and when he started giving you attitude, I wanted to put him in his place. I know that's not an excuse, but—"

With a loud huff, Ziggy closes his hands over the front of my shirt, and he hauls me closer.

I'm expecting a punch, but what happens next rattles me even more than that.

Ziggy's mouth slams against mine.

Pleasant surprise shoots through every limb. His lips are soft and at complete odds with the two tiny metal bars digging into my chin. There's a whole moment where we're both completely frozen, and then my brain goes offline.

I cradle his face and press forward, tongue sweeping into his waiting mouth. I'm freezing from the rain, but his mouth is hot and delicious, and when my tongue brushes something unexpected, the excitement shoots straight to my cock.

He's got a tongue piercing?

Which leads to my next question:

Does he have any other secret piercings?

The groan that slips from me is out of my control, and Ziggy answers it with a shaky inhale. He's kissing me back like it's the first meal he's ever had, and I'm happy to meet his enthusiasm.

I'm happy to kiss him back.

To keep kissing him.

I had no idea he had this in him, and I'm sure I'm supposed to stop it, but I can't.

I've been trying to lock down my attraction to him, but now that I've had a taste?

Impossible.

CHAPTER
FIFTEEN

ZIGGY

can't breathe.

Kennedy's tongue is filling my mouth, and his kiss is so deep and so powerful, I'm not sure my feet are still touching the ground.

I'm spinning with how something can feel this good. How one single thing can bring every nerve in my body alive to the point where I'm confident I could do this forever. The kiss is so Kennedy in a way I can't put into words. His passion and the way he's not holding anything back transfers into the kiss, and all I can do is hope that it's as good for him as it is for me.

As far as first kisses go, this one has to be the best.

It's made me so goddamn hard I can't think straight.

But for as incredible as it is, it doesn't keep that little voice quiet for long.

That little voice that took over when Kennedy and that guy were speaking. The one that told me Kennedy is and always will be too much for me.

Too bright.

Too happy.

Too friendly.

It's no surprise that we can't even come into a small town without people wanting him, so if he has all of these options, why the hell would he pick me?

I'm not worth the clothes on my back, and kissing him like this isn't fair. He'll want to know why, and those aren't words I can give him.

It's the hardest thing I've ever done, but I rip myself from his mouth and stagger back out of his hold. His lips are stupidly red, and my top one is scratchy from his mustache, but as our eyes meet, his widen, and everything we did sinks in.

"Ziggy … what … what was that?"

I wish I knew. The only thought running through my head was how desperately I wanted to make him mine. How I wanted all those other people to stop looking at him, and him to stop looking at them. I want to be the one who gets his smiles and his closeness and his kisses.

So I took one.

And it's only hitting me now how deeply stupid that was.

If I want Kennedy to pick me, he has to *pick* me. I can't go around always taking what I want. His surprise melts into concern, and seeing him look at me like that is too much. I don't want him to worry about me. I don't want him to kiss me out of some misplaced pity. He thought I was mad at him, and I couldn't tell him that the only one I was mad at was myself. Mad that I couldn't have an easy conversation with him. Mad that I couldn't hold his attention. Mad that I'll always be the *shy* one he has to make excuses for.

I wanted the kiss to take away his guilt, and for him to know that I'm not mad. Not at him.

And he kissed me back.

It's only now hitting me that he did it to make sure I wasn't upset.

Fuck.

What have I done?

Before he can reassure me or try to make everything okay, I turn on my heel and run. As soon as I leave the safety of the awning, rain buckets down over me, seeping through my hair and my shirt. The storm is so close that the thunder is directly overhead, and it's impossible to see anything through the rain until lightning flashes across the sky.

This storm won't last long—they never do—but I need to put as much distance between myself and Kennedy as possible before it ends.

My head is swimming with the alcohol I don't usually drink, and I cross the parking lot to come out on the road on the other side. I'm panting, my heart rate is still up from that kiss, and I want to find somewhere that I can curl up into a ball and never show my face again.

At the very least, Kennedy doesn't know where I live, so once I'm home, I won't have to face him.

I almost stop running at that stray thought.

Before Kennedy, I knew I was missing something in my life. I could feel it, like the misplaced haze of a dream where you're in one place when you know you're supposed to be in another. I didn't know what it was that I was missing, but now that I've met Kennedy, everything I thought I liked about my life is empty.

Why did I have to go and kiss him?

This is why I hate leaving Wilde's End. There's nothing in the outside world except for big, scary chaos, and now I've created the biggest and scariest chaos of them all.

No surprise for someone who can never do anything right.

All my life, I've been the screwup. Even when I was working with Dad and becoming a qualified electrician, I was too scared to do anything in case I made a mistake. Which led to making *more* mistakes. The anxiety gets so consuming it's like it takes over my body. I can't move right, I can't talk right, and when I force myself through the things my body doesn't want to do, it rebels against me.

I've learned to stop fighting it, but tonight …

I don't know what that was.

My hands are shaking, and it's hard to tell if my face is wet from the rain or if I've finally given in to the urge to cry. I'm not a crier—it's too loud and has never gotten me anywhere in life—but the pressure behind my eyes is quickly winning out.

Why do I ruin everything?

The best I can do is crawl back into my cave and stay away from the outside world.

It's stupid of me to want more. To think that I can interact with someone like Kennedy and have it turn out okay.

Instead, I'm poisoning him. Turning his laughter into worry. His friendliness into solitude. That big, open heart is shrinking down to fit the tiny world I've created for myself. I should feel terrible that I'm dimming his light, but all I selfishly want is for that light to keep shining on me.

Sometimes, when I'm with Kennedy, I feel like a whole person again.

He makes me feel seen, and now that I've had that, I don't want to let go of it again.

If I really cared about him like I claim to, it would be easy to walk away.

Selfish.

Pathetic.

Needy.

Turns out my parents were right. I do only care about myself.

The sound of tires slowing on a wet road comes from behind me as headlights fill the street. I'm scared to look, but after a moment, the car pulls into sight, and Kennedy's voice sounds through the rain.

"Ziggy, get in the car."

I keep walking.

"Dammit, Ziggy, you don't get to kiss me like that and then disappear. Get in the fucking car."

I freeze at his tone. Kennedy's never used that voice with me before, and when I get the courage to peer in at him, rage is written all over his face.

I'm stiff as I reach out and click open the door. Rain has come in on the passenger-side seat, so I'm not worried about dripping all over the leather as I climb in. Kennedy puts up the window from his side, and then I sit and wait for him to either keep driving or to yell at me.

He doesn't do either.

"Shit, you worried me. Why the hell did you run off like that?"

It takes a full minute of silence before I realize he's actually waiting on an answer. Staring at my lap, I shake my head.

"Look at me."

That's the last thing I want to do. My chest is squeezing too tight, my throat trying to close over, and this whole night feels like an out-of-body experience. Nothing about this is normal, and adding a pissed-off Kennedy to that only sharpens the experience.

I hate the way he sighs.

"I checked the weather, and this storm is supposed to be here for another few hours. I'm not driving back in this."

That's fine since I was prepared to walk all the way back anyway.

When it's clear to him that I'm not planning on answering, he pulls back onto the road. We're only driving for a minute or two before he turns into another parking lot.

I squint through the window at the glowing sign, blurred by the rain.

"We're staying here tonight. I'll book us a room." He unclips his seat belt and sets his hand on the door to open it when he pauses. Kennedy turns serious eyes on me. "Be here when I get back. Understand?"

As much as I want to bolt again, I'm shivering, soaked through, and wanting nothing more than to make Kennedy happy. So I stay while he ducks inside, dreading whatever comes next.

CHAPTER
SIXTEEN

KENNEDY

'm tuned in to every noise from outside as I check into a room and leave my credit card details on file. I'm dripping all over the floorboards, and I don't remember a check-in ever taking so damn long, but the seconds drag by with me expecting to walk out of here and find Ziggy gone again.

I'm not sure what's going through his head, but I've got whiplash, and between him running off and me finding him again, it's been the most confusing half hour of my life. I've gone from worried I offended him, to being kissed senseless, to thinking I fucked-up *again*, to pissed off that I'm feeling that way at all.

Whatever that was, I enjoyed it, and if Ziggy didn't, well, he needs to tell me that. It doesn't have to be out loud, but it's time we started to understand each other for real. I've spent most of my time trying to interpret his silences, but I'm not sure he's ever tried to interpret my words. It needs to go both ways.

"Enjoy your stay," the middle-aged man says, handing over a

room key with a large number fourteen stamped onto the wooden tag.

I thank him and hurry back to the car, only feeling like I can breathe properly again when I see Ziggy still sitting inside it. He's not looking my way, so I venture back into the rain and open his door. "Let's go and get dry."

He doesn't look at me as he climbs out, and I don't know if he's mad at me for something or if he regrets everything tonight as much as I do, but I'm going to find out. Maybe this storm will be good for us.

He follows me up the rickety stairs and to one of the second-floor rooms. We catch some stray rain being blown in sideways, but it's not like it matters at this point. I'm drenched, feeling heavy in my limbs, and still spiraling over how the hell we got to this point.

The room is basic with navy carpet, white bedding, and one queen bed standing proudly in the center.

I probably should have paid more attention at check-in. Saying there were two of us could have been more specific. I sigh and toss the keys onto the chipboard desk, eyeing the tiny chair in the corner to work out if it's large enough for me to curl up on or whether I should head back out there and request another room.

Ziggy closes the door behind us and dulls the sounds of the storm.

Fuck it, I'll sleep on the floor if I have to. I just want to get dry.

I switch on the lamp and cross to the small closet, hoping to find towels or spare sheets, but instead, we get ridiculously lucky. There are two white robes hanging side by side.

I take one and hand it to Ziggy. "Go shower and warm up. We'll talk once you're done."

He hesitates, gaze warily sliding from me to the robe. Then he takes it and closes himself in the bathroom.

I really should shower next, but the thought of dragging out this talk any longer is rattling me, so instead, I peel out of my wet clothes, hang them over the hanger in the closet, and then dry off with a towel as much as I can.

I've just pulled the robe on when the bathroom door cracks open, and Ziggy walks out in his. Considering I didn't hear the shower, I'm guessing he couldn't wait either.

"S-sorry," he whispers.

That knocks all the annoyance from me.

I drop down to sit on the edge of the bed. "I just want to understand what happened."

He takes a shaky breath, then nods. His hair is still damp, and chunks of it are hiding his eyes, but I know he can see me when I pat the spot beside where I'm sitting. It only takes a moment of debating with himself before he joins me.

"We were having fun," I start. "Then that guy got involved, and I thought I fucked it up because I left you out of the conversation. I didn't mean to, but I was getting annoyed with him and wanted to put him in his place, which, when I think back over it, there's no way for you to have known. I'm … protective of people. It's not only a *you* thing, but I didn't like the way he dismissed you." I scratch at the side of my thumbnail. "I felt horrible, then you kissed me and I felt incredible, and then you ran off and I felt worse than I did before that. I don't like being confused, and I hate the thought that I upset you. So if we're going to be friends, we need to know more about each other." I finally get the courage to look over at him, and he's watching me from the corner of his eyes. "It's okay if talking isn't possible. You never have to say another word to me if you don't want to. Maybe we can get by with yes or no questions. Or you can write shit down." This restlessness prickles in my gut as Ziggy wraps his arms around himself. "I like to think I'm good at reading people, but considering what a failure all my relationships have been, maybe that's not true. I'm tired of guessing. I'm tired of never knowing where I fuck up." It's possible that I didn't realize until this moment how messed up I've been over all the rejection.

I try and try so damn hard, and the more I'm pushed away, the more determined I am next time. Something tells me that most people don't go into a new relationship with the aim of proving the last person wrong.

Ziggy looks like he's about to faint, and his breathing is louder, quicker than usual.

"Not now," I add, turning to him. "It's okay if it's not now or soon. I'm not going to push. As long as you promise not to be mad at me if I make a mistake, I can wait as long as you need. *Anything* you need, Ziggy."

It takes almost a full minute of him struggling to control his breathing. All I want is to know how to help. How to react in these conversations and make things better for him. But he gets himself there, and once he does, he rests his hand on the bed between where we're sitting and runs his pinky over my thigh.

I watch him for a few seconds. "Does that mean you'll try?"

He's not looking at me when he nods.

I can work with this.

Small steps.

"Are you feeling up for some questions now?"

Another steady breath and another nod.

I tap one of his Band-Aids. "Do you hurt yourself a lot?"

He shakes his head.

"You have been lately."

He nods again.

"Can you tell me? What you've been doing?"

No.

I was ready for the response, even if it's not the one I wanted. "Did ... did you like hanging out today? Up until ..."

Yes.

"That's a relief. Because you can say no if you don't want to do something. I don't care what we're doing as long as we both have fun."

He brushes some of the hair from his eyes and turns to me. I'm still a work in progress, but that's a pretty clear sign he's not trying to distance himself from this conversation anymore.

"I *really* want to know why you ran out on our game," I whisper. "Could you write it down, maybe?"

His expression gets dark. "No."

The fact that he forced himself to speak when he could have shaken his head is proof he doesn't like not being able to answer me, but he's trying to give me something. "Okay. Can you at least tell me if it's because you were mad at me?"

No.

"You weren't mad?"

I wasn't.

Well, that rules out one of a million things it could have been. But it's a start.

"Ziggy …" I should probably shut up, but when have I ever been good at that? "I don't know what I'm doing here. All I know is that when I met you, I could tell you're a good person. I like when we hang out, and I like every time I learn a new thing about you. It's fun. *You're* fun. And for the first time in maybe years, I have someone I can be myself around. There's no pressure to be cooler or funner or sweeter. I don't have to impress you with expensive things." My mind is spiraling, and I have no idea where I'm going with any of this. "I guess what I'm trying to say is that you make me feel safe. There's no judgment." Slowly, I reach for his hand, and I'm relieved when he doesn't pull it away. "And I want you to know that you're safe with me too. Not sure why, but it feels important to say it. Out loud. You can talk with me, or you can not talk with me, whatever you want. I will never, ever judge you. Ever."

His hand tightens around mine. "Thank you."

The weakness to his words flickers my protective side. "Have you always been like this? Afraid to talk."

His eyes widen, and I don't break contact as he studies me.

"Did someone make you afraid?"

"Y-yes."

This time, I'm the one gripping him harder. I had a suspicion, but suspecting something like this and having it confirmed are two wildly different things. I'm trying to keep my anger down, trying to protect this safe space I want for us both, but *fuck*. "Since you got to Wilde's End?"

No.

"Before?"

Yes.

Another piece of his puzzle slots into place.

I brush his hair back some more and lean closer. "I'm a pacifist. I like people. I like making people happy. But if I ever meet whoever did this to you … I'll beat them to a pulp."

He swallows thickly, and it's hard not to do the same.

"You didn't deserve that. And I'm so damn sorry."

Ziggy's expression is too hard to read, but whatever is going through his head looks like a struggle. He lifts a shaky hand to my cheek, and his fingers, still cold from outside, scrape over my stubble. I lean into his touch, hoping he feels as close to me as I feel to him.

"Kennedy …"

I almost choke at the sound of my name. "Yeah?"

"You said … earlier … that you … liked our kiss?"

Nerves tickle my gut before he has all the words out. "Yeah. Wasn't it obvious?"

"I thought you kissed me because you felt guilty."

Understanding over why he ran away hits hard. I cover his hand with mine. "I would never. The second you started kissing me, it was like I completely forgot how to think. I was only focused on how good it felt."

The warring emotions in his face slip away as his lips tug up on one side. He opens his mouth twice before he can get the words out on a rasp. "Want to forget how to think again?"

CHAPTER
SEVENTEEN

ZIGGY

Kennedy's looking at me like he doesn't know where those words came from, and I'm feeling the same way. Considering I practiced them over and over before I spoke, I should have been more prepared for how they'd sound out loud, but I'm still in shock.

All I know is that Kennedy does make me feel safe. It's not the kind of safe that shuts up all of my irrational thoughts, but it is the kind of safe that makes me want to try.

"Did you like kissing me?" he asks.

It was the greatest moment of my life. I have no idea if he interprets my nod that way or not, but an exhale rushes from him.

"Stop me thinking, Ziggy."

I'm nervous as hell, but the second my lips touch his, that surge of power comes back to me. Like if we keep kissing, I can forget everything that's ever happened up until this moment. I'm just a man kissing another man.

He parts his lips, mustache scratching my skin in a way that sends pleasant ripples down my neck, and I follow his lead. His tongue strokes into my mouth. I'm buzzing at the contact, buzzing at the way he licks my barbell, buzzing at the overwhelming warmth as his mouth seals to mine.

My hand drops from his cheek to the hollow at the base of his throat that his parted robe has been teasing me with. It's right above that sexy crease between his pecs and hints at the hair that covers his chest. I want to push the stupid robe off his shoulders and spend the night exploring his body, but I'm lucky to even get this.

Talking might not be something that comes easily for me, but I've never thought of myself as unconfident. I'm capable, I've built what I thought was a good life, I have friend-type people and a useful skill … but I've never had sex before. It's not like I could go out and strike up a conversation with someone I was interested in, and living with my mom and dad made sneaking out for a hookup impossible.

Now, I'm kissing a man I've fantasized about every day since I met him, and I have no idea how to take things further. How to show him that I want more.

It was hard enough to ask him if he wanted to kiss me again, but I was determined to use my words this time. Asking him if he wants to have sex? There's no way.

And knowing what I know of Kennedy, he's not going to be the one to make the first move.

The longer we kiss, the harder I get though, and I'm worried that if I don't do something about it soon, I'm going to come just from kissing.

I refuse to let it end that way.

I break my lips from his, struggling to breathe, scared I'm about to ruin everything as I let my fingers slip from his throat and set my hand on his knee. I'm so nervous I feel sick, but I wait for his unfocused eyes to sharpen on mine, and then I slide my hand up an inch and stop.

The brown speckled through his green eyes is deepened in the motel lamplight, and they bounce from one of my eyes to the next, like he's trying to pull the thoughts from my mind.

His large hand covers mine. "If you want it, I want it. But there's no pressure from me."

I'm trying to work out whether he's too nice to turn me down.

"I swear," he continues. "I'd be happy to kiss all night if that's what you wanted."

The rasp in his voice gives me confidence.

I slip my hand under the robe, and before I can stop again to check in with him, Kennedy's head tips back to the ceiling. "Oh, fuck," he gasps, tendons in his neck tightening. "Touch me, Ziggy."

Touch him … I can't believe I'm about to.

The robe bunches around my arm as my hand slides over his fleshy thigh, loving the strength in it and marveling at the way the light hair is tickling my palm. I've wanted to do this for so long that the fact that it's happening has my cock *aching*. My tip is brushing the rough cotton of the bathrobe, and I'm sure I'm leaking all over it, but I don't care. I only want to know if Kennedy is doing the same.

I'm holding my breath as I reach the top of Kennedy's thigh, and my hand doesn't stop. It dips between his legs as he spreads them wider, and then … his balls fill my grip. My dick pulses, and I almost lose it myself, but somehow, I manage to hang on through what is hands down the sexiest moment of my life.

His balls are heavy and warm against my cool skin. Cradling them, rolling my hand over them, exploring every hair and crease and vein is something I want to carry with me to my grave. My vision wavers for a moment, and I remind myself to *breathe.*

I'm not sure my stuttered inhale could be considered breathing, but it brings me back to the moment enough to enjoy it. I explore higher, leaving his balls behind and trailing my fingers over his hard shaft. The relief that hits me over him being as turned on as I am is ridiculous, but I don't let it stop me.

My hand closes around his cock, and I'm touching more than I've dreamed of touching, but all it's doing is making me want more. He's thick, long, bigger than me, but that's all I have to compare it to. All I know is that it feels amazing, and now when I jerk off over him, this is going to be burned into my brain.

At least that's what I think until Kennedy's whine fills his chest and he thrusts into my grip. "More," he begs, and then, before I know what he's doing, he tugs at the tie on the bathrobe, and both sides of it fall open, revealing everything.

My jaw actually drops.

I'd gotten an eyeful of his body the other day, but seeing the way his stomach curves down to his groin, the way the light blond hair beneath his belly button trails down to his pubes, and the way my pale hand is wrapped around his angry-looking cock is almost too much.

I give him another firm stroke, and Kennedy falls back against the bed. He's biting the knuckles on one hand while the other buries into his hair.

I want to ask him if this is good. If he's enjoying himself.

But Kennedy doesn't leave me guessing for long.

"Bit tighter," comes out muffled around his fist. "Just like that." He thrusts into my hand again, and this time, I'm ready to stroke him through it. A speck of precum builds at his tip, and I watch it get larger as my hand moves over him.

Every inch of him is incredible, but I'd be lying if I said I was looking at more than his dick. It's paler than the rest of him, but still a few shades darker than my hand, and there's a prominent vein running along the underside. He looks painfully swollen, and I feel the same. I'm tempted to touch myself too, but I know the second I get some friction, I'm done for. My balls are already tight to my body, and I'm fighting with everything I have to keep this going.

I'm so horny, and I have no idea if this gets better with prac-tice, but I refuse to be embarrassed. I'm finally getting to experience this, and the only thing I'm allowing myself to think about is Kennedy and how perfectly his cock fills my hand.

Well, that and the way my gaze keeps returning to the teasing drop of precum. His tip is dark red, and stroking him isn't bringing the relief we both need.

My mouth waters, and I need more. More him. More memories. More moments I can take with me after now, when I question whether this happened at all.

So I lean in and run my nose over his balls. They twitch, and when I glance up, Kennedy's mouth is hanging open. I give in to the urge to bury my face into him and inhale deeply. He smells like sex and him, and this time when my cock begs to be touched, I listen. Not for relief, but to strangle that thing and get it back from the edge.

Fuck, I want to come. I want to come so badly. I'm a mess with how much I'm leaking, but I'm goddamn making this last, and I squeeze my cock almost to the point of pain.

Then I press my face into him again.

His scent is like a drug, the way it makes my brain so cloudy. I swipe my tongue over his tightening balls, then relax my grip on his cock as I rub my face over it as well. I want to live here. With Kennedy begging and my cock begging, and me indulging in all the ways I want.

I reach his tip, and my tongue darts out to catch that bead of cum.

The sound Kennedy lets out almost sounds like a whimper. "You're killing me, Ziggy."

I hold his eye contact as long as possible while I wrap my mouth around his tip. I suck it in, eyes falling closed at the lightly salty taste that hits me. I'm running off pure instinct, and I know I'm supposed to be fitting as much dick into my mouth as possible, but I can barely make it halfway.

I turn off the stupid voice telling me that I'll never be good enough and remember this is my first time. Maybe, if we do this again, he can teach me what he likes, but for now, this is enough. This is real. Raw.

Perfect.

Spit dribbles down his length and makes it easier for my hand to move and meet my lips. To make up for the lack of depth, my tongue doesn't stop moving over him, and when I use my barbell to run over his slit, both of Kennedy's legs twitch against me.

"Again," he pants. "Piercing. Again."

I do as I'm told and open my eyes to watch goose bumps break over his skin. He's tugging at one of his nipples, and I want to reach the other, but between breathing and licking and stroking, I'm all tapped out.

The taste on my tongue gets stronger, and Kennedy gives short, shallow thrusts into my mouth.

"So … close …"

I'm prepared for whatever he gives me, and I squeeze my dick in warning that it has to wait a tiny bit longer.

But when I think he must be about to fill my mouth with cum, Kennedy pulls out suddenly, grabs me, and flips us so my back hits the mattress.

He hovers over me, supporting his weight on the forearm at my side, while his free hand reaches for the tie on my robe.

"I want to see you naked before I come. Can I?"

I'm too stunned to do anything more than nod. Kennedy's intense gaze, his hand opening the knot, peeling back the material, revealing me to his greedy eyes …

Shit.

Shit, shit, shit.

All it would take is a light breeze to come at this point. I'm so ready.

He chokes deeply, "You're pierced," and before I can stop him, Kennedy moves down the bed and sucks me all the way into his mouth. The sudden heat and suction engulfing me is impossible to fight against. My hands grip fists into the bedding, and the simmering pleasure building in my balls explodes.

I come hard and fast, vision blinking darker and lighter as I unload into his mouth. The high sweeps from my head to my limbs, and I ride it out until my cock stops throbbing in his mouth and my body turns to Jell-O.

I'm completely wiped out. Bubbly and happy in a way I've never been before.

Then reality crashes into me.

I cover my face, unable to believe I was barely in his mouth before I came. Rooney's always open to talking about his hookups, and while I might have been a virgin, I've picked up enough from him to know that no guy is impressed by it being over so soon.

I don't even notice Kennedy has moved until his husky voice fills my ear.

"That was so fucking hot." His body blankets mine, and he grabs one of my legs to wrap around his waist. Kennedy grinds down into me, rutting his hard cock against my softening one. "You have no idea … how crazy … you make me …"

His thrusts get faster, firmer, and I tug his mouth down to meet mine again. When his tongue dips between my lips, I taste myself, and the satisfaction that brings catches me by surprise. There's something deeply possessive about knowing he just drank my cum.

He feeds me the kind of unhinged groan that only comes from being close, so I fumble my way to his nipple. As soon as I find it, I pinch it gently, over and over, until Kennedy stiffens above me.

His moan is long and loud as he comes, his release painting my stomach and landing in my groin. The wetness seeps into my skin as I lie there, and Kennedy, instead of breaking the kiss, only deepens it. His weight sags against me until I'm being swallowed by the mattress.

And I love every second of it.

CHAPTER
EIGHTEEN

feel incredible. The happy, buzzy feelings are making me sleepy, and while it would be easy to drift off, I need to clean up after myself first.

A satisfied sigh leaves me as I roll my legs off the bed and then disappear into the bathroom for a washcloth. As I'm rinsing it under the tap, I catch sight of myself in the mirror, and I couldn't be happier with what I see. Messy hair, bright eyes, relaxed expression—all markers of really good sex.

I have no idea where that sex came from, but Ziggy was into it, and I was into it, and *goddamn*, I was caught off guard by how hard I blew my load.

When I walk back into the bedroom, Ziggy is still spread across the bed, robe open, streaks of cum glistening on his skin, and the whole scene in the dim lamplight makes my mouth go dry. He's beautiful.

He tips his head my way, hair falling over his face, and watches me approach. Like always, he's silent as I reach across him and drag the cloth over his skin, his stomach twitching at the contact. I take my time, making sure he's clean, spending probably more time than I need to at the piercing through his tip. I'm not opposed to doing this all night, but he's clean too soon, and then I have to move on to cleaning myself.

I know I need to tell him that it was great and make sure he's not overthinking since he won't say anything himself, but my brain is bobbing around in happy vibes, and my mouth won't move.

Did I intend to be friends who fuck with Ziggy? Not at all. I think he might be the first attractive person I've met who I didn't immediately try to date. Normally, I meet someone, fold myself backward to impress them, ask them out … and then crash and burn shortly afterward.

With Ziggy, it's been easy. Spending time with him isn't something I overthink. He's him, and I'm me, and it works.

So how does sleeping together change that?

This high I'm enjoying slowly fades to a normal level. I ditch the washcloth in the bathroom, and after hesitating in front of the mirror again, I do up my robe before heading back out there.

He still hasn't moved, so to avoid me being tempted into a round two, I lean in and kiss him softly while I close his robe as well.

"I can't think while your dick is out," I murmur.

His soft laugh brushes my lips as I pull back again. Then I settle on the bed, and he moves up to sit next to me.

We look at each other for too long to be normal, but it's unnervingly comfortable with him.

"That was very fun and very surprising," I say, testing to see if he'll give me more information.

His smile is brief, and I'm shocked when he speaks. "It was my first time."

His first … I stare at him as those words sink in. Well, *sort of* sink in. "In a hotel room?"

"All of it."

All. *All* of it. The kissing and the sex and the hotel room and and and … Ziggy is fucking gorgeous, and he didn't come across as inexperienced. I mean, he came as soon as my mouth was on him, but I assumed it had been a while. Not *twenty-eight years.*

"Huh." My brain isn't coming up with more words than that.

"Sorry."

I can't stand the disappointment in his tone. "No, you have nothing to be sorry about." I struggle to bring my brain back online. "I'm surprised because I wouldn't have guessed it. Seriously. That was … wow."

His cheeks get redder as he tries to hide the way that lights him up. But I don't want him to hide it. I want to see that light shining out of him all the time.

"I'm also very confused because how the hell haven't guys been all over you? What was wrong with the queer men in Lincoln?"

Ziggy taps his lips, and I get what he means.

"You don't need to talk in a glory hole." By the disgusted face he pulls, I guess that answers that question. "Hey, don't knock it until you try it. I mean, I only tried it once, and I was very, *very* drunk and heartbroken, but it was sex. Sex is good."

His lips twitch. "Very good."

I stretch across the bed, trying not to let that go to my head. "Outstanding." And as much as I'd love to spend the night complimenting his skills, we've reached the part of the conversation I know needs to be had, but I'd rather avoid.

"What now?" he asks, proving that Ziggy has way more confidence than I give him credit for.

It's also not a question I have an answer to.

My gaze strays from him across the room, and I try to separate my thoughts. On the one hand, sex like that is something I'm not turning down in a hurry, but … it's *Ziggy.* He feels like my first real friend. The first person I've had a real connection with since my brothers grew up and closed off.

I'm worried that if we sleep together again, and again, I'll fall into old habits. That my feelings will take over, and common sense will go out the window, and Ziggy will break my heart like everyone else inevitably does.

"I don't want to lose you." It's the only truth I have for him. "I look forward to seeing you and spending time with you. I like having a friend who's all mine."

Ziggy's hand covers mine.

"But also … it's not only my choice," I point out. "You have an opinion too."

His glare doesn't have much heat behind it, more like he was hoping I wouldn't ask. I wait him out, hoping that with enough time, he'll find the words he needs. Just when I'm about to give up, his mouth moves. "I don't want to lose you either."

"Okay." That reply boosts me. "Then we don't."

Okay.

"We stay friends."

Good.

I'm interpreting his nods with no idea if I'm getting it right, but he doesn't correct me. It feels like we're both on the same page, so that's good … I think. "And we just … don't do this again."

I'm not sure if that's a question or a statement, but Ziggy doesn't answer. His large eyes are watching my face, more like he's curious than offended or pissed off.

"Right?" I check, needing him to give me something.

His hold on my hand tightens briefly before he lets go, dragging his gaze with him. He pulls his knees up to hug against his chest as he looks at the bed. "You want to fall in love."

I have no idea where he's going with that. "Yes."

"For the last time."

I know I told him that only a few hours ago, but it sounds odd repeated back to me. No less true though. I can feel how tired my heart is of constantly being stomped on, and I don't think I can put myself through that again. "Yeah."

"How will you know?"

"What do you mean?"

It looks like he's chewing on his tongue, maybe thinking about how to reword his question. "How will you know it's the last time?"

That's a question I'm not expecting, and in Ziggy's soft tone, it somehow hits harder. "I won't. That's the hard part." My chuckle is self-deprecating. "I'm a terrible judge of something like that. I'm hit with so many *this is it* moments, and it's never been it. All that talk about listening to your gut is useless on me because my gut is obviously drunk and wearing lust goggles." That's the sad reality, isn't it? In my desperation to find the one, I'll settle for *any*one. What if Ziggy is the one person who doesn't get sick of me, and then a year down the track, I realize I'm only with him because I had no other options?

Ziggy deserves better than that.

He deserves to be *the* only option.

And aside from the sex we had, I don't know if Ziggy is an option for me at all. He's never given me any reason to think he might be interested before now. Maybe he sensed my attraction and figured this was his chance to lose his virginity? I'm glad he picked me and that I made it good for him, but he's not exactly pushing for a repeat.

Actually, he didn't really give me an answer at all.

Can I blame him? All he's heard me whine about is finding my forever person and smothering them when I do. It's not like I've been selling myself to him, and if our positions were reversed, I probably wouldn't be in a hurry to tie myself to this sinking ship either.

"I assume," I start, wanting to pull myself out of this funk, "that I'll know when I see it. That when I fall for the last time, it'll feel different to all the times I've fallen for someone in the past." I look over at him, feeling hopeful, and slowly, Ziggy lets go of his legs and lies down opposite me.

He's on his side of the bed, and I'm on mine, but when I roll to face him, it feels as intimate as if we were touching.

"It would have to be like that, right?" I ask.

"I have no idea."

It really is ridiculous that every time I hear his voice, this little *meep* goes off in my chest. "I'll let you know if I ever find out."

That doesn't get a response, not that I'm expecting it to, but Ziggy does reach for my hand again. His fingers link through mine, and he holds it like he has a right to be holding it. The lack of hesitation is hot.

"Tomorrow, I'll drive us back to town, and then you're not allowed to disappear on me. Understand?"

The sly look I get back isn't an agreement.

"I'm serious. You said you don't want to lose me either. Once we're back there, it's back to being friends again. Friends who sometimes tease each other about the time we had sex."

I get a real laugh, and I swear that makes the whole night worth it.

"Deal?"

He shakes our joined hands, like we're entering into a contract.

That's good enough for me.

We talk—well, I talk—for a while longer, until my eyes grow heavy and I have to fight for every word. I don't want to fall asleep. I want to take as much time with him as possible, but it's been a long day, and the more I battle my tiredness, the deeper it takes hold.

Each long blink cements more details into my mind.

The glint of his piercings in the low light.

His chest teasingly on display by the robe.

And his hand anchoring mine to the bed, the warmth of it staying with me all night.

CHAPTER
NINETEEN

ZIGGY

We wake up and get back into our slightly damp clothes, and then Kennedy feeds me breakfast before we get on the road home.

But I'm distracted the entire time by one thought:

Kennedy doesn't know what love is.

At least, that's the conclusion I've come to after last night. He's a funny one. The way he can be so sure it's a thing he wants, even though he's never experienced it. I assume. From what he says, no one he's dated before has appreciated what they had with him, and their loss is my gain.

Because I'm going to do it.

I'm going to win Kennedy over.

I glance at where he's singing along to the radio as we speed back toward Wilde's End and promise myself that I'm going to give Kennedy the love he deserves.

There's just one problem.

I need to figure out what love is first.

A recluse with absentee parents vowing to shower this guy in love? Ridiculous. It sounds like the start of a bad joke. People underestimate me all the time though, and I'm not about to do it to myself.

We reach Old End, and I'm expecting him to pull over, but he passes the houses and keeps going.

When I turn my confused look on him, he's already watching me, grinning like he's up to something. I have a hunch that I know what that something is.

My eyebrows rise a little, prompting him to share the idea he's so obviously proud of.

"I'm going to keep driving," he says like he's warning me. "So you might want to tell me which way to go to your place, or we'll end up very, very lost."

I don't point out that it's impossible to get lost in Wilde's End. The real risk is ending up in the Dale, but Kennedy doesn't need to know it exists.

Not completely sold on his idea, I tap the dash for his attention, then point to a trail to the left.

"Here?" he checks. I know why he's hesitating. It's deceptively small, but we get trucks through here fine, and those are much bigger than this SUV. "Okay ..."

I could have easily had Kennedy drop me anywhere in Wilde's End, but I also *want* him to know where I live on the off chance he'll come to me for once. But while that idea is appealing, I'm nervous as hell because I love my place. It's warm and comforting and gives me everything I need.

It's also a mine shaft.

I couldn't stand it if Kennedy looked around at my entire world and decided it was beneath him.

I don't own much, but what I have is *mine*. I'm proud of it, and I'm proud of the life I've built for myself. I might be lonely, but that doesn't change the fact that I've fought hard to get here. Exactly where I want to be.

I direct him the whole way, getting more nervous the closer we get to home. Kennedy's back singing along to the music, and I remind myself, for the millionth time, that it doesn't matter either way.

I'm able to hold on to that thought until we clear the tree line and he pulls to a stop on the dirt clearing in front of my place.

Kennedy looks around. "Where is it?"

Directly in front of us, but I'm not about to tell him that.

Instead, I make a show of tapping my knuckles against his jaw before climbing out of the car. Unfortunately, Kennedy follows me.

"Hey, wait. Aren't you going to show me around?"

Before it can dawn on him that the *mine shaft* is my home, I take him by the shoulders and spin him back toward his car, then give him a little push.

He lets out a heavy sigh. "Fine. Next time, then."

Oh, yeah, sure, of course.

I wait for him to climb back into the car and turn on the engine, and then I wave until he disappears into the trees and I can't see him anymore.

Ahh … Kennedy. These last twenty-four hours have been … they've been … I'm all jittery and squirmy and fluttery in my gut. I can't believe we kissed. I can't believe we had *sex*. Sex that apparently won't happen again, and I don't have the energy to sulk about that because I got more than I ever thought I would.

Is this what happiness tastes like?

The titter of a bird in a tree close by brings me back to the now. The sky is still patchy with clouds, but the rain is gone, and it won't take long for everything to dry out, including me. It's also way too quiet for the big feelings I'm having, and because I know there's no way I'll be able to go inside and rest, I figure I'll spend the day working on my present for Kennedy. I stayed up late watching him sleep last night, and I don't regret a minute of it.

The breeze picks up briefly, already heavy with the coming heat, as I make my way toward the train carriages that hold our supplies. I need a few things for this bird, since I want to try out an idea I had to fix the beak, and I'm distracted going over the design in my head. I reach the first carriage and pull open the door—then freeze.

It wasn't locked.

My gaze darts to where the padlock normally hangs, but it's not there. Did Wilde come up here while I was gone? He's normally so careful about locking—

Something shiny in the thick grass gathered around one of the large metal carriage wheels snags my attention. I stoop down, pick it up … and my pulse takes off.

The padlock has been smashed open.

This wasn't Wilde.

I quickly close the door, tuck the damaged padlock into my pocket, then head inside my mine for my keys. It's the second time this week I've had to use my truck, and I can't remember a time that's ever happened.

Wilde's End works because we look after each other. We don't take more than we need, we don't hoard goods, and if someone needs something from the supply carriages, all they have to do is let Wilde know, and he'll get it for them.

We keep our shit locked up in case of strangers and the rare times people from the Dale have raided us. Considering how many matches Foley has won in Peril lately, they shouldn't be wanting for anything.

So while it's unlikely, I can't rule out that possibility. But I also can't rule out the possibility that it was one of our own. This is one of the many, many times I'm glad I'm not in charge. Wilde can work out what to do about it.

He's not at home, so I check in a few of the usual places and find him walking out of the Lair. He's sweaty, carrying his post, and looks like he's just finished training.

The second he sees my car, he's immediately on alert.

"What is it?" he calls as I climb out.

I pull the padlock from my pocket and hand it over.

There's a pause while Wilde turns it over, inspecting the damage, and then he holds it up. "This from the carriages?"

Yes.

"Shit. Where's Rooney?"

"I haven't seen him." Which means he's either sourcing or at home.

"Think you can find him for me? He needs to call a meeting."

Thankfully, he's at home, and when I show him the lock and utter the word *meeting*, Rooney jumps in my truck and directs me to where everyone should be. He has an uncanny knack for knowing things, and I've never been completely comfortable around him. It's not like with Booker, where I assume he's waiting for me to drop dead so he can see how much blood's inside me, but it throws me anyway. Sometimes I think Rooney knows things about me before I know them myself.

By the time we get to the Cutty, everyone's waiting for us. Wilde has been home to shower and change, Nox and Booker are sitting at the table furthest from the door, Lynx has his arms folded, leaning by the entrance like he'd rather be anywhere else, and Viv is bustling around in the kitchen out the back.

She doesn't technically have to be here, but whenever she knows there's a meeting on, she shows up with snacks. And I love her for it.

Booker doesn't technically need to be here either, but he's nosy and is the one with connections across all the towns within driving distance.

"Someone broke into the supplies," Wilde says, jumping straight into it as always. "We need to find out who, and we need to do it quickly."

That catches everyone's attention. Rooney joins Wilde by the jukebox as Viv brings out a plate of cookies and hands it off to Nox.

They're confused as they look from Viv and back to Wilde again. "You think it was someone in town?" they ask.

"I don't think anything. Someone broke in, and I want to know who."

"I'll tell you who," Lynx says. His machete is strapped to his belt, and even with Bob waiting outside, he looks no less menacing. Thankfully, I know better.

"Who?" Rooney asks, playing along, though I have a good idea what he's going to say next.

"The brothers. They need supplies, so they figured they'd help themselves to ours. Like they have done with everything else in this town."

"It wasn't them," Wilde pushes back.

"Did your boy tell you that during pillow talk?"

Wilde grunts but chooses to ignore him. "Ziggy, was anything missing?"

I freeze with everyone's attention on me. Heat slowly seeps into my cheeks, and I know that Wilde doesn't expect me to talk, but having attention is too much. The pressure to say or do the right thing grows, ballooning out until it's so big it fills the room.

I want to provide a detailed list for him of all the things that were gone, but I didn't even think to check.

"Right." His sharp voice has every pair of eyes swing back to him, and I stutter out a breath. "We'll go and take inventory and tell you what's gone. Ask around, keep on the lookout for—"

"Do you think someone came up from the Dale?" Nox asks.

Booker and Lynx answer at the same time. "No." There's a pregnant beat as they eye each other. Booker's smile lights up his face, but he goes on saying nothing, so Lynx continues.

"I've been by that border all day. No one's crossed it."

"Then it's someone in town," Wilde concludes. "Bring me a name, and I'll handle it."

Handle it could be anything from reestablishing the rules to running them out of town. All I know is that I'd hate to be the person on the end of Wilde's temper.

He makes it clear the meeting is over and crosses to me as conversations break out. Lynx leaves, door thudding closed behind him, and Wilde glares at the now empty spot.

"He's on thin ice."

I give Wilde my most doubtful look. He and Lynx have always had friction, but we need them both. Lynx is prepared to do the work no one else wants to, and I'd struggle to survive without him stopping by with food every few days.

"Sorry to put you on the spot like that," Wilde says. "I wasn't thinking."

He shouldn't have to be sorry; it should be something I can handle. I've known the people in this room for years, and logically, I know they're not going to belittle me for trying, but my brain doesn't work like that. When everything that's ever come out of your mouth is treated like it's stupid, you start to believe it's true.

Even eight years here hasn't undone the damage. It probably doesn't help that I don't have a lot of opportunities to try. Except with Kennedy. He's been giving me the space and patience I need.

Wilde goes to continue, and I pull the same move with him that I pulled with Kennedy. My hand seals over his mouth, and I give him a determined look, warning him to give me a minute. I *want* to do this.

I might not have been able to do it in front of the whole room, but Wilde is safe.

"It's okay," I finally manage. There are times the words come easily and times where I have to fight for every one. I *know* it's all mental. I know it's something I need to push through, but my brain and my mouth don't always link up.

He pulls my hand away and nods once. "Good."

The best thing about Wilde is that he never questions me. He trusts me to give him the truth.

"When did you find the lock? Right before you brought it to me?"

Yes.

"So it happened this morning?"

That, I don't know. I'm hesitant to give him the truth, but it's important. "I wasn't home last night."

"Where the hell were you?"

"In Wayward. With …" I need an extra breath for courage. "Kennedy."

He processes that information as he studies my face. He's the only one who knows about my feelings for Kennedy, so I'm sure he's putting things together. "Has he been good to you?"

"We're friends."

"Didn't answer my question."

I like that he cares, and I duck my head with a smile, caught off guard by that thought. Wilde has always been the closed-off protector, but since he started his relationship with Hudson, I'm getting glimpses of another side to him.

A side that might have answers.

"Wilde … what's love like?"

That shocks him so much that his gray eyes fly wide. "Love?" His expression closes off, like he's far away, something brewing behind his eyes that's the complete opposite of what fills Kennedy's when he talks about it. "Love is pain and disappointment. The second you love someone, you have something to lose, and more often than not, you're going to lose it."

He shoves through the Cutty front door, and I watch him go, wondering if he's ever voiced those thoughts to Hudson. I can't imagine anyone related to Kennedy would feel the same way.

Then again, what would I know?

Wilde was speaking from experience, and given the mix of

good and bad highs I have with Kennedy, he might be right. I can't say the way I feel about him doesn't hurt sometimes.

I join the others, sharing Viv's plate of cookies and letting their voices wash over me. My gaze flows from one of them to the next, trying to guess who out of us has been in love before.

And knowing that there's no way I'll ever ask.

CHAPTER
TWENTY

KENNEDY

"It still makes absolutely no sense to me," I confess. When Ziggy didn't show up the day after our, uh, *moment*, I was worried we were back to him avoiding me, so when he walked in this morning, I didn't play it anywhere near as cool as I should have.

Ziggy trails his finger back along the wire, then points at where one of the lights will be. I've still got nothing. I widen my eyes at him, trying to convey my confusion without words. Communicating without talking really isn't as easy as he makes it look.

Case in point: the *really?* look he sends my way.

I give him a halfhearted shrug that I'm hoping says, *I'm clueless, what can you do?*

He studies me for so long I worry that he didn't read me right, but then his gaze dips back to the red wire, and he runs his finger down the length again. "It's a trail. Leading the electricity from one point to the next."

"Ohh …" There are a lot of trails though, and while Ziggy obviously knows what he's doing in here, I'm clueless.

Hammering comes from next door, where Hudson is working, and I think he's picked up enough to know that when Ziggy's here, he shouldn't be. I'm hopeful that it won't always be like this, but after how they met, there's a distinct change in Ziggy when Hudson's around. Like he closes himself off even more.

This, right here, is the Ziggy I like the most. Confident and teasing. It's killing me not to know the thoughts going through his mind after the other night, but he's doing exactly what we agreed to. Back to friends. Totally normal. Nothing out of the ordinary.

Except that's a fucking lie because every time he's not looking at me, I'm looking at him. And I'm *looking* looking. He doesn't give much away under his clothes. They hang off him, almost like he's raided Wilde's wardrobe and never bought a thing for himself. The T-shirts hang off him like a sack, and his pants are bunched up and pulled in tight at his waist. Even that doesn't stop me.

Because I can still glimpse the smooth dip of his neck every time his hair shifts, can still see his capable hands and remember the way they felt wrapped around my dick. And whenever I catch a glint of that tongue piercing, it's like I can feel the smooth metal rolling over my cockhead. For a man who was certain that friends were the way to go, my brain has a lot to answer for.

Especially when he groans, hands pressed to his lower back as he arches it, and all I can see is the way his hips tilt forward and picture the cock I know is nestled inside.

I really need to get over this. I yank my eyes away from him and pace toward the back of the house, looking out toward the hill towering over the town. The hill is pretty. Special. Lots and lots of trees. A very great, wonderful thing to look at. That isn't Ziggy.

Because I've gone and overestimated myself. I might have been able to be friends with him for this long because I didn't know he was interested in me, but now I know, it's like the chains are off. Everything he does is designed to make my brain get stuck on him. He's beautiful, inside and out. The kind of man I could see myself settling down with and—

No.

No, no.

Fucking stop it.

I'm half a second away from thumping myself in the forehead to wake up any sleeping brain cells. I always do this. There's interest, so that must mean it's forever. I'm not diving into those thoughts again.

Just because I want to walk up behind him, press him against the wall with my body, and trail kisses down his neck doesn't mean I *have* to do that.

No matter how happy and bubbly it makes my gut to think about it.

Being friends with him is important to me because I think I could learn a lot from him. Not about electricals, because I'm hopeless there, but his calm energy, the way he doesn't force his thoughts into every opening, and how he lives completely in the moment are all things I respect.

They're also things I'm terrible at myself. I always have to be moving, or talking, or making things happen around me. The loudness hides the loneliness, and it's been working for me so far.

Ziggy's lonely too though, and he doesn't feel the need to do all that.

Besides being insanely attracted to him, I also admire him a whole hell of a lot.

So I can't screw this up. Knowing me, I *will*, but the least I can do is put in some effort to keep things friendly. To make sure that we have each other, because I wasn't lying when I said I didn't want to lose him.

A hand on my arm makes me jump a mile, and I turn to find Ziggy's bemused expression.

"I was thinking," I say, defending my over-the-top reaction.

Sure you were.

At least, that's what I think he's saying, and it's nice to be getting more confident at reading him. It's also nice to see less hesitation and nervousness around me. If I had to guess, I'd say that having sex has loosened him up when it comes to me. I guess once you get naked with someone, there isn't a whole lot left to be self-conscious about.

"How's the wiring going?" I ask to move on from the jump scare.

Good. Ziggy points to the wall that has wiring running through it.

"All done?"

He nods and points to two others, indicating that he hasn't started them yet.

"When do you think you'll have time to do them?" I'm conscious of not pushing or asking for too much. The last thing I want is for Ziggy to think we're taking advantage of him, even though he's the one who didn't want to be paid.

When he doesn't answer, I'm about to jump in and remind him that he doesn't have to, but the determined expression he's wearing makes me pause. His mouth moves, and it occurs to me, way too slowly, that he wants to answer.

Which means I have to give him time.

I'm not good with being patient and letting silences happen, but if I want to be as good a friend to Ziggy as he is to me, I need to learn. What he needs matters as much as what I need.

"Hopefully tomorrow," he mutters.

"Tomorrow works for me."

His deep brown eyes meet mine, and they're shining with something I can't place. "Good." I'm not sure what gives me the impression, but there's something almost cocky in the way he watches me. Like he's waiting for something.

The longer we hold eye contact, the drier my mouth becomes

until it's like I'm trying to swallow the Sahara. I'm very seriously starting to doubt that I'm built for friends, because I know keeping things platonic is for the best, it's the smarter option ... but I don't want to be smart.

I want to remember what his lips taste like and how he moans and squirms with my hands on him.

"Kenny ..."

My gut twists with my name, loving how he says it. "Don't say my name."

He blinks through confusion, and I hurry to clarify.

"Because it makes me want to do things to you that I shouldn't." To be even clearer, I add, "Again."

I'm not expecting the slow smile that stretches across his face. He steps closer, one hand finding my arm again as he leans in so his lips are hovering by my ear.

A shiver races down my back before he's even said a word.

"*Kennedy.*"

His scratchy, soft tone has a pool of want building in my gut. It would be too easy to take his hand and tug him closer, chest-to-chest, face-to-face, my hands cupping his throat as I pull him in for a kiss.

Alarm bells sound like a family of birds at sunrise, and I groan as I pull away from him.

The stern look I give him isn't as effective when my cock is this hard. "You're not helping."

His innocent expression looks genuine, but I know better. At least, I'm starting to.

Ziggy isn't the sweet, shy guy I first thought he was.

And *fuck*, it makes me like him even more. I want to explore that side of him and see how far it goes.

I don't realize I've stepped forward again until his eyebrows lift in interest.

"Wait. No. Dammit. You're messing with my head."

His laugh is almost enough to make me say screw it, but I hold strong. It's only been two days since we slept together, so of course my wires are bound to be crossed. And twisted. And knotted beyond recognition. My body remembers his body being responsible for one hell of an orgasm, so biology—probably—is trying to make it happen again.

After a little bit of distance, friends won't be an issue.

We enjoy each other's company enough to wait it out. To get through this rocky patch. So long as I manage to survive my instincts.

This will be the one relationship I don't mess up by being tunnel-visioned on the future.

Friends.

We're friends.

Good friends.

If I say it enough, maybe in sixty years, it will stick.

CHAPTER
TWENTY-ONE

ZIGGY

'm not a sexy guy. I'm not even an *exy* guy. The way Kennedy looks at me almost makes me think I can pull it off though.

I'm working more than ever in a thinly disguised effort to spend time with him. He's nice enough not to call me out on it, but I know he knows. Kennedy isn't an idiot, and he proves it every time we're together. Which has been almost all day, every day this week. And the more time that grows since we slept together, the more the tension between us is suffocating.

I lean against the side of the house, taking a breather, and as usual, he finds me a few minutes later.

"Look at you, slacking off."

I flip him the bird, smile painted on my face.

"If I didn't know better, I'd say you were trying to get away from me. Way to hurt my feelings." He presses his hand to his wide chest like he's emphasizing the point. "I thought we were friends."

He's not trying hard to act convincing, which is good because it wouldn't work anyway. One, because I enjoy the attention, and two, because while most people don't notice me, I notice them. I've gotten really good at reading people.

I'm not sure if it's a leftover survival instinct from reading my parents' moods and knowing when it was safe to appear or safer to hide, but the smallest things are obvious to me. I usually know within minutes of meeting someone whether I can trust them or not.

Kennedy has always had trustworthy written all over him.

He leans against the house beside me, shoulder against the shiplap paneling, his focus on me. Giving in to his begging for attention, I turn my head his way, and this wash of nerves floods my gut when we make eye contact.

This. This is why I love spending time with him. He makes me feel good from the inside out, and he's probably unaware he's doing it, but the subtle shift from friendly Kennedy to ... *this* person couldn't be more obvious.

I feel the way his eyes always find me. The way he gravitates as close as possible—like now—and his vibrating energy for more matches my own.

Like I know if I leaned in and kissed him, he'd kiss me back, but I made the first move once.

Next time is on him.

If he's really determined to ride out this no-dating rule that he's set for himself, then I'll ride it out too. All the while making it as hard for him as possible. It's his choice, but I never agreed not to tip the odds in my favor.

"What do you have planned for the rest of the day?" His voice is half a pitch deeper than usual, and the familiarity of it makes me want to lean in closer. Who am I kidding? Everything about him makes me want to lean in closer.

It can't be me though.

I lift my shoulders, trying to look cute while I do it. I'm not sure that I'll ever pull off flirty, but I'll do whatever I need to in order to keep Kennedy hooked.

It's almost predictable the way he opens his mouth to suggest we hang out, but the sound of a car reaches us before he can speak.

And like that, our cozy bubble pops.

"Hart back already?" he asks, leaning forward to see the entrance to Old End, and it doesn't take long for the white SUV to appear. "Weird. But I guess that's our cue to—"

He cuts off when Hart isn't alone. A shiny silver thing trails behind, and when Hart pulls off the road, it parks alongside him.

Kennedy and I exchange a confused look before he breaks away from me to see what's going on. And I'm left frozen to the spot, not sure if I'm supposed to follow him or wait here.

Hartwell is hard for even me to get a read on, then add a complete unknown to that, and walking over there feels impossible. Especially with the further Kennedy gets from me.

Approaching a group of people? Having them *watch* as I get closer? No, thank you.

I'd rather electrocute myself.

But then, is it any more awkward than hovering here, at a weird distance, and staring at them?

Fuck me. The only thing that stops me from tugging at my hair is the fear it might draw their attention. Why am I like this? Why am I so set to sabotage myself that I *know* walking over there won't be a big deal, but in my brain, it's a very, very big deal?

I clench my jaw at the building frustration and duck back between the houses before I'm seen. Hudson's likely to join them soon, and I can just picture him walking past and questioning why I'm spying on people.

Error. Error. Error.

In a split second of self-preservation, I duck back inside. I'll pretend like I wasn't interested in the mystery visitor, and if Kennedy wonders where I've gone, he'll find me here working, and it will look like the most normal thing in the world.

After all, it's the whole damn reason I'm in town to begin with.

I'm supposed to be here.

It makes sense.

It's not until I'm sheltered from view inside the building, the dull murmur of voices outside too low for me to make out, that I remind myself to breathe. Kennedy won't be gone long. Then we can pick up where we left off.

Minutes pass, and I try not to get antsy. Or curious.

Who the hell did Hart bring with him?

Another tradesperson to help with the houses? They have me to cover the electrical, but maybe a plumber? What if they're an asshole?

While I wait, I might as well get my curiosity under control. I check down the side of the house to make sure that Kennedy isn't back yet before I creep through the inside, stepping around the frames of partially built walls. The windows on the front of the house are mostly boarded up, but some of them aren't flush, and sunlight peeks through the gaps.

I choose the biggest one to spy from.

Like I'd suspected, Hudson has joined them. He's got his back to me with Hart beside him and Kennedy side on. The three of them are surrounding someone who's blocked from view by Hudson.

Because of course.

That brother always has to make things difficult for me.

While I'm watching, a laugh bursts from Kennedy, the tops of his cheeks patchy and red as he scuffs a hand back through his hair.

His body energy is … nervous?

Who the fuck is it?

I turn my glare to Hudson, willing him to shift out of the way. Something about Kennedy is throwing up alarm bells, and I'm cursing my stupid wreck of a brain that wouldn't let me walk over with him.

It would have been easy. So easy. For anyone but me.

And then I'd be right in Kennedy's line of sight, so there's no way he'd forget about me while he laughs and blushes at someone else.

There's a whole house between us, but I know for a fact that's what it is.

He's *blushing*.

My tongue piercing runs over the back of my teeth, and I have to hold back the urge to bite it. This is fine. I'm probably misreading everything, and any moment now—

Hudson shifts to point at something, and my heart drops like a rotten tree branch in a storm. Torn away and then in free fall.

It's the woman from the diner.

Her hair is out, and she's not wearing that ugly uniform. She looks … pretty.

I hate her more than I did the first time I saw her.

I know this would be a perfect time to walk away, to go back to work and stop thinking about her and distract myself with literally anything else.

My feet are stuck though. Stuck like when all the worries kick in, but this is something different this time.

This time, it's straight-up jealousy.

Hudson playfully pushes Kennedy's shoulder, and I watch as he takes a step toward Caroline, then pauses. His gaze swings back this way before he leans in toward his brothers, says something, and then follows Caroline down the street.

My heartbeat is so loud in my ears, it makes my head dip out of focus.

Where. The hell. Is he going?

His form gets smaller the further they walk, and I'm so focused on him, it takes me too long to notice his brothers are heading toward me.

I hear them by the side of the house and only manage to scramble to my feet before they walk in and look around.

"Ziggy?" Hudson calls.

"Back here." I speak without even thinking about it, but my head is scrambled. There's this deep ache in my chest that's got me dangerously close to throwing up. I'm trying to hide it as I reach them, but I have no idea what expression I'm wearing because when I step into view, both Hudson and Hart immediately look worried.

"You okay?" Hudson asks.

I nod, jerkily and too fast, but I'm losing the will to care.

Hudson doesn't look convinced, but Hart buys it.

"Kennedy wanted us to let you know he's taking the rest of the day off," Hart said. "He had a visitor."

A visitor.

The rest of the day.

The day that was supposed to belong to me.

Good to know I'm so easily traded out, I guess.

I try not to storm away but mustn't pull it off because Hart's arm flies out in front of me. "Hey, don't mind him. She's Mrs. …" He trails off, thinking, "Nine hundred and seventieth The One." He rolls his eyes like that's supposed to make me feel better.

"Yeah, he gets like this," Hudson adds. "Meets someone, then for a week or so, it's all about them, until they dump him and he's a mess over it." He snorts. "So much for not dating."

I'm not sure if this is supposed to be comfort or rubbing it in that Kennedy had me as an option but chose not to take it.

"Should stock up on the gin now," Hart drones.

Hudson sighs, crossing his arms to lean against the wall. "Maybe this could be it? I wasn't expecting Wilde. Maybe Kennedy will find—"

"No." Hart already sounds bored. "He's not finding the love of his life up here. This will end the way they always do."

"True …"

It's like they've forgotten I'm still here, so I make it easy for them and leave. I jump off the open back of the house, cross the short distance to the tree line, and start the walk home.

He's not going to find the love of his life up here.
Kennedy didn't want me waiting for him.
So I won't.
He knows where I live.
Let's see how long it takes him to remember I exist.

CHAPTER
TWENTY-TWO

KENNEDY

I really, really don't like this. I'm walking along with Caroline, but everything inside of me is screaming to go back to the house. I should have checked in with Ziggy. I should have told him I wouldn't be long.

But my brothers were pushing me to go with her, and Caroline was looking at me with all this expectation after driving two hours to get here. *Two hours.*

I'm still spinning over the complete one-eighty the day has done so quickly. How was I supposed to tell her that I already had plans—which I didn't—after she made the effort to come all this way?

At least I told my brothers to apologize to Ziggy for me. As long as he knows that I'm not blowing him off, that's the main thing.

Now I have to figure out how to blow off Caroline without being rude.

"I can't believe you're restoring this entire town. That must be so much work."

"It is." I glance back at the towering houses, happy with the progress we've made. "We're at the stage now where nothing feels like it's progressing forward, and it's hard work but a lot of patience too."

"I could imagine." She reaches over, playfully giving my shoulder a squeeze. "Feel how tense you are. That can't be good for your body."

I subtly step out of her hold and don't have the heart to tell her that I'm tense because she caught me off guard. It's mean to tell someone who's obviously interested in you that you'd rather be with someone else.

Maybe her coming here was the distraction I needed though.

All week, Ziggy's been within arm's reach, and it's only going to take so long before I cross those invisible lines between us. The time I thought I needed still hasn't come, and the longer I deny myself, the more I want him.

Ziggy knows it too.

At least, I think he does. If I'm reading him right, he can see the way I'm struggling, but he hasn't made a move to put me out of my misery. Which only cements he's as serious about this friendship as I am.

I glance back down at Caroline, and the interest is clear in her blue eyes. In the way she made an effort to come here. How she's putting herself out there again, even though the last time didn't work out so well for her.

She's *really* pretty. I can't deny that. Sexual attraction isn't the issue, but it's not her personality either. We've never had a problem holding a conversation, and I genuinely do like her.

So where's that spark?

The spark that I get for literally any other person who'll give me the time of day? It's not here. It wasn't there when the bartender flirted with me the other night either. I'd like to think I'm maturing and finally kicking the habit of emotional patheticness, but after thirty years, there's no way. It's who I am. I'm stuck with me.

And I have a sneaky feeling I know where that spark has gone.

Ziggy stole it.

It would be so much easier if Caroline pulled all those feelings from me. Trying a relationship with her would be zero risk. Sure, it'd be awkward at the diner, but losing her from my life would be a nonevent. Ziggy though? It's just my luck that the one person outside of my family who I want to keep has the biggest risk attached to him.

If I lost Ziggy, I don't think I could breathe.

"Why are you here?" I ask suddenly, and it's only after the words are out that I realize how rude they sounded. "Not that I don't appreciate the visit, of course, but it's out of the blue."

I've knocked her off guard, and she pauses, almost at the tree line, and offers me a hesitant smile. "Thought you might like a friendly face and an excuse for a few hours off work."

"I don't need an excuse though. No one's forcing me to do anything."

Her light brown eyebrows curve downward, and I immediately feel like a dick.

"Sorry, I'm … feeling a bit off today. It's nothing personal, but … you remember what I said last time, don't you?"

"I remember you giving me some story about the distance and having to work."

"It wasn't a story. You made the drive; you know how far it is."

"Two hours." She shrugs, shoulders tan from the sun, with the thin straps of her dress holding on for dear life. "It was nice and scenic."

"I have nothing to offer a relationship right now—"

"And I'm not asking for one." She plants her hands on her hips. "I thought we could get to know each other better. Away from the diner. Maybe become friends and see if there's anything here."

Friends, I can do. It's not like you can ever have too many of them. "Friends?"

She nods quickly. "Exactly."

"As long as you know that I'm not looking for anything romantic. That's not on the table."

"You've said. It's fine. I get it."

"Okay …"

Do friends drive two hours to see other friends on a whim? I have no idea. Apparently, I've never been a great friend to people, which checks out when I've always been so focused on that dream of getting married and settling down. Maybe learning how to be friends with Caroline will help me when it comes to Ziggy?

Even I can admit that sounds like grasping at straws, but I'm up for anything.

"So …" She sways side to side, making her dress go all swishy around her. "Want to show me around this place? Hart said you guys own the whole thing. That's impressive."

Ownership is a loose term, given all the headaches we went through with Wilde. "Sure. Follow me."

I'm cautious of it getting late when I put Caroline in her car and warn her to drive safely. She should make it back to Wayward before dark, but up here, surrounded by hills and trees, nighttime sets in fast.

I watch as the brake lights disappear into the trees, feeling thrown by the last few hours. For someone who's always sucked at romance, there's no doubt in my mind that Caroline was flirting with me, after the agreed friends thing, and it's not sitting right.

I'd hate to think I'm leading her on, but I was up-front about where I'm at.

I don't know what else to do.

My brothers are sitting in the camping chairs outside the main house we've been using to sleep in. It's the only one we haven't started pulling apart, but once one of the others is livable, this one will be going too. Until then, it's almost starting to feel like home.

"Surprised she didn't stick around for dinner," Hart calls as I get closer.

"Didn't want her driving in the dark."

"She could have stayed the night. We wouldn't care."

I bristle at how easily he throws that out there. "Why would I want her to stay?"

Hart's cynical gaze slides to Hudson. "Ah … because that's sort of your thing? Smother them in attention, wear their skin …"

"Gross."

"He's got a point," Hudson unhelpfully adds. "Normally when you start seeing someone, you don't let them out of your sight."

"The difference is," I say, trying to keep my tone even, "I'm not seeing Caroline."

He waves my comment away. "Dating. Wanting to date. Same thing."

"Did it occur to either of you that I don't want to date her at all?" My tone gets louder with each word, but I'm met by silence. "Hartwell? I *told* you I didn't want to date her."

"Yeah, because of the stupid deal you made with Hudson."

Before I can answer, Hudson cuts in. "Which I'm not holding you to, by the way. I know that getting together with Wilde sort of negated—"

"It doesn't negate anything. And you don't need to hold me to it." I turn to the cooktop and act invested in getting it as clean as possible before I start dinner. "I brought up the idea because I wanted to do it. I'm sick of having my heart stomped on."

"If it helps, I don't think she's planning to do any stomping." Hart scowls. "I bumped into her in Wayward, and to get her to shut up about you and stop talking to me, I offered for her to follow me up here."

"Yeah, well, thanks for that," I throw back sarcastically. "Next time, don't offer. I was busy and then had to spend the afternoon playing tour guide."

"Tour guide to a pretty girl who's interested in you?" Hudson mocks. "The *pain.*"

"Shut the fuck up." It's not like me to snap, and I know I'm making them uncomfortable, but the longer I have to think about it, the more I don't like that no one is listening to me. Is it really that unbelievable that I'm not interested in someone?

"Wait …" Hart drags out the word. "Are you … *mad* at me?"

Am I? Hudson and I lock horns about the important stuff, but Hartwell never gives anything enough attention for me to bother getting mad at him. Right now though? I actually think I am.

"All I'm saying is that it would have been nice if you called first."

"With her in my face? You wanted me to call and see if I was allowed to bring her over for a playdate?"

"I had plans."

"Doing what?"

Nothing, actually, and I'm too slow to think up a lie.

"What's really going on here? Any other time and you'd be high-fiving me for setting you up."

"I don't *want* to be set up."

He makes a sound like he's blowing me off.

"Fine, we get it," Hudson says, taking over. "No more setting up. We'll let you do your own thing."

"Thank you."

I ignore the way Hart sneers at us both.

Then, because I don't want to draw more attention to myself, I pull out the utensils and check them over as I casually ask, "Did you pass on my message to Ziggy?"

"Yep."

"What did he say?"

Hudson's laugh is bitter. "Since when does he ever say anything?"

"He says a lot. You just have to pay attention."

"Uh-huh. Right. Well, we told him you wouldn't be back, and then he just awkwardly walked off. I assume he'll be here tomorrow."

I freeze. "You told him what?"

"That you had a visitor."

I slowly turn to Hudson, anger rolling in my gut. "That's not what I said."

"It's close enough."

"How is *he has a visitor* anything like what I told you?" My blood is bubbling hotter as it occurs to me that Ziggy didn't get my message. Not the one that was meant for him. That I very specifically worded *for* him.

This is not how I wanted my day to go. I'll make it up to you.

"Why does it matter?" Hart snaps. "You guys got everything you needed done, and he had an early mark."

"Keys."

He blinks up at me.

"Give me the goddamn keys."

I could kick them. Or myself. All I know is that while I was out here with Caroline, Ziggy probably thought I was blowing him off. With any luck, I'll get to his place and he'll be fine and think I'm ridiculous for worrying.

Worst case, he'll think I did what I swore I'd never do.

Forget about him.

No one who knows Ziggy could ever do that.

Sunset is close to kicking in as I snatch the keys from Hartwell and storm toward the car.

My gut is twisted tight, and every minute it takes to get to him feels like forever.

CHAPTER
TWENTY-THREE

ZIGGY

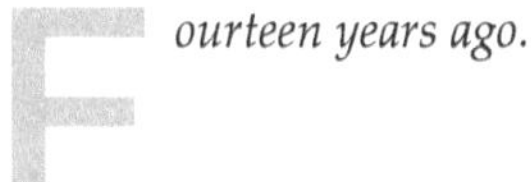 *ourteen years ago.*

I'm barely breathing as I shift my door open, one hand pressed to the wood while the other grasps the handle in my sweaty palm, easing it open inch by painfully slow inch. I strain my ears for any sign of life downstairs, but there's nothing. There never is.

I don't even know if they're here or working, but I've waited as long as I can.

Praying my empty stomach doesn't give me away, I slip into the hall in my plumpest, softest slippers that I picked out specifically for this purpose and follow the path engrained into my memory. I'm completely silent, strangled breathing a familiar pain in my chest, and I don't exhale until I've passed their room and reached the stairs.

Then I gather the air in my chest again and make my way down. All the weight is kept on the balls of my feet; every shift, every step, every redistribution of my weight is measured and incremental. I'm careful. So careful. The stairs have become a pattern of left, right, front of the middle, back, foot sloped sideways with as little pressure as possible, and it's not until I reach the bottom without a single sound that my muscles start to unlock.

Other than hearing, it's like the rest of my senses go into hibernation. The dread of leaving my room is heavy, but my heartbeat is steady, my hands don't shake anymore, and I slip through the living room toward the kitchen with renewed purpose.

I can't cook anything because that will definitely bring hell down on me, so I debate what's the biggest risk. Opening the fridge and risking the puff of the seal being that fraction too loud, or hoping the pantry door hinges are the right temperature not to squeal. With the fridge, I can grab a handful of bananas that are easy to carry and silent to eat. With the pantry, I can load up my pockets with snacks and bread that should last a few days before having to do this again. But the plastic wrappings have given me away before.

A bird lands on the kitchen windowsill.

Its twittering fills the kitchen, wings bumping the window as it jumps along, and my veins turn to ice.

Go!

I wave my hands at it, ears strained back up the stairs to my parents' closed bedroom door.

The bird ignores me.

Move.

Leave.

Shut the fuck up.

I'm gesturing so wildly, trying to startle it, that my pulse has kicked up its rhythm.

Please, please, please don't ruin this for me.

Like it can sense my begging, it disappears as quickly as it came, throwing the house back into silence. Silence, except for my heartbeat in my ears.

It's going to have to be the fridge. Maybe their shifts will line up today, and they'll both be gone at the same time, so I can restock my room.

I focus on calming my breathing, my heart rate, and getting my hands to settle before I risk the fridge. The door releases with a *puh*, and I freeze again, listening … listening …

My stomach growls.

Fuck.

I open the drawer, grab two bananas, and close it again, the plastic reconnecting sounding like a gunshot in the silence. I'm so close. Halfway there. I close the fridge a bit too hard in my rush, and the glass bottles inside shudder together.

I'm panting from the effort, the sickening adrenaline, stomach in angry knots that I beg just to work with me until I'm back in my room.

A noise comes from upstairs, and panic floods me. I lock up. Freeze. Knowing I should run and hide, I can't do anything to make myself move. I wait for the inevitable footsteps, the anger, the screaming, the names …

A minute passes before the noise replays in my consciousness.

It was a pipe.

Just a groaning pipe.

Even if it did wake them, no one could blame me for that.

Still, it takes me another few moments before I can move again. Before I unlock my muscles, shaking more than I can control, and risk taking another step.

I make it back upstairs. Down the hall. Into my bedroom, where it takes me a full minute to close the door again.

Then I collapse onto my bed with relief.

Something prickles at the backs of my eyes, but I grit my teeth against the feeling. It's okay. I'm okay.

But even though they didn't wake up, I can hear Mom's shriekingly loud voice anyway. *Why are you so ungrateful, Ari? Why can't you ever let us sleep? So selfish, so thoughtless, so disrespectful.*

I pull my knees to my chest and breathe through it.

It's okay. *I'm o-fucking-kay.*

Four years. Eleven months. Twenty-two days.

As soon as I'm eighteen, I'm gone.

I just need to make it until then.

I'm lying on my bed, staring at the ceiling of darkening rock, shadows filling all the carved grooves running through it. The stiller I lie, the easier it is to keep the feelings and jealousy in check. It's only once I move, knocking them from the carefully built box in my heart, that everything *hurts*.

I'd been so sure I could feel something building with Kennedy, so what happened today feels like Velcro being ripped apart. Sharp, loud, and fast, leaving me with nothing but confusion. Hart's words keep playing over, and as much as I want to believe I'm good enough for Kennedy, I have a lifetime of evidence that proves I'm not.

Why would he want someone selfish and pathetic when he can have literally anyone?

I squeeze my eyes closed, pushing back my parents' voices. I don't care how today made me feel; I haven't been imagining the way Kennedy looks at me. I didn't dream up his kisses or us having sex.

It all happened.

And if he can look at me like that—someone who I'm

convinced is the greatest person alive—it makes me question the tight grip I've had on all the truths I've been fed.

Because Kenny wouldn't be interested in someone pathetic. Would he?

I thump my mattress, frustrated with myself. These thoughts aren't getting me anywhere. Kennedy is still with Caroline. I'm still here alone. I can hope for my person all I like, but it doesn't mean he's going to be delivered to me in a pretty bow. No matter how much I want it.

The worst part is that I know I'd treat him good, and that's what he's looking for in a partner. Would he treat me good though? Or is his interest only because I'm *here*?

The way he was blushing at Caroline makes me certain of that answer, but I don't want to come up with it myself. I want him to tell me.

Not that I'll ever get the confidence to make it happen.

My ears prick up at the sound of a motor, and slowly—so I don't knock over that jealous, bitter box I've built—I throw my legs over the side of the bed and go to investigate. I can already tell it's not Wilde's truck, and my pulse picks up when that severely narrows the options.

Either someone's back to raid the storage cars again, or …

The flash of white before the SUV pulls into view fills me with this deep, nervous excitement that's stronger than my jealousy. I'm still annoyed and still feel sick over Caroline, but Kennedy's already seen me spiral once, and I refuse for him to witness it again.

I'll suffer in silence.

Something new and different for me.

He's barely stopped the car before he throws open the door and staggers out, slamming it behind himself. "Fuck, Ziggy, I'm so sorry." His green eyes are wide with guilt, and his mouth is sagging under his thick mustache. "I gave my brothers a message to pass on, and they didn't. I feel like a complete dick."

Those happy nerves creep cautiously higher as I tilt my head.

"I didn't plan for her to come up here. It caught me by surprise, and the more I think about it, the more I'm not happy about being ambushed like that. I didn't want to blow her off because it felt rude, so I told my brothers to apologize to you and that I'd make it up to you. And they didn't. I should have done it myself. I screwed up. I'm sorry." He pauses a few feet in front of me, panting like he ran up here instead of driving. His large chest and shoulders move with every breath, and the more I take in his expression, the more I believe him.

He really didn't want Caroline here.

We're staring at each other for a long time before I find the words.

"You were blushing."

"I was?" Confusion crosses his face. "I don't remember blushing. I was frustrated and trying not to lose my shit."

Could that have been what made him go so red? The way I swell inside is trying to convince me, but I'm cautious. Worried that I'll buy every word, and it will all be bullshit. I don't like hurting. I've been able to mostly avoid it for eight years now, and the second Kennedy stumbled into my life, all those feelings flooded back into me.

"Then … how?"

He takes a careful step forward. "How what?"

"How will you make it up to me?" My voice comes out huskier than I planned.

Kennedy's eyes lock on mine, startling the butterflies in my gut that I do my best to ignore. I fail, of course, because being trapped in Kennedy's gaze is magical. "Ahh … hadn't thought that far ahead yet."

Right. My lips are so fucking dry just looking at him, and I run my tongue barbell over the bottom one to shake the feeling. I'm not going to make the first move. I promised myself. Not even when his gaze dips from my face and starts a slow track down my body.

"Maybe ..." He clears his throat. "We could hang out?"

Always. I try not to let my disappointment show while I nod quickly.

He steps closer. Clears his throat again. "Are you okay? Like ... really?"

Am I? There are so many ways I'm very not okay, and I could probably write a list for him. But that's not what he means.

He means are *we* okay.

I'm not sure of the answer to that either. He's barely feet from me, and the pull I feel, like a hook ripping through my heart and yanking me toward him, is sickening. I crave Kennedy like I've never craved anyone, and I don't know if it's because I've let myself want him or if there's something deep and intuitive that's decided he's mine, but it's not exactly a feeling I can call *okay*.

Nothing about this is okay.

Everything is exciting and terrifying and the reason to keep breathing.

I want Kennedy in so many ways I'll never have the words to explain.

"Ziggy ..." He steps closer, right into my space, and it's not until he drags his thumb under my eye, catching a tear, that I even realize how blurry my vision has become. I blink quickly, instinctively looking away, but Kennedy's fingertips on my jaw bring me back again. "I know," he whispers. "I feel the same."

It's the last thing I expect Kennedy to admit.

He shuffles forward again until his feet knock mine, and I'm too scared to breathe and ruin this moment. My tears dry up from the shock of it, and I focus on every detail in his face. Including his lips. Especially his lips.

"Tell me not to kiss you," he rasps.

"Never."

It must be what Kennedy was waiting for because his mouth

slams down on mine. Like the first time, my whole body comes alive. Ripples of excitement race over my skin, and I focus all my energy on fighting the need to shiver. I press closer toward him, parting my lips and hoping Kennedy will take it for the invitation it is.

He knows me too well. He licks into my mouth, hand leaving my jaw to bury in my hair as the other one finds my side. His thumb rubs circles into my hip bone, and I want to soak in every detail of this moment.

Kennedy's need, his lips, his touch. The way his mustache scrapes roughly over my lips. Or his tongue flicks over my barbell. Or my piercings crush between our chins.

I give in to the urge to tremble.

His hips meet mine, hard cock rocking against my trapped erection. This sizzling, unbridled need has been unleashed, and I can't get enough.

Kennedy grunts, backing me up so quickly my back slams into the rock wall. It forces the breath from my lungs that Kennedy catches with his mouth as his hand sneaks up under my T-shirt.

"So sexy," he mutters against my tongue as his thumb circles my nipple. "Prettiest little nipples."

I exhale sharply and lift my shirt over my head, forcing his mouth to break from mine, and before he can kiss me again, I work on his. The open button-up is stripped from his shoulders and his tank top yanked upward and discarded somewhere along with mine.

His big, warm body boxes me against the rough wall at my back, and skin on skin, I've never felt more incredible.

"Hold on."

I tilt my head, not sure exactly what I'm holding on *for*, when he reaches for my headband. Of course. He pulls it out and sets it back in place, the scrape against my scalp like a warning not to touch, clearing the hair I like to hide behind. I feel exposed without it, but when Kennedy's gaze settles on my features, it's filled with hunger.

"How am I supposed to look at that face and behave myself?"

My smile feels wicked as I curl my fingers into the sides of his jeans. "You don't."

His intense gaze is studying mine, like he's trying to convince himself to hold back.

If he thinks I'm going to help him with that, he doesn't know me at all. I tilt my face to his ear. "Show me what I do to you."

Kennedy drops to his knees, tearing at the front of my jeans. I'm not expecting it, but I'm also not about to complain when he rips my fly open and tugs my boxer briefs down below my balls. His appreciative exhale is cool against my aching dick. Then his mouth is there. Warm, wet suction closes over my tip, and I have to ball my hands into fists and shove one of them between my teeth to stop from coming. The pain I'm biting into my knuckles helps me fight it, but every inch Kennedy takes is testing me. His tongue is working some kind of magic, and while this is the second time my dick has been in his mouth, the first was nothing like this.

I'm not even sure that could be considered a blow job with how quickly it ended.

This time I'm determined to last.

Even if every one of my muscles is straining.

Even if my teeth have broken skin.

Even if his fingers brushing my balls make me forget how to breathe.

The warm stroke of his tongue, the light scrape of his facial hair, the way he hums around me like he's as turned on as I am.

Fuck, fuck, fuck.

I tug his hair, and Kennedy pulls off, looking at me through lust-drenched eyes. "What is it?"

"I'm ... about to ..."

"You don't want it to be over yet?"

I quickly shake my head, because how the hell do I vocalize something like that?

He ducks down and drags his flattened tongue over my balls. "You taste so damn good though."

He's going to kill me.

"I want to taste every inch of you, Ziggy."

Actually, scratch that. At this point, I'm convinced I'm already dead.

CHAPTER
TWENTY-FOUR

KENNEDY

think I was made to be on my knees for him. The way he's standing over me is hot as hell. He's thin, very lightly muscled, piercings glinting on his face and at the head of his dick, and all I want is to feel it rubbing against my tonsils again.

His dark eyes are watching me, not bothering to hold back the need he feels, and I know for a fact that he's choosing to show me since Ziggy has no problem closing off when he wants to.

He wants me to know how much I turn him on, like I want him to know he does the same to me. Not only is he hot, smart, interesting, with a dick I could suck all day, but the fact that no one else has ever touched him is a massive turn-on.

I'm not a possessive guy. I might come on too strong in relationships, but it's never in an ownership way. I'm getting a thrill of excitement from exploring parts of him that no one has ever seen before.

With a huff, I push to my feet, shed my restrictive jeans, and kick my briefs off after them. His gaze drinks me in like he never wants to stop looking, and fuck me, I feel the same.

I give my cock a good tug to take the edge off.

"I can't make up my mind how I want to get you off."

He sets his fingertips on the center of his chest and slowly trails them down his body. I try to swallow my groan, and I fail.

"Touch yourself."

Ziggy hooks my gaze as he wraps those long, capable fingers around his shaft.

"Damn, you're so hot. Jerk off."

He does, touching himself with the intimate strokes of familiarity, and I want to learn his body the way he knows it. Want to know exactly what he needs to make him come.

My own dick is aching, desperate to touch, but I can't make up my mind. I want to take over, but I also want him back in my mouth, and I really want him to turn around and give me a better view of that ass I can't stop thinking about. Maybe sink my cock into his hole until he's crying out for more.

My dick gives a warning throb, and I hurry to squeeze it again.

I need to make up my mind.

"Turn around."

I don't sound anywhere near as demanding as I'm trying to. Not a surprise, though, when I'm weak for this man.

He sets his forearm against the rock wall and keeps jerking off. His jeans are around his ankles, and his underwear is stretched tight around his thighs, but they're low enough to expose his ass, and I step forward, needing to touch it.

He fills my hands, and I grab him hard, squeezing the soft flesh and picturing how it would jiggle with him bouncing on my cock. The image is sinful. I want it so much, but I don't have lube or condoms, and fucking him without them isn't an option. If I'm the only person he's ever had sex with, I'm going to make sure I set the standard.

I give in to the urge to touch him, pressing myself against his back and slipping my cock between his legs. My tip is nudging his balls, and Ziggy shivers in my arms.

I box him in and drag my tongue up his neck until I reach his ear. "You are too sexy for words."

That gets a husky laugh from him.

"I want to devour you." My hips thrust forward, not able to stop myself. "Touch you. Suck and lick every inch of your body."

"What else?"

His voice hooks something behind my navel that tugs us together. Seals my need for him in a way I've never experienced before. Like separating from him isn't an option. "I'd make you fly, Ziggy. Make you feel so good you wouldn't be able to stop from screaming my name." I spit into my hand and coat my cock with it. Then I slide it back between his thighs.

"Close your legs," I beg, lips right by his ear. "Squeeze my cock as tight as you can make it."

He does exactly as I asked, and fuck, it makes me hot. How well we work together, how eager he is to please, and how damn eager I am to make him feel good. This has been building all week, to the point where I had to walk away today before I pinned him to the wall, and the fact that he thought I could possibly be interested in Caroline when he's been teasing me with all of this is ridiculous.

"You've been driving me out of my mind all week," I tell him, starting to thrust.

"You can talk."

If he thinks I have anything on him, he's dead wrong. "Nuh-uh," I breathe. "Just watching your hands move. Remembering them on my dick. The cute, shy little looks you give me from under your hair. The way your jeans tease at that ass they're hiding. How sometimes your shirt pulls up and shows off a little slip of skin. You have no idea how much my mouth waters every time I see it. I've got nothing on that."

His shaky exhales bounce off the wall as he pushes back against me, muscles in his thighs shifting and flexing around my dick in a way that feels indescribable. "What about when you look at me like you're about to break? The way your eyes go dark. How your jaw tenses. The way you use any excuse to touch me."

"You noticed that, huh?"

"Kenny …" He laughs darkly, voice thick with arousal. "I *live* for that."

Shit. He's so on edge, it gets me closer. Even naked, the night is warm, and I'm building up a sweat as I move against him. Our bodies are sealed together, skin slapping against skin as I lose control of my thrusts. The scent from his hair is filling my nose, his heavy breathing is on a direct line of access to my balls, and the feel of his body under my hands—his nipples, his chest, his sides and stomach—I've lost the ability to process it all.

My balls have tightened, ready, and I need Ziggy to get there first. He's stopped jerking off to press both hands against the wall in front of him, so I drop one of mine to do it for him.

"Please," he hisses. "I'm close. Too close."

"Good." I drag wet, messy kisses down his neck. "Come for me. Show me how good I make you feel."

He shudders, the friction around my dick almost too much. He's sticky with my precum, and he's pressing back as desperately as if he were riding me. Fuck, I want that so bad. My teeth dig into his shoulder as I hold back the need to come.

He's going to be first.

I'll edge myself all night if I have to.

"I still can't believe it," I murmur.

"What?"

"That no one else has ever touched you."

He makes a dismissive noise as he thrusts into my fist.

"I mean it." My words come out harshly. "They have no idea what they were missing out on. I'm going to hear your cute little moans for the rest of my life."

And like he's trying to seal my fate, he moans. Hoarse, soft, in the back of his throat, like he's trying to stop it but can't.

"That's it. Just like that." I suck on the closest stretch of skin I can reach. "Let me hear you."

"No, no, no-no, *no*." His dick pulses, and he covers the wall with his release. Every twitch, every throb, every muffled sound of his pleasure has mine crashing down over me. I come so hard, blackness kicks in for a second, but I grip his hips hard and don't slow down until my balls are empty, and a rush of calm passes through me and makes my limbs light.

I fold forward against his back, breathing deeply, face pressed to smooth skin, and never wanting to move in my life.

He speaks too soon. "Well, fuck. Was really trying to last longer than that."

He sounds half-drunk, half-asleep, and a surge of satisfaction ripples through me.

I did that.

And I want to keep on doing that.

Well, our friendship lasted all of five seconds. I know I'm supposed to regret my lack of self-control or whatever, but Ziggy with flushed cheeks and messy hair and bright eyes only makes me thankful to have shit all willpower.

"I think we have a problem," I say, stepping into my briefs and pulling them back up.

The confusion that ripples across his brow is adorable, and I lean in to press a kiss to it.

"I don't think we can be friends."

"You don't want to be friends with me?" he mutters, soft as a breath, but when I meet his eyes, the teasing in them is impossible to miss.

"I'd *love* to be friends with you, but considering the things I want to do to you are incredibly unfriendly, I don't see how it would work."

"Felt friendly to me."

I catch my laugh, looking around with an uncontrollable smile on my face. "So. Where's your place?"

His eyes dart to the side, expression immediately closing off as he tugs his jeans up.

"Wait … why do I get the feeling you don't want to show me?"

He opens his mouth, then quickly closes it again. Wary eyes search mine, and then with a huff, he turns on his heel and walks into the mine shaft right by us.

I wait a beat for him to come back, and when he doesn't, I follow him. As I creep around the corner, I'm half expecting a bear or a mountain lion to jump out at me.

I'm not expecting to walk into a whole-ass *home*.

"What is this?" I ask, then a second later want to kick myself. It's obvious what it is. It's where Ziggy lives.

There's a couch and a TV on one side, then what looks like the pieces of a bathroom on the other. Behind it all is a bed, and behind *that* … nothing but darkness. I'm torn between finding it cool and creepy as hell.

"You live here?"

He's paused in the middle of the room, hovering there and watching me like he's waiting for something. It's getting dark, so his face is harder to read than usual, but as I look around, I can feel his expectant stare. The way he's begging me to say *something*.

"It's … nice." Thankfully, I manage to inject conviction into my voice.

He scowls, tucking his hands under his arms, like he's hugging himself.

"No, really. This is cool. Umm, different, obviously, but …" I fall silent when annoyance clouds his features. "Fine, it creeps me out a little. But I'm not used to it, that's all."

He turns, taking in his place, gaze straying back to all that darkness. His hair falls over his face, and I know what he's doing. He's withdrawing to protect himself.

I don't ever want him to need protecting from me.

"Nuh-uh …" I close the distance between us, and even when I sling my arm around his waist, he's tense. "Ziggy, don't be mad.

Please." I tuck his hair back, and he drags his dark eyes up to meet mine, a determined spark deep in them.

"I like it."

"Good." I have no idea how, but I'm not stupid enough to say that. "It's your place. You should."

"But you don't."

I sigh, because I don't want to lie to him. "It's not that I don't like it. It's unconventional and cool. But …" I nod toward where the shaft disappears into nothingness. "How can you sleep, picturing something coming out of the darkness and eating you alive?"

"I don't picture it."

He's giving me so much more openness than I could hope for, and I don't want to lose it. "You are a thousand times braver than me. But … this is your place, and I sort of hope I'll be spending more time here, so I know it'll grow on me like it grew on you." At least that's what I hope, and I'm going to try.

"You're spending time here?"

He's going to make me clarify, because of course he is. For a guy who doesn't like words, he's not shy about facing difficult conversations. And I don't care how many relationships I've had, admitting feelings is never an easy thing to do. I think it's *because* of how many relationships I've had that it's harder than it should be.

Because I know what comes next.

I tell him how I feel, and he lies and says he feels it too, then he immediately starts pulling away. And the distance only makes me try to cling tighter.

The alternative is being caught in this endless loop of pretending to be friends until the pressure breaks, sleeping together, and then faking friends again.

Both options sound fucking painful.

"I like you, Ziggy," I confess. "More than a friend."

"I know."

That simple acknowledgment helps snap my nerves in two. "Of course you do."

"Your thoughts are very loud."

Maybe that should bother me, but it doesn't. "Even without speaking them?"

"*Especially* without speaking them." His lips barely move, but they're still puffy from kissing, and with the worry gone, his whole face is content. I like that look on him.

"You're so beautiful."

He chokes on a laugh, and I know he disagrees and wants to deny it, but I don't let him.

"Don't shake your head at me. You can think whatever you like, but so can I. And I think you're the most beautiful man I've ever met."

One corner of his lips holds a smile. "I like you too."

The relief—and fear—that crashes through me is almost too much. "Okay. Good."

Good. His arms loop around my neck.

"Umm … what does this mean? Are we dating or … or boyfriends?"

He sucks in a sharp inhale. "Boyfriends."

"Yeah?"

Yeah.

"Okay." My hand shakes as I brush his hair back again. Screw holding out for my forever person. Screw the six months with no dating.

Ziggy's exactly who I want.

Now I have to shut up that voice telling me that I'm making the same mistakes I always do.

CHAPTER
TWENTY-FIVE

ZIGGY

I jolt awake, confused by the pressure against my front, and blink down at the person sleeping next to me. Kennedy's crushing my arm under his weight, and his scent has filled my pillows and sheets in a way that makes me lightheaded for a moment.

He's here.

I … am so confused.

Drips of memory from last night come back to me, and unlike last time, it's a fraction easier to believe it happened. Easier, because we're both tangled together, almost naked. And my arm is getting pins and needles.

I try to slide it out without waking him, but when he only cuddles it tighter, I give up. I clear my throat loudly, giving my arm a solid tug, and while I'd love for him to keep sleeping sweetly, my arm is *really* fucking sore.

Except apparently, he's impossible to wake up. He goes on sleeping while I lose all feeling in my arm.

"K-Kennedy?" I try, but it's so soft I have no hope of waking him that way. Why can't I have a deep voice? A loud, confident one? The kind of voice where no one would have anything to tease me about anytime I opened my mouth.

When it comes to Kennedy, I know I trust him. I know logically that I'm safe with him, and he'd never be someone who'd ridicule my flaws. But it's so goddamn hard to forget all the times I tried to speak up for myself, and it only made things worse.

To me, speaking has always been stressful. It's always been a land mine of abuse. Even with all this distance between me and my tormentors, speaking is associated with pain. Fear. Embarrassment.

It's easier to rewire an entire house than my own brain.

I'm so tired of being scared.

I wouldn't talk either if I sounded like that.

I know I've come a long way from the boy who wouldn't say a word, but I hate that it's still so hard. That I can't even wake the man I feel safe with and not feel like my throat is closing over.

He asked why I'm not scared of the dark.

The dark has always been where I've escaped.

My demons don't exist out there. They all live inside me.

I hate that I've allowed them to do that.

I catch an inhale in my chest and force my voice louder. "*Kenny.*"

He jolts, and I immediately tense up, freeze, wait as his eyes blink open and his gaze moves from my arm up to meet mine.

Then a grin fills his face.

"Morning, boyfriend."

Like that, warmth floods through my anxiety, and my muscles let go of their tension. "Boyfriend," I echo.

He leans in, lips meeting mine, and I sigh into the kiss.

I'm okay.

Everything is okay.

Then everything goes from okay to incredible when Kennedy

tugs me on top of him, pushes down the waistbands of our under-wear, and I rock against him while he begs me to come on him.

So I do. We both cover his solid stomach with our release that he happily rubs into his skin.

"I was tossing up between that and having you sit on my face," he says.

And my shock must take over my expression because he laughs.

"It's okay, we'll do that next time. I want to suffocate in your ass."

I don't think it's possible for my eyes to get wider. Or my body to feel hotter. That's … a deal I can make.

"Oh, look, I'm making you blush. That's hot."

I dip my head. I think it's less of a blush and more me over-heating. I have a boyfriend. And we had morning sex. And now he's promising more sex.

This whole thing is so strange.

Amazing, but strange.

Almost like I can't believe that it's real.

I glance over at him as I climb out of bed and catch the worried look he's throwing deeper into the mine. I don't know what he's worried about. There's no way at all for someone to be down there. It caved in a billion years ago, so other than this shallow entrance, there's no way to access it. No one is coming from that way.

It's what could come from outside that we have to watch.

This is why I was worried about him seeing my place though. I don't want to see it as anything other than my safe space, and I know he doesn't like it. There's a reason he slept with his back to the mine last night and had me wrapped around him.

I guess having to snuggle into him isn't the worst outcome, but I want Kennedy to love this place like I do.

He follows me out of bed and heads to my sink to wash up.

"I need to head home and get some work done, do you—wait.

You have *hot water*?" The look he gives me is like he's been slapped in the face. "Screw it. I'm showering here before I go."

Kennedy shoves his underwear off, bare ass and broad back teasing me with the view as he walks over to my shower and turns it on.

I'm hovering in the middle of the room, just staring as he slips under the water and lets out a long groan.

"Not fair," he says. "I've been suffering through cold showers for months now." Then he squeezes out my soap into his hand and lathers himself up with it.

My soap.

He's going to smell like *me*.

Phwoar. Okay. I like that? Apparently so.

I don't move the entire time he's washing himself, whistling happily, and completely unaware of how I'm impersonating a statue. He's filling my home with sound, and all that life radiating from him is addictive.

I don't want him to leave.

The shower switches off suddenly.

"Ahh … any chance of a towel?"

Towel. Yes. That thing.

I only have two, but I hurry over to my drawer where my spare is and hand it to him. I watch as he scrubs it roughly over his hair, swipes it over his limbs, and then reaches down to drag it over his cock. It's hanging soft and thick over his balls, and I've always known dicks are hot, but I never actually processed how much I actually *like* them.

Especially when the dick in question is attached to Kennedy.

"Am I allowed to put clothes on now?" he asks, bouncing his eyebrows.

I scoff like I don't care and head out the front, but there's a good argument to be made for having him here, naked, permanently.

He joins me a few minutes later, and the soft way he kisses me feels like a promise. "Will I see you today?"

There's still more I could do down there, but house two is fully wired, so they're not waiting on me for anything. As much as I'd love to obsessively stick to his side, I won't. We might be jumping into boyfriends, but I've been listening to his worries about things going too fast, and I'm not going to play into them.

Besides, there are some things I want to look into.

Not today.

"Damn." He rubs his thumb softly over my top lip. "I would have enjoyed admiring my handiwork."

His handiwork?

"Your top lip is all red from my mustache. We'll have to be more careful next time."

Next time. There'll be a next time. And if my top lip is all red, I can only imagine what my ass will look like once he's done with it.

"Will I, uh, see you tomorrow?" he checks. "It's okay if that's too soon. I just …"

"Tonight."

It looks like he's fighting a smile. "You want me to come back tonight?"

Yes.

"Okay. Yeah. I'll be here."

This time, I kiss him before taking a step back. He looks like he doesn't want to leave, and I could get used to this feeling. This deep need for us to be tied together. For it to feel wrong when we're apart.

But his feet get unstuck, and he makes his way across the grass and back to the car. I watch as he leaves, knowing tonight can't come fast enough.

"Ah, well, I have ideas," Rooney says, rubbing his chin. "Obviously, we could install a tarp door system thing like you have at the front, but that took us a while." He paces deeper toward the darkness. "Another option is that we fill it in. Like, permanently."

I stare at the wall of shadow looming over us. It's not something I even really pay attention to anymore. It just is what it is. I'd planned to put in lights at one point, trailing all the way to where the cave-in happened, but after a while, it didn't feel important.

A permanent wall means I won't be able to extend my place if I ever want to, but the trade-off is giving Kennedy some peace of mind, so it's an easy choice.

I click the pen and jot down "wall" on the paper, then hand it over.

Rooney nods, then reads the next item. "Hot water system? Does yours need to be replaced already?"

I shake my head.

His confusion hangs between us, but I don't address it.

"Okay, I'll run this by Wilde. A few of us will help with the wall, but the funds for the hot water system will be something I might have to argue for."

I'd expect nothing less. I have a feeling that once Wilde knows what I'm planning with that, he'll magically find the money somewhere.

"Cool, was that everything?" he checks.

When it comes to supplies? Yes.

But as we walk side by side out of my mine, I can't help the words forming on my tongue.

"Have …"

He pauses, waiting me out.

"Have you ever been in love?"

"In love?" My question has thrown him. "Yeah, of course. I was married too, for a minute."

He was *married*? I have so many questions to ask him, but I don't know where to start or how to make them come out. I'm worried I'll ask the wrong thing and make him mad because when it comes to Wilde's End, we have one rule. Don't ask.

Rooney waves a freckly hand my way. "It's a long story. But yeah, I assume we were in love."

"What … what was it like?"

"Being married or in love?"

"In love."

"It was …" He tucks his hands in his pockets along with my paper. His mismatched colored eyes squint as he thinks. "Confusing. It was like there were all these rules I was supposed to follow, but no one told me what they were beforehand. I had obligations. Things people expected of me. Love is … effort. And losing yourself."

Well, fuck. That's not too far off what Kennedy hinted at either. How love would consume him until he wasn't acting like himself. Between that and Wilde's answer, I'm starting to question why anyone would want to fall in love at all.

"I thought …" What did I think? I have no experience with any of it. "That it's supposed to be … good."

"Eh …" He lifts his shoulders in a shrug. "For some people, it might be. Ask Wilde. He seems head over heels for his man."

I don't answer, and Rooney tilts his head my way.

"Did that help? With whatever you're trying to figure out?"

Love is pain and confusion. And losing yourself.

Rooney leaves while I'm still trying to figure out the answer to his question.

CHAPTER
TWENTY-SIX

KENNEDY

"And where the hell have you been?" Hart asks, leaning against the side of the house, arms crossed over his favorite black tank top.

"Places."

"With Ziggy?"

"Maybe."

He swears and kicks at the dirt. "So I've lost you too?"

I turn his way, hand frozen on the car door that I haven't pushed closed yet. "What?"

"First, Hudson ran off with Wilde, and now you're all up in Zig-zag."

Of course he'd know exactly what I was doing. I'm not a good liar, but Hart would let me get away with it if I tried, so I consider actually doing it.

But I don't want to lie.

Lying isn't going to help me get my brothers back.

I push the door closed with a *thup* and approach Hart slowly. He looks resigned to dealing with another one of my relationships, and I don't want it to be that way this time. "I really like him."

Hart doesn't outwardly react, and I can't blame him. He *has* heard all this before. So many goddamn times he could probably set a watch to my relationships.

"You couldn't at least wait until he finished working for us? When shit blows up, who's going to do our electricals then?"

"*If*," I correct him. "If we break up."

"Oh, come on, Kenny. You know how this goes."

Yeah, and I'm terrified. Instead of arguing with him like I normally would, I bite that impulse back and admit it. "I do. Which is why I want your help."

That takes some of the bite out of his bark. Hart looks me over, arms crossing tighter like he refuses to let down his guard. "With?"

"Where's Hudson?"

"Inside."

"Okay." I can't believe I'm going to do this. "Then let's go. I need relationship advice from my brothers."

For the first time ever.

Hart doesn't respond, but I hear him on the stairs behind me as I head into house three. It's in a similar state to two, but without any of the wiring done.

"You're back," Hudson says, the *ziiip* of the tape measure returning to its roll filling the room.

"Yup."

"Where were you?"

"With Ziggy."

"Right." He tugs on the tape again. "Is he okay?"

"He's fine."

"Good. And we're sorry. We should have passed on your message. I just didn't realize it would cause issues."

Before I can answer, Hart cuts in.

"That's because neither of us knew they're fucking."

Hudson laughs and turns back to the wall. "Yeah, okay."

"No. They're *actually* fucking."

The fact that my brother thought that was a joke can't be a good sign. He pauses, then turns slowly, and I brace for the Hudson who explodes first and thinks later.

"Is that true?"

I drop my eyes to the ground, but after a moment, he's still waiting. And it takes a moment after that for me to remember it's because I didn't actually answer him. At least not with words. "Yes. It's true."

"What the fu—" He cuts off and drags a loud inhale through his nose. "Right. How long?"

"First time was the night I spent in Wayward with him, but I think it's been coming on for a while." My heart gives this little blip as I think of him. "He's really …"

"Silent?" Hart supplies.

"Fuck you."

"What? How can he be anything when the guy literally doesn't talk?"

"He does talk when he's comfortable or wants to. He doesn't talk around people who are assholes to him."

Hart points at Hudson. "Exhibit A. A is for asshole."

I wave my hands to cut through their shit. "This isn't what I wanted to talk about. I really like him. A lot. And as Hart was so nice to point out, that means I'm doomed to mess this up."

My brothers both fall quiet.

Hudson's the first to break. "Mess things up is a little harsh."

"Then what would you call it?"

"Coming on too strong?" He pinches his thumb and forefinger together. "Just a bit?"

"Stop lying to him," Hart drawls. "Surprising someone you've been dating for two weeks with a couple's holiday *is* messing things up. Telling a guy you've been on three dates with that you're in love with him *is* messing things up."

I slide down the wall to sit on the floor. "He's going to dump me before I even get a chance to see him again."

"Well, that's not physically possible." Hart lowers himself to sit beside my feet. "Unless he sends someone else to do it."

Hudson kicks Hart's thigh and joins us on the ground. "Don't listen to him."

"He's right though."

"He's not. Ziggy is a whole new relationship. You can't compare him to everyone else. First, that's not fair. And second, because, well, he's not like everyone else."

Hart snickers. "Yeah. The good thing is if he doesn't talk, it'll probably take him longer to dump you."

"Not helpful," I point out.

"Are you sure? I'm almost certain that's what they call a silver lining."

"Ziggy's special."

They exchange a look, and yeah, yeah, they've heard it all before. But I haven't felt *this* before.

"Look, believe me or don't believe me," I snap. "I still want your help. I want you to tell me what to do so that I won't scare him off. I want a real chance this time."

"In that case," Hart says, "I recommend you do literally nothing that you want to do."

"What?"

"All of your instincts, stamp them down. Want to see him? Don't. Want to declare your every loving devotion? Walk away. Want to wear his blood in a vial around your neck?" He makes a buzzer sound. "Abort. Next."

"When have I ever wanted to wear someone's blood?"

"Just getting in before you do."

Hart might be trying to sound like he doesn't care, but he actually made a suggestion. One that, under the derision and sarcasm, he actually meant. He's here. Supporting me.

Maybe we're not as broken as I thought.

"What do you think?" I ask Hudson, who's watching me carefully.

"I think …" He sighs and pats me on the knee. "I love you, Kenny, but I think Hart might be onto something."

"With the blood?"

"With the playing it cool. Tone it down. Remember that you guys are only at the beginning of your relationship, and stop trying to jump to the end. Because once you're there, what else do you have to look forward to?"

"Happiness?"

His lips droop. "You're not happy?"

"With Ziggy, I am."

"Yeah, but you can't rely on someone else for that."

I can't believe he, of all people, is saying that. "Really? When are you *ever* happy?"

"Almost never. But I'm working on it. And that included walking away from Wilde when I didn't think he could give me what I needed."

That gives me the boost I need. Hudson has always been content to accept being treated like crap in relationships, and if he can draw the line and change, then maybe I can too. Maybe it's possible for me not to smother Ziggy and actually get to keep him.

I really don't want to hope and be disappointed, but optimism is as easy to me as breathing.

"I can do this."

Hudson gives me a thumbs-up, and Hart's expression closes down like he's bored with us both, but before he can disappear on me, I reach over and pluck his sleeve.

"Thanks. Who knew my brother was a genius?"

"Yeah, well, out of the two of us, someone had to get the brains."

"Thank you for giving me all the looks."

He sneers and flips me off. "We're identical, moron."

"Then why am I the one who gets all the dates?"

"Oh, I dunno." He pretends to think. "Maybe because you like people, and I like them anywhere other than near me?"

I swing my finger between me and Hudson. "I know of two people you'll never get rid of."

"Kill me now," he mutters, standing up as I blow kisses his way. "I'm going into town."

Some of my good mood fizzles. "You don't want to stay and hang out here for a bit?"

"I'd rather stab myself through each individual finger than be in this town a second longer than I have to be."

He leaves, and the bond I thought was feebly stitching back together between us snaps. Again.

I slump against the wall. "Think we'll ever get through to him?" I expect Hudson to say he can go and fuck himself, but I'm surprised.

"I really hope so."

My gaze catches his, unprepared to see the same wistfulness staring back at me. "Sometimes I miss what we used to have."

"Well, there's only one thing we can do then, isn't there?" He taps the floor we're sitting on. "We build something better."

A lot of the time, I'm sure Hudson is only telling me what I want to hear, but there's something about his words that feels different this time. Almost like he's starting to let himself believe them too.

For the first time in … years, maybe? It really feels like healing things might be possible.

Hudson goes back to work, and I grab my phone, determined to start work on myself. I'm going to be the coolest, calmest, most collected boyfriend that Ziggy could ever dream of. Starting now, no more over-the-top Kennedy. No more wanting sleepovers every night. No more craving to see him smile. No more trying to make everything about his life perfect.

I will be chill.

I will be—

My Internet Explorer takes forever to load, but when it does, it opens to my last search.

And it's not a search I made.

What is love?

Huh? I scratch my head as I scroll down through the options, noting that a few of them have been opened. This wasn't an accidental search. It was on purpose.

But it wasn't me.

I have more than enough experience with love, which is literally my whole problem.

So who was this?

Hudson? Is he falling for Wilde?

Hart? He'd be most likely since I don't think he's ever experienced a feeling in his life.

But they both have their own phones. Why would they use mine?

I search my brain, trying to pinpoint a time where I've left my phone around them and coming up blank. No one uses my phone, especially out here where the service is blood-boiling slow. We do most of our work in Wayward, but even then, I can't think of a time when they would have used my phone.

Then it clicks.

The last time in Wayward.

Me on my computer, and a slim, pale hand sliding my phone face down on the table beside me.

Ziggy.

What is love?

Knowing it was him puts so much more weight behind the question. How could he not know? He's mentioned a family before. If he has one, how doesn't he know what love is? Even my dysfunctional, negligent one has had its moments. But not all of them do.

That thought trails off as I remember the guardedness in his eyes every time he talks. The way he flinches away from Hudson ever since they met and Hudson threw him into a wall.

Was it his *family* who did this to him?

Rage rushes through me so fast and hot that I can't think straight.

What is love?

My heart breaks for him.

CHAPTER
TWENTY-SEVEN

ZIGGY

have exactly zero complaints about Kennedy showing up and feeding me. He noticed I don't have an oven, so dinner came precooked, and we sit on a log together outside and eat it while the sun sets.

The whole time, I'm overly tuned in to him. His muscular arm brushes against mine every time one of us moves, and my heart is still in overdrive from him catching the sauce by my mouth with his thumb. He keeps shooting me smiles like he can't help himself, but they're more restrained than the ones that set off fireworks in my gut.

It's taken me all through dinner to land on a question that doesn't sound stupid.

"How was your day?"

He finishes chewing and swallows, eyes squinting a little as he thinks. "Interesting, I'd say."

"Why?"

"I mean, Hart was gone for most of it, but before he left, I think I had a moment with my brothers."

I lift my eyebrows, encouraging him to continue.

"We don't really talk. Or … they don't. I don't stop talking, but trying to get a real conversation out of them is like pulling teeth. I hate it."

"Sorry …" I whisper. "I'm not good at it either."

Stupid, pussy, useless.

He turns to me, and I'm confused how he can look surprised. "You're so good at it. What do you mean?"

I give him the driest look possible, but he waves it off with a flick of his hand.

"You give me the real stuff. You let me in; that's all I want. I just want to know people in here." He reaches over to tap his finger against my chest. "My brothers have their feelings on everything locked down tight. It wasn't always like that. But this morning, it almost felt like old times for a second."

The hope in his voice is so Kennedy. The man who wants to see the best in people. I have no idea how he's related to his brothers when they're both so … let's go with different. I suppose there has to be a moment where a guy decides to be nice to his boyfriend's brothers.

I reach up and slide my hand over the back of his neck, giving it a supportive squeeze.

"Thanks. It felt good." Like he's remembering himself, he straightens, putting some distance between us. "How was your day?"

Planning a hot water system for them and a mine remodel for me? I steal his answer. "Interesting."

"Good." That's all he gives me, and I wonder if he's as nervous about our relationship as I am. It's all new for me, and like Rooney said, the rules are a mystery. I'm prepared for Kennedy to turn into an overbearing love monster, and I know I'll be able to handle it, but as for what he wants from me? It would help to ask him, but an almost thirty-year-old man questioning how to be a boyfriend is almost as pathetic as googling love.

I'm going to have to follow Kennedy's lead and trust my instincts.

You know, those same instincts that ended up with me in the middle of nowhere, lonely and living in a mine.

Forcing courage that catches even me by surprise, I slide closer, until our hips touch, and then I pull his face to mine. For all the weird hesitancy I've been feeling tonight, there's none of it in the kiss. I could spend all night like this, but there's something I want more. Something I've been thinking about most of the day.

I suck on his tongue while my free hand slides up his thigh and settles over the straining bulge between them.

His chuckle fills my mouth. "I was about to say I should head home, but we've got time for that first."

Home?

I'd thought he would spend the night again.

I have to shake the disappointment from my head. Of course it makes sense he wouldn't sleep over every night. He has his own place, his own bed, and neither of them comes with the creepiness of mine. Apparently.

So this is all completely normal.

"I've been thinking about it all day," I confess in a whisper.

It must be the right thing to say because Kennedy cups my face and kisses me deeper. He pours all the need I've been feeling into the kiss, and even with my tender top lip, I don't want this to end.

He pulls me with him as he stands. "Have you showered?"

"Before you got here. I, uh, wanted to be ready."

His low groan sends ripples of need through me. There's nothing I've ever experienced in my life like when we're together. It's addictive. Kennedy makes me feel so wanted, and I'm scared to get used to the feeling in case I lose it again.

He kisses me as he backs me inside, grass turning to tile flooring underfoot until my calves bump the side of my couch, and he finally breaks the kiss.

His hands find the bottom of my shirt, and he pulls it up over my head. His goes next.

I love Kennedy's chest. He's muscular, all across his pecs, shoulders, and arms. His stomach is thick, but softer, and covering it all is a layer of blond hair.

I'm so fucking hard as I run my hands over his chest, thumb catching one of his nipples. A sharp inhale rushes past his teeth, and Kennedy's darkened gaze locks on mine.

"Take off your pants."

I don't drop his gaze as I reach for them. I want him to see what he does to me. I want him to see that I need this.

As soon as my fly is undone, the heavy denim drops to the ground, and I kick it aside.

His focus finally dips, and he licks his lips like he's starving for me.

I reach for his pants. They're thick work material, but perfectly sculpted to his ass, his thighs, his cock. I've inspected them so many times while we work together that it's committed to memory.

I tug his fly down, and his cock follows his zipper, spilling out like it's eager to reach for me. He's not wearing underwear, which only goes to show he was hoping for this as much as I was. Kennedy should know by now that this is always on the table for him.

Because I can't help myself, I push his pants from his hips and wrap my hand around him. He's hot and heavy in my palm, a feeling I'm convinced I'll never get used to, and as he thrusts into my grip, his eyes flutter back.

"That feels so good."

Pride prickles in my gut. The way I can turn him on is the biggest high, and half the time, I'm convinced I need a mirror to check it's really me standing here.

"Here's what we're going to do," he says, voice hitched as he fucks my fist. "I'm going to sit on the floor and put my head back on the couch cushion. Then you're going to face the back of the couch and lower yourself until I'm wearing your balls like a hat. Got it?"

My brain is too stuck to answer him, even if I wanted to.

He slants a grin at me. "Think that sounds good? Wait until my tongue is in your ass."

I think I choke on air.

Kennedy pulls away from me and gets into position. My heart is racing sickeningly fast, and the thought of doing what he wants to do is making me equal parts hot and self-conscious. He's going to see everything. I want him to see everything, but I'm also scared of him seeing everything, and it's the strangest mix of emotions, but my dick is aching, so I don't stop to think about it for long.

Especially when Kennedy props up one of his knees and reaches for his cock. He's stroking himself as he watches me.

"Ziggy, just looking at you is enough to make me blow. So if you don't want me to get myself off, you better give me something else to do with my hands."

Oh.

Fuck.

Okay.

The blood drains from my head to my cock, and I forget to overthink this. I climb up onto the couch, gripping the back of it, and then I take a deep breath and straddle his head.

The puff of Kennedy's exhale near my hole is almost too much for me to continue. Chills race down my spine. My balls rest on his forehead, and then his tongue slips out and licks a stripe along my crease.

My hands clench tight to my couch as my dick throbs with sensation.

I can do this. I can get through it. Even though my eyes are trying to roll back into my skull.

"Fuck, Ziggy." He lashes his tongue over me again. His

mustache is scraping the skin between my legs, but instead of hurting, it's a delicious burn against his warm, wet tongue.

I've played around back there myself, but it's usually when I'm getting close to coming that I'll help myself out. I've never taken my time, never stopped to enjoy the sensations when my dick is the priority, but when Kennedy's tongue massages the area around my hole, softening it and helping me relax, I realize what I was missing out on.

This feels incredible.

His tongue presses against my entrance, then dips inside and breaches the tight ring of muscle. My thighs shake. I'm struggling to hold myself above him as it is, but with every plunge of his tongue in and out of my hole, I don't know how much longer I can do this.

Then he slaps my ass with a massive *thwack.* The pain spreads across my skin, so sudden and hot, precum blooms from my tip. I choke back the pain, and I'm about to give him space when he wraps both hands around the dip where my thighs meet my hips, holding me in place.

"Ziggy ..." he gasps. "You're not going to suffocate me like this."

"W-what?"

"Show me how much you want it. Smother me."

Every word out of his mouth is turning my brain to Jell-O. I'm not in control anymore. I'm not even aware of where all my limbs are. My cock is aching, my hole is twitching for more. I can't take this.

"I told you to sit," he says, warm hands tickling the crease on either side of my groin. "Now, *sit.*"

Kennedy's hold on my legs tightens, and he pulls me down hard. His face buries between my cheeks, and the deep moan he lets out vibrates from my ass to my scalp.

The grip I have on the couch tightens until my knuckles go

white, and when Kennedy's tongue presses into my ass, I can't stop from grinding back onto it.

He knew exactly what I needed, and while I crave touching him, there's a special kind of torture in him being out of my reach. In being powerless to what he's doing. All I can do is hold on tight while he has me ride his face, like I'll die if I stop.

His tongue slides in and out of me, filling my hole with a delicious stretch, and the coarse hair of his mustache ripples against my skin. I can't work out what I want more of, just everything, and my hips are rocking more aggressively against him, but Kennedy's hands stay planted where they are, not letting me give him room to breathe.

He's kissing and sucking my hole like he's afraid I'll disappear, and the sounds he's making as he eats me out are as needy as the ball building in my chest.

My head drops back, eyes screwed tightly as I clear my brain and let myself feel. I've missed out on this for way too long, denied myself something that feels this good, and now that I have it, I'm going to take advantage of everything he'll give me.

His hands release, just for a second, then one closes around my cock while he presses a finger up my ass beside his tongue. I go from enjoying myself to close to the edge, and I grit my teeth against the need to come.

I want this to last.

I want to enjoy this all night.

But I know that very soon it won't be my decision.

I'm leaking and close, body burning up, head so full I'm dizzy.

Kennedy finally pulls away, panting loudly, then pulls me down further so when I look down, we make eye contact between my legs. "Put your balls in my mouth."

I don't stop to think. Just do as I'm told, lowering my balls onto his waiting tongue. His lips close around them, the wet suction almost too much as he strokes two fingers in and out of my ass and jerks me off with the other hand.

Everything is getting oversensitive. Too much. Too good. Too fast.

The swollen head of my cock disappears and reappears in his fist, right over where his eyes have fallen closed as he sucks on my balls.

I always knew Kennedy made me feel good.

Platonically. Romantically.

But I never would have picked this.

This deep hunger that's settled in my gut as I willingly let him do whatever he wants to me. I trust him to make me feel good, to know what I like, to hold me and build me up and help me discover all these amazing things I've never experienced before.

The pressure in my cock swells, my brain cuts out, and then twitches take over my whole body as I come. I pant my way through it, riding out wave after wave that pass over me, hovering in that sheen of an orgasm for a moment before it slowly seeps away.

Kennedy releases my balls and disappears from between my legs. Before I can look back at what he's doing, he presses gently against my lower back until I'm leaning over the couch.

"Yeah, like that," he gasps, the sounds of him jerking off filling the room. He grips my ass with one hand, spreading it open, and his exhale hitches. "So fucking hot."

I look back over my shoulder, watching as he jacks himself, hard and fast, gaze locked on my ass. He grunts, muscles tightening, then redirects his cock right as he releases. Warm ropes of his cum cover my back, and the sigh he lets out when he's finished is full of satisfaction.

His thumb skims my sensitive hole, and then he pulls me up so he can wrap his arms around me.

"How was that?" he murmurs by my ear.

Mind-blowing. I take his hand and help him rub my release into my front, head resting back on his shoulder. I'm so relaxed and satiated that I don't want to move.

Ever.

"I ran out of breath at one point and still didn't want to stop," he says, hips nudging forward until his half-hard cock nestles between my cheeks. "You have the sexiest little hole I've ever tasted."

I might be inexperienced, but even I know this is all just sex talk. It doesn't stop me from feeling amazing though.

My clean hand reaches back to slide through his hair as his lips trail down my neck.

"Next time." His voice has taken on a husky tone. "I want to fuck you." He rolls his hips against mine. "Can I?"

"*Yes.*" I don't need to think about this one. Even being here with him doesn't take away that deep ache for him. To be closer. To claim him.

The answer will always be more.

"I can't wait." He leaves one last kiss on my shoulder, then pulls away. It's a warm night, but without his body against mine, everything feels cold. "Come on, I'll wash you before I head home."

And with his hands on me under the water, I forget to feel disappointed.

It's not until much later, under a darkness that not even the moon can cut through, that doubts find their way back in.

Everything floods back to me, and without the fog of horniness, I question every little thing. Every sound I made. How I straddled him. If I was good enough.

I'm *sure* he enjoyed it.

But the loneliness strangling me questions that certainty until morning.

CHAPTER
TWENTY-EIGHT

KENNEDY

As soon as I wake the next morning, I get up, change, then head downstairs for the keys. It's not until the cool metal is in my hand that I remind myself to stop.

I only saw him last night.

I won't be too eager.

I can do this.

Even if all night, I've been haunted by the memory of him riding my face.

I've always, *always* wanted to do that, and it makes sense in a way that Ziggy was the first person to let me. We're meant to be. I just know it. Most of the people I've been with haven't been into ass play, and the ones who are either weren't comfortable with potentially murdering me with their ass, or we weren't together long enough for me to suggest it.

Ziggy climbed up and gave me exactly what I wanted.

Like he's made for me.

My head drops back on a groan, and I make it as far as the front door this time before I force myself to stop. The pull I have to him is indescribable. Sure, I've been off in horny land before with people, but this is next-level. It's not only that I want more sex; I want to see *him*.

His snarky little expressions, that soft, raspy voice, the way he hides behind his hair, and the even hotter moments when he doesn't. When he meets me head-on. When he reminds me of what a confident person he is by making the first move and taking what he wants.

He's perfect.

I pause, hand on the driver's-side door of the SUV, with no memory of walking out here.

Fuck.

I let it go like it shocked me.

The whole time I'm waiting for my brothers to wake up, I try making coffee, try making breakfast, all of it broken up by me pacing back to the car every few minutes and then having to tear myself away from it again.

Ziggy's probably not even awake yet.

I'm obsessing over nothing.

"Did someone finally fuck your brains out?" comes Hart's dry voice.

I whirl toward where he's walking down the front steps. "What do you mean?"

"You're lurching around out here like a zombie. I didn't know whether to grab a gun."

"You have a gun?"

He snickers. "No. You wouldn't let us get one, remember?"

I'm not sure whether to believe him or not. Unlike me, Hart is a fantastic liar.

"What are you doing?" he asks.

"Ignoring my instincts." When it's clear he has no idea what I'm talking about, I elaborate. "I'm not going to see Ziggy."

"Okay."

"I mean it."

"I believe you."

"In fact …" I toss him the keys. "Keep those on you."

"Got it."

We stand there watching each other, my hands twitching together. "You know what, this is ridiculous. I can hold on to the keys without going there. Give them back."

"Yeah … no chance."

I almost roll my eyes. "Come on. I'm not some uncontrollable monster."

"Uh-huh."

"Keys."

"Nope."

I scowl at his stubbornness, and Hart almost manages a smile.

"Tell my future niblings to thank me one day."

"I can't believe you think so little of me."

"Sure you can." He pockets the keys. "Because I think even less of myself."

Having the option taken away from me only makes me want to see Ziggy even more.

"I really am pathetic, aren't I?"

Hart squints at me. "This feels like a trick question."

It's the longest day in history.

Hart keeps the keys hidden from me, and I get through a whole day without seeing Ziggy. I pull out my phone more times than I'll willingly admit to message or call him before I remember he doesn't have a phone.

Ziggy shows up to work the day after, and it takes every last scrap of willpower I have not to follow him around like a puppy. I leave him to do the work he needs to do, while I get on with mine. Well, mostly.

I'm so distracted all day that I'm useless and even end up managing to put a nail through my thumb. I'm lucky that it only catches skin and I haven't done any real damage, but it's a wake-up call. A very painful wake-up call.

My instincts are assholes.

If I hadn't listened to Hart's advice about whether Ziggy would have gotten sick of me by now. Would things already be over if I could call and text him anytime I wanted? Maybe Wilde's End and its shitty reception is a good thing. Maybe I actually have a chance out here. In the wild. Where Ziggy has no other options.

That does *not* make me feel good about myself.

I tug at the bandage I've wrapped my thumb up with, annoyed that even though I know how stupid I'm being, I still want to see him anyway. I kissed him hello this morning, gave myself some time to flirt, and then forced myself to walk away.

I thought it would be enough.

I should have known better.

Knowing Ziggy is *next door* is eating at me.

"You okay?"

I jump hard at the soft voice and whirl around to face Ziggy. "You scared the shit out of me."

That gets a sly half smile from him.

"Sorry, I was zoned out."

The look he gives me says he already knew that.

"What are you doing? Done already?"

He doesn't answer, just searches my face from behind his thick hair like he's the one who asked the question.

I give in to the urge to move close. To reach up and brush all that hair back from his eyes.

The tightness in his expression fades, and it settles something in my chest.

"Hey, Zig."

"You busy?" he asks.

I should be, but with how I've been working today, I think I've caused more issues than I've fixed. "Not really."

"I ..." His eyes cut away while he swallows, and then he meets mine again with determination. "W-will I see you tonight?"

Hope strangles me. "Do you want to?"

He quickly nods, and the relief I'm hit with makes me feel like I might float away. This is what I was waiting for. I'm letting him lead. Letting him decide when he wants me around. "Then yeah, of course." I try not to sound too eager, but I don't know if I pull it off. "At your place?"

Sure.

"Cool." I go on grinning because my face doesn't want to do anything else. I'm mesmerized by him. That sweet, angular face, his abnormally large brown eyes, the thick hair, and the guardedness he only ever lets slip around me. Hart's rules can go fuck themselves for a second because I can't resist cupping his chin and brushing a soft kiss over his lips.

Ziggy pulls back, cheeks red, tongue piercing tapping against his teeth. He checks behind himself like he's worried we're being watched.

"Ah, don't worry about my brothers. They already know we're together."

His eyes fly wide.

"Ah ... I mean ... is that okay?"

Ziggy does nothing but blink at me, but I haven't yet figured out what a whole lot of blinking means. Is he mad? Upset? Surprised?

"Blink three times if it's okay and you don't hate me."

Unfortunately, that makes him stop blinking at all.

Then, a laugh hiccups from him.

"I don't know how to translate that."

"It's okay." He steps forward, taking my hand and wrapping his fingers through mine. "Explains why they were staring."

"Staring? I'm going to kill them."

He's not exactly smiling, but his eyes are happy when they meet mine.

"You can't blame me," I point out. "You're hot. I had to make sure neither of them started getting ideas."

His lips purse tighter, and I can read him this time. *Yeah, right.*

"Don't argue with me. You're a catch, and I won't hear another argument against it. Got it?" I cup my ear, but I'm too fast for him, even if he wanted to argue. "Got it. We're agreed. Good. Now, where are you taking me tonight? If it's not a five-course meal with fireworks after dessert, I'm not interested."

Doubt clouds his eyes, but I don't let him get away.

"I'm kidding. If you're there, I'll be happy."

I could say so, so much more than that, but I force myself to stop. I'm being cool. Collected. Nothing to see here.

His brow crumples, and he grabs my other hand, turning it to see my bandaged thumb.

"Hazards of replaying our memories from the other night," I say, just to see him blush. Then I tap the Band-Aids around his fingers. "Looks like you had the same problem."

He pulls his hands back and tucks them behind him. "Tonight?"

"I'll be there."

Even if I have to tackle Hart to the ground to get those keys, nothing will keep me away.

CHAPTER
TWENTY-NINE

ZIGGY

I glare at the basket Queenie left, almost certain this is a bad idea. No matter how many times she told me that romance is sweet and thoughtful, when I'd asked if she'd ever been in love, her confused "why bother?" didn't fill me with confidence.

I didn't have an answer for that.

The thing is, while Queenie might enjoy being social and dating whoever she wants to date, that isn't me. I'm having enough trouble dating *one* man. The anxiety that fills me over trying to juggle partners makes me want to burrow into the ground.

If things don't work out with Kennedy, I don't see them working out with anyone. Not necessarily because I don't see myself trying again, but because I don't want to try again. Kennedy feels right. He feels like the person I've been waiting for. There's no way that type of connection comes along regularly, and I don't know what I'll do if I lose it.

I cast another doubtful glance at the basket. It's getting late, and after a day of silence yesterday, and him being weird and standoffish today, I'm getting worried that I'm already close to losing it. I'd been prepared for a boyfriend I couldn't get rid of, and now it's like I have to preschedule time with him. I'm not sure if Kennedy was exaggerating with his past relationships or if it's all a me problem.

All I know is that I refuse to let this eat at me too.

My emotions are constantly buried, bound into a tight package and hidden so far back in my mind that I can't focus on them. It's helped protect me, but it hasn't helped me live.

Kennedy makes me want to live.

Just as I'm about to give up on him coming, a figure lurches out of the trees and makes me jump.

"I'm so sorry!" he pants. "I was waiting on the car, then it was getting late, so I called Hart, and he was still an hour away, so I figured I'd walk, but I took two wrong turns and ..." Kennedy shakes his head as he crosses the grass toward me. "All I knew was that if I kept taking the paths *up*, I'd find you eventually, but I can't lie and say I wasn't getting worried when the sun disappeared." He pauses in front of me and takes me in with soft eyes. "Hey."

I'm so happy to see him, I catch him in a kiss. I hope he knows I'm saying hello and I'm glad he's here and thank fuck he didn't get lost all at once. Relief is seeping through me as well, and when he pulls back and smiles at me, it's the one I'm so used to seeing from him.

"So, what are we ..." His gaze falls to the picnic basket. "Are you taking me on an actual date?"

I wrinkle my nose, not sure how to answer that, and pick up the basket. Then I head for the trees while Kennedy trails after me.

I'm so nervous over this stupid idea, and all I can do is hope and beg that I'm not coming on too strong. I'm halfway along the trail when I remember I'm not supposed to be charging ahead on a mission and slow my steps. When Kennedy draws level with me, I reach over and take his hand, fingers slotting between his, and continue on.

After so many years of solitude, it's new being with someone at all. Having a person to hang out with and spend time with is an adjustment, but one I want to be making. I'll do whatever I need to in order to keep him here.

We're walking for a few minutes before Kennedy talks. "You do know where we're going, don't you? Because I have no clue."

It's really not hard to find your way around Wilde's End. He'll get it one day.

We reach the almost vertical rock wall at the end of the trail, and I have to let go of his hand to scramble up it. Then I turn and take the basket from him while he follows.

From this lookout, we're above the tree line, half-nestled in the hills, and Old End is too far away to see. I always feel untouchable up here.

"Wow …" Kennedy mutters, wiping his hands off on his pants as he joins me. "This is cool."

It's a usual, clear summer night, and the stars stretch from the hills on one side, all the way over to the tips of the blackened trees on the other. I let him admire the view while I get to work setting up everything exactly the way Queenie instructed me to. First, the rug, then I switch on all the battery-powered candles, lay out the baking Viv did for me, and hold my breath.

Kennedy's staring at the setup like he's as out of words as I usually am. If there's one thing I know, it's that speechless is not a good thing.

"You did this for me?"

I clear my throat and force out the answer. I promised myself that I was going to talk tonight. Anxiety or not, I need to know what this is and if I'm doing it right. I need him to know how unsettled an actual relationship makes me. "Yes. Is this good?"

"I ..." He steps closer to the blanket, staring at it like it's a puzzle. "I have organized too many picnics to count for people."

That nonanswer doesn't clear anything up for me.

Then his eyes find mine, sparking like little gems under the moonlight. "No one's ever planned something for me before."

"Never?"

His lips twist into what's supposed to be a sly smile but just looks sad. "I guess I don't really give people a chance."

"Do you need to?"

"Well, if I'm always around, then ... what are they supposed to do?"

"Plan it anyway." The answer is that simple to me. "When you're with someone who deserves it, you do it."

"Yeah, but ... I don't think anyone's ever thought I deserve it."

I could kill the people he's been with. "They were wrong." We watch each other, and I'm almost sick with nerves. Sick that I'm going to say the wrong thing. End this moment before it can start.

But making sure he knows how special he is is worth fighting my anxiety.

I force my way through it. "Why haven't you been smothering me?"

The question catches him off guard. "What?"

"You've been ..." I don't even know how to describe it without sounding like a loser. "Different."

He doesn't deny it. "Ah, I just, I'm trying to be cool. Not jump in too fast."

"Why?"

"Ziggy ..." He tries to pull back, but I grab his hands. If I'm doing something wrong, I need to know.

"*Why*, Kenny?"

"Because I'd hate it if you got sick of me."

I stare at him, processing the words that sound ridiculous all together. Get sick of *him*? Kennedy Bellamy? The guy who puts himself last and everyone else first? Who doesn't question all my weirdness and just jumps in and tries to match me at my level. Who's sweet and kind and happiest when he's around others.

"Sick of you?" I echo, because I'm still trying to work out how he can mean that.

He gives me a halfhearted smile and tugs me over to sit down with him on the blanket. "You ask that, but it happens. Easily. I've told you how it always goes."

"You don't trust me?" The question is painful to ask.

"What? *No.* I don't want to put you in the position where you wish I'd fuck off but don't know how to tell me. And then it gets to be this huge issue I have no idea about until you lose it and say you can't do it anymore." His voice cracks. "I can't go through that again."

"And you won't," I promise him. "Those breakups weren't your fault."

He's about to argue, and I frown at him to shut up a minute.

"You gave it everything. And they didn't. If I annoy you, you'll tell me. If you annoy me, I'll tell you. I don't want you holding back. So stop it. Because the more you do it, the more I feel like you're getting sick of me."

"I could never."

"Then prove it," I beg him. "Overwhelm me. Never leave me alone. Be clingy and needy and *yourself.* Then I get to tell you what I like and what I can handle."

His lips part, and he searches my face. "You're serious."

Yes.

A long rush of air leaves him. "Want to know what I like?"

"What?"

"You getting bossy like that. Feel free to do it whenever you want to."

Heat rushes to my cheeks, but Kennedy grabs me and pulls me closer to him. He folds my legs across his and runs his hand over my cheek.

"I also really like when you blush. And make me picnics."

"I was so scared you'd hate it."

He sighs and rests his forehead against mine. "I have a feeling we're going to be two complete idiot boyfriends who mess up and overthink and have no idea what we're doing."

"It'll be nice not being the only one."

CHAPTER
THIRTY

KENNEDY

"Wait. I have something for you," Ziggy says, untangling himself from where I was very comfortably holding him.

I'm still in awe over, well, *everything* tonight. From the cute date to him telling me point-blank that he doesn't like me not being around. The hurt side of me doesn't believe he means it, that as soon as I give in to who I am, he'll run screaming, but the side of me that's in awe of him is hopeful. I know he doesn't like to talk, so him using all those words on me has got me right in the chest.

Maybe, finally, I won't have to fight for someone to see me.

He opens the basket and pulls out—

"What the hell is that?"

The smile he gives me is part cocky, part proud. I watch as Ziggy moves a few feet away, sets the firework on the ground, then lights it. A firework. Just like I'd joked about wanting.

He backs up as the string burns, and then it shoots into the sky.

There's a bang and an explosion of light, but I miss the whole thing.

I'm too busy staring at the side of Ziggy's face.

At the way the red light brings his features alive.

And feeling the way my whole world narrows into the man standing in front of me while one thought fills my mind.

I've never been in love before.

Every moment up until a second ago, I would have sworn I had. I've felt it, I've dived into it, given it my all. But with one firework, Ziggy has cleaved my life in half.

Now I can't work out what was so great about it all.

He laughs as he joins me back on the blanket. "Sorry, I could only get one last minute. That was fun though."

For the first time ever, caring about someone doesn't hurt.

"When I was younger," I whisper. "I'm sure I remember Mom playing with us. Building forts, and teaching me to ride my bike and ..." The memories always make my throat close up. "Something happened. I can't even pinpoint when, but it was like ... I had her, and she was my mom, and then one day, it hit me that I hadn't had her for a very long time. She was still there physically, but the person in her body wasn't anyone I knew. Dad was always sort of distant, so when he left one day and didn't come back, it didn't hurt as much."

Ziggy slides his legs back over mine, and I pull him close to my chest. I don't even know what I'm trying to say, but I need the cover of my face buried into his hair before I can say it.

"It's always been me and Hart. He's my twin. My other half. Then Hudson was the one I looked up to. But I lost them too." My eyes sting, and every word tears at me. "All I've ever wanted was to not be alone, Ziggy. To have someone care about me like I care about them. Someone who won't abandon me just because I want to be needed." My body shakes, and I'm goddamn crying. I don't know when it started or how to make them stop, but I'm so relieved to finally be getting these words out. "I have felt like the biggest failure for so goddamn long." I sniff back the tears and pull away so I can see him. He's got that pinched look he gets sometimes, like he's trying to bury his thoughts, but I need him to see how much this means to me. "Thank you. I've forgotten what it's like to be seen."

He dries my tears the same way I dried his, and I know I'm fucked. I know he's going to ruin me. I know, without a doubt, that if things don't work out with Ziggy, it won't be the same.

Our failure won't be a notch in a long line of past regrets.

I'll carry it with me forever.

And staring at Ziggy, watching the way he fights against the same pain I'm living with, I have a feeling he knows exactly where I'm coming from. He might not want to tell me right now, or ever, but he doesn't need to.

Like I told my brothers, Ziggy communicates without words. His family have messed with him too.

So fuck Hart's plan.

If this is going to work, we have to trust each other.

I'm going to give Ziggy all of me.

Give me a hot date, Ziggy, and sex under the stars, and I'll be a happy, happy man. I get back to town with a smile on my face, ready to get a full day's work in before Ziggy shows up later.

I've never felt this optimistic about the future, which is saying something, considering that's my default. Ziggy has made my heart sprout wings, and if he ever clips them, I'm going to be devastated.

"Fun night of sex?" Hart asks, hunched over the paperwork on the floor in front of him.

"I got taken on a date."

He eyes me suspiciously. "Like … to a restaurant?"

"Nope. Picnic under the stars. Where Ziggy told me to stop being weird and backing off and that he wants the obsessive, over-the-top side of me."

"Well, you know what they say about being careful what you wish for."

Normally, that kind of comment would put me on guard and question my decision. Not today. "Or maybe I've found someone —finally—who actually wants my company." Then, because I'm still raw from last night, I add, "You know. Like you used to."

Hart looks at me through hooded eyes. "When did I ever want your company?"

"Be a dick all you want, we used to be close. Same with Huddy."

He doesn't answer, and normally I'd let him get away with it, but not this time. Apparently, letting everything out at once has ripped off the guardrails.

"Actually, fuck you."

That gets his attention.

"And fuck Hudson too."

"What did I do?" he asks from the doorway, and it looks like he's joined us right on time because I'm done with the both of them.

"It was bad enough when Mom and Dad left us to fend for ourselves, but at least I had you guys. Then you left me too, and I don't know what I did wrong, but I needed you both. And maybe I blame you a bit for me going into relationships too strong, especially when you tease me for it, because I'm just trying to not feel so lost and alone." I jab my finger at the ground. "And it was the two of you who made me feel this way."

"Shit, Kenny ..." Hudson starts, but I actually don't need to hear it. I don't need anything from them unless it's genuine, and I don't think yelling at them until they apologize will get me what I need.

I'm breathing like a bull, but the sound of a car outside saves me from talking about it any further.

"I'll go see who it is." My voice cuts through the silence, and the heavy stomp of my boots through the empty house follows it.

When I get outside and see Caroline's shiny silver Prius pull up, my footsteps don't slow.

"Morning," I call to her as she climbs out.

The smile that reaches her eyes is bright, hopeful, and it's like a gut punch. No matter what I've said in the past, Caroline is stuck on something between us. It tells me I'm making the right call. "Hey, Kennedy, I brought you breakfast. Your favorite."

"Nice. Come walk with me."

She hurries to lock her car and catch up with my broad strides. "You're in a good mood."

"Mostly." She doesn't need to know about me losing my shit back there. It's like everything I've known has unraveled, and it feels both exhilarating and terrifying. Like playing jump rope with a live wire.

"Well, I'm happy to see you."

"Yeah, I'm happy to see you too." I stop and turn to face her so suddenly she has to backtrack a step. "I need to tell you that I'm seeing someone."

"You're …" The light behind her eyes dims. "What do you mean?"

"I've met someone, and I've fallen for him. It sort of snuck up on me, but since I know how you feel, I wanted to make sure I told you first."

"But I thought you weren't dating. That you—"

"I thought so too. That wasn't bullshit."

She takes a step back from me, chewing on her bottom lip like she can't work out what to say. "It sort of feels like it was bullshit."

"I know. Trust me, I know how it sounds. I really am sorry,

because I do like you, but there was always something holding me back. Now I know it's because I fell for him first."

It's like I can see the wheels turning behind her eyes. "Ziggy. It's him, isn't it?"

"Yeah. How did you know?"

Her eyes fall closed on a defeated sigh. "When I saw you in the diner together. I couldn't explain it, but something about you together made me uncomfortable. That's why I came here last week. I thought if we could get more time together …"

"I'm sorry."

"Yeah …" She swallows thickly. "Me too."

"If it helps, you knew before I did. Which, if you knew me at all, you'd understand how weird that is."

"No offense … but I really don't want to talk about you and some other person."

"Sorry."

She braces against the word. "I'm just going to go."

And this is exactly what I didn't want to happen. Her, leaving here upset. Thinking there was a chance when there wasn't.

But that's not on me.

I've been clear from the start, and if Caroline didn't want to listen … I can't even blame her for it. Because I've been in her position too many times to count.

I know exactly how she's feeling. Every relationship, every potential, each time someone showed interest, I clung to it until it was torn from my fingers. It's also how I know that I've done the right thing for her.

I force myself to keep my mouth shut as I walk her back to the car and watch her leave.

Hopefully, one day, we can be friendly again, but at least I know I've done everything I could.

CHAPTER
THIRTY-ONE

ZIGGY

aroline. Caroline. Caroline. Caroline.

Why can't she ever leave us the fuck alone? I'm panting hard by the time I get back to my place, fists clenched tight, this unsettled anger rattling through my bones.

The second I saw her pull up and Kennedy walk off with her, I felt like I was going to explode. If I'd gone down into Old End, I would have confronted her, maybe yelled at her a little. Kennedy doesn't need to see that, just like I didn't need to see him happily taking a stroll with her.

I kick the rock wall outside my mine as hard as I can. Pain shoots up my shin, and I have to catch my instinctive cry. This. Isn't. Fair.

All I want to do is fall apart and sulk, and maybe throw something at her. Kennedy is mine. He's *mine.*

I fist both hands in my hair, the sickly churning in my gut almost enough to make me double over. I hate this. I hate it so much.

Wilde's right. Love is pain.

I turn my back on the rock wall and slide down until I'm sitting in the dirt. I force myself to be still, to keep gritting my teeth and not let these nasty feelings take over.

Kennedy didn't ask her to come.

She might be pretty and flirty and easy to talk to, but he also hasn't done anything to make me think he's interested. He had the chance to date her, and he turned it down.

I suck a deep inhale through my teeth. Jealousy sucks. It's worthless. And annoying. Like a bruise hovering over my heart, I keep nudging at it for the pain, because it's easier to do that than be objective. Because if I'm objective, maybe a teeny tiny part of me worries I've overreacted.

I let the tension seep out of me, and even as my brain keeps trying to feed me images of the two of them together, I fight back against it.

After our date last night, it isn't fair of me to doubt him. He opened up against all his worries and trusted me with them. Kennedy was real, raw, and the way we connected after that was more than I ever hoped I'd get with one person.

Things are *good*. So instead of playing into my anxieties, I need to let them go. For him.

Because it's not fair on him to stress that he's done something wrong—again—when the real issue is me.

Relationships are new, and apparently, jealousy isn't something I can just get over. It feels as much a part of me as the loneliness, but I owe it to Kennedy not to let it take hold.

Because if it takes over, I don't trust him.

And if I don't trust him, we've lost.

I refuse to lose.

So I push back to my feet, trying to leave my bruised heart alone, and wipe off my jeans. I'm going to go to work, and everything will be fine. I'll pretend like I didn't see Caroline, no matter how desperately I want to know what they talked about, and I'll just … get on with it.

There's nothing else I can do.

I walk back down into Old End for the second time today, trying to ignore how I'm braced for what's waiting for me. Kennedy and Caroline being all happy, with his brothers speculating about whether they will or won't get married. It's hard to acknowledge that maybe I'm taking this deeper than I should because I do think Caroline would be good for him. She'd probably treat him well and be all cute and sweet and make him picnics too.

But I'm never going to give her the chance.

The anticipation is sending my pulse skyrocketing. I don't want attention. I've wandered into all of those unspoken rules Rooney was talking about.

I'm unsettled and on edge by the time I get to the small town with its half-massacred houses looming over me.

But down the other end of the street, Caroline's car is gone.

With everything crossed that Kennedy hasn't gone with her, I pick up the pace. My tongue piercing plays at the backs of my teeth, and I listen closely for any hints as to where someone might be.

The white SUV is still parked on the road, so unless they *all* went with Caroline, at least one of them must be here.

I make a right, intending to slip between houses two and three, when I almost slam into someone. Hart grabs my shoulders, like he's steadying me, but I manage to keep my footing.

"Sorry," he says, as surprised as I am.

I nod his way and go to step around him.

"Kennedy's in his room."

That makes me pause, and I turn to Hart, questioning if he's setting me up to see something I really don't want to see.

"He's mad though," Hart continues. "Might not be the best company."

Mad? What's happened between him leaving this morning and now for that to have happened?

I give Hart a long, searching look, and when that gets me nowhere, I turn on my heel and head for the only untouched house on the street. I know the brothers have been living out of this one while they work, but I've never been inside.

It's unlocked, and I push into the old house, not sure what to expect. There isn't much to look at. A lot of it is untouched and dusty, but here and there are signs of life.

Supplies clutter the kitchen counter, a sheet has been laid out over an old sofa, and dishes are sitting in the sink. I glance around at the cracks between old shiplap walls and the boarded-up windows. How the hell can Kennedy call my place creepy when he lives here? It feels like a casket.

It's silent downstairs, and I'm not comfortable exploring on my own.

"Kenny?" I call, having to try twice so my voice is loud enough.

"Up here." His voice comes from near the stairs.

I climb them, listening to the groans of the treads underfoot, and thankfully, when I reach the top, I catch a glimpse of him in the first bedroom.

He's on a mattress on the floor, gazing up at the ceiling.

Alone.

I keep walking until I reach the doorway, then lean my shoulder into it.

"Ziggy?" His eyebrows reach his hairline, and then he pats the mattress beside him.

I take the spot by his hip and look down into his face.

"It's been a morning," he tells me.

I wait for him to be comfortable sharing. Considering this is Kennedy, it doesn't take him long.

"I got into a fight with my brothers, then Caroline showed up."

I try really hard to stay casual, but I mustn't pull it off because he pinches my chin gently.

"I told her we're dating."

"You … what?"

"I hope that's okay?"

It's more than okay. I want everyone to know.

He chuckles. "I want everyone to know as well. I felt bad, but I've always been honest with her. I guess some people only hear what they want to hear—I have experience with that."

"She's gone for good?"

"Maybe. I'd like to be friends, but I know that's asking a lot. Would that be okay with you?"

"Would there be flirting?" I hate how small I sound.

"No, never. If I saw someone flirting with you, it'd eat me up inside. I'm not about to make you feel like that."

"I felt like that when I saw her here."

"You did?"

I could easily lie and say it was nothing, but I don't get to pick and choose honesty. "Yeah. And I left, thinking I was spiraling again."

"Were you?"

Knowing that what I'm about to say will sound stupid makes it really hard to get the words out. "A bit."

"Ziggy—"

I wave my hand to cut him off. "It's not your fault. And I got myself out of it."

"Of course you did." His smile spreads, warm and happy. "You can do anything."

That's a reach. Anything except speak up for myself, and be social, and confront my parents over everything they put me through.

"Stop doubting," he tells me. "Whatever happened to you wasn't your fault."

"How do you know?"

"Because I know *you.*"

I'm frozen under his gaze, but I fight my instinct to retreat and wriggle out of my shoes instead. Then I crawl over next to him and rest my head on his broad chest.

"I don't think my parents wanted to be bad people," I whisper. "They worked really hard, but I don't think they ever planned to have a kid come into their lives and ruin it all for them." It's easier to talk with my face buried into the cotton of his T-shirt.

"It was still a choice they made."

"Maybe. I was on my own a lot. Mostly left up to my own devices. When they weren't working, they were sleeping. When they weren't sleeping, they were yelling. At each other, but mostly me."

Kennedy's arms tighten around me. "That's fucked-up. You didn't deserve that."

"I thought I did for a long time. If I wasn't silent at home, I was punished. If I was silent at school, I was bullied."

"I wish I'd known you then," he murmurs. "I would have beat up every one of them."

He wouldn't have, and I like that about him. Kennedy is a good person who wants good things for people. Including me. "I'm getting there," I whisper. "I might have needed a savior then, but I don't now."

His chuckle is warm under my ear. "That's lucky. Because I think you're the one saving me."

Him?

I push up onto my elbow to see his face. Expressions give away more than people want them to, and when I look at Kennedy, all I can see is defeat.

"From giving up on people." He manages a bitter laugh. "Because I have to say, some days, I am really, really close."

I've never seen this side of Kennedy before.

"Your *parents*, Ziggy? How is that fair? You were a kid. And then my parents, and my brothers, and the kids you went to school with … some days, I worry that we're all put on Earth to make things worse for each other." Kennedy reaches up to tuck my hair behind my ear. "You remind me how things are supposed to be."

With a sigh, I sit up and cross my legs, then lift my hands, splay out my fingers, and move both hands away from each other in a half circle.

He's frowning, but he sits up, too, and copies the movement. "What is that?"

I do it again and point at him.

"Me?" He looks excited as he repeats the motion. "What does it mean?"

"Sunshine. You've always been my sunshine. So you can't give up. Because I need you too."

CHAPTER
THIRTY-TWO

KENNEDY

Hudson disappeared with Wilde a few hours ago, and now I'm waiting for Ziggy to pick me up. It's getting late, but I'm happy to wait because I'll never get over how big and bright the stars are out here. Interestingly, he's driving, and considering he walks everywhere, it's got me curious where we're going tonight.

Tonight. Exactly one night since our date. And he's the one who suggested it, not me, which is new and different for my dating self.

Ziggy's truck comes down the street, and the sound of it must draw Hart's attention. The front door opens, and he hovers on the step, watching as Ziggy gets closer.

I don't have anything to say to him right now, so when Ziggy slows, I make for the truck.

"Hold on," Hart says, jogging down the stairs. "You're leaving too?"

"Yeah?"

"So what? You both disappear with boyfriends, and I'm supposed to be a sitting duck, waiting for that guy with his bobcat to come back and kill me?"

From inside the truck, I hear Ziggy laugh.

"Lock the doors. I'm sure you'll be fine."

"Good to know you care." He crosses his arms, glaring at me as I climb into the truck.

I lean over to kiss Ziggy hello and feel his lips curve under mine as he smiles.

"Tell him to come," he whispers.

"Hart?"

"Yes."

"But aren't we going on a date?"

He lifts his narrow shoulders. "Sort of. But your other brother will be there."

Okay, now I'm really curious. I'm still not feeling warm and fuzzy toward either of them, and as much as I'd love to tell Hart to stay and be freaked-out, I also hate the idea of him actually being freaked-out.

Maybe Hudson's right that I'm a pushover.

With a sigh, I push open my door and lean out. "Get in."

"Why?"

"Because I said *get in*."

His stubborn ass stays planted where it is for a moment before he grabs a piece of timber and starts for the car.

"What's that for?" I ask as I slide into the middle, and he takes the passenger seat.

"Protection."

"From?"

"Anyone out there that I need protecting from."

Ziggy smiles across me at Hart and surprises the hell out of me when he talks. "The dangerous ones are all preoccupied tonight."

Hart blinks at him. "That doesn't fill me with confidence."

"No, but I'm doubly curious now," I say. "Where are we going?"

But Ziggy's back to not talking because he throws a U-turn and heads back toward the trees. In the dark, it's impossible to keep track of where we're going. We make it along trails that his truck really shouldn't be able to fit down, and other than the halo of light cast by his headlights, everything else is pitch-black in the trees.

"Maybe I should have stayed home after all," Hart mutters, but almost as soon as he says the words, pinpricks of light appear up ahead.

"Is that where we're going?" I ask.

Ziggy nods, and a few minutes later, we leave the trees behind and pull up beside an enormous building. It's all timber, highly polished, and looks like someone goes to a lot of effort to take care of it. Ziggy climbs out first, and Hart and I exchange a look.

"Where have you dragged me?" Hart's trying and failing not to sound interested.

"Hell if I know." I'm still not giving in to my urge to let my attitude slide, but there really is only so long I can go on being mad. I'm not built for negative emotions, even toward the people who bring them out in me.

"Well, we *were* born together. Might as well die together too."

"No one's dying," I snap, nudging him to get out of the car.

A small group of people walk by toward the left of the building, where a slash of light is thrown out over the grass.

Hart finally climbs out, and I follow him. This isn't at all what I was expecting, and I'm still not even sure what it is. When I reach Ziggy, I'm hesitant as my hand slips into his, testing to see where we're at with our relationship. I'd rather we had that conversation without others overhearing it, but it didn't even occur to me before we left.

His hand tightens around mine, and I have my answer. He's not embarrassed by me.

We let Ziggy lead the way to the lit-up section and find a man stationed at the entrance. He has a childlike innocence about him, probably from his bright eyes and chubby cheeks, but there's something in the way he smiles our way that I don't like.

"Look at this," he says as we draw closer. "The little mountain dweller and two harbingers of destruction."

Hart goes to respond, but I set the back of my hand against his chest in warning.

Ziggy taps the clipboard the man is holding.

"Oh no, I don't need to check this for your names." He steps closer to me. "I wrote the list, you see. The paperwork is all for a dramatic flair. I only pretend to check for names on it. If I really don't like the person, I'll even pretend not to see them for a moment." He laughs at something in Ziggy's expression. "Oh, yes. I leave Foley waiting the most." The man's eyes sharpen as they find my face, then slowly move on to Hart's. "Twins, Ziggy? Who would have thought you had it in you."

He scowls, and I'm about to reject the gross assumption when Hart gets there first.

"Incest," he says dryly. "Such a cute thing to joke about."

"Ah, you're the angry one. Good. I have a feeling we're going to be close, you and I."

"Who *are* you?" I cut in.

"Where are my manners? I'm Dr. Booker. You come and see me anytime you need putting back together." He grips Hart's shoulder and runs his hand slowly down his arm. "Any little scrape, bruise … you could never be an imposition."

Ziggy sighs loudly, catching Booker's attention, and points at the door.

Booker laughs. "Of course I can't let them in. They're not on the list."

Ziggy swings his thumb between us.

"They might be with you, but you're not on the list either.

There are only so many times you can reject my invitation before it starts to feel personal."

I have no idea what's going on, but as easy as it looks to step around Booker and walk in, I get the feeling that's an illusion. If he's really as protective of his list as he says, he's not risking any walk-ins.

"What's going on here that's so special?" Hart grunts.

"Peril."

"As in, it's dangerous?"

"It's Peril. Of course it is."

I'm so confused. "You do realize we have no idea what you're saying."

His fingers drum a deep rhythm against the wooden clipboard. "Outsiders rarely do."

"Kennedy? *Hart*?"

I turn toward my name and where Wilde and Hudson have just arrived. "Do you know what this is?" I ask them.

Hudson glances at Wilde like he's not sure what to say, and I can't help notice the new bruises beneath his tank top. Most of them are thick and long, suspiciously the same shape as the stick Wilde is holding.

Shock floods me. "Did you *hit* him?"

Instead of giving me an answer, Wilde smirks and turns to Booker. "Let me guess, they're not on your list."

"I don't make the rules, Wilde."

"You literally did." He steps around Booker, heading inside, but Hudson stays put.

"We're not leaving my brothers out here."

Wilde freezes, but doesn't turn back.

"I'm serious," Hudson pushes, crossing his arms. "You want me to watch your match, they need to as well."

"Sorry, my sweet Hudson. As intimately as I know you, a list is a list is a list." Booker taps the clipboard again. "There's nothing I can do."

"Let them in, Booker," Wilde snaps.

Booker's face fills with a grin. "Make me."

That's a bold request, considering Wilde looks like he could kill a man. I have the muscle mass to possibly take him on, but Booker is half a head shorter than me, chubby, and looks too sweet to hurt a fly. But he goes on innocently smiling, and the longer he holds it without Wilde taking a swing at him, the more something *off* creeps up my spine.

Wilde glances back, taking in Ziggy, me, and Hart, before he huffs. "Let them in and I'll break something of Foley's for you."

Booker's gaze drops back to the list. "Oh, look at that. Ziggy, Kennedy, and Hartwell. Here all along."

And when he tilts the clipboard, I catch sight of my name.

We're actually on there.

Hart scoffs and takes off after Hudson, but I'm confused.

"If you had our names, why didn't you just let us in?"

"I like to play games." He waves a hand at the giant structure behind him. "I'm the maker of games, and you and your brother are unknown pieces. Word for the Wilde: permission isn't given freely around here. It's demanded. Better luck next time." Booker turns his back on me, and I'm left blinking at the back of his head.

Part of me wants to push this, but Ziggy gives my hand a tug, and I reluctantly let it go. Booker's nonsense isn't going to ruin my night.

Especially when we step inside and I see what's waiting for us.

Tiered seating rings the room, and in the middle is what looks like an … obstacle course? Sort of?

There's safety flooring under nine metal platforms all at different heights, and above them is what looks like monkey bars.

"What is this?"

"Peril," Hudson answers.

"That still doesn't tell me anything."

The four of us follow Wilde into a row of seating as a horn goes and two people climb onto opposite, low platforms.

Ziggy turns, mouth pressing to my ear. "Peril is a type of fighting. Like a mix of stick fighting and martial arts that all takes place on the platforms. The goal is to push your opponent off, however you can. The only limit is that there are no blows to the head allowed."

"I've never heard of it."

"You wouldn't have. It mutated here. It's how Wilde's End and the other towns that compete earn money."

"That's so ..." Weird? Aggressive? Dramatic? But while I'm searching for a word, Hart sits forward in his seat between Ziggy and Hudson.

"This is so fucking cool."

"Is it?"

He shoots me a bewildered look. "Look how fast they're moving. How hard they're hitting each other. No safety equipment, no padding ..." His gaze moves back to where the two people are fighting, and the loud *thwack* that comes from someone being hit reaches us. "I want a turn."

"No," Hudson and Wilde say at the same time. My brother continues. "It's dangerous."

"*You've* clearly been doing it," Hart says, jabbing at his chest. And the bruise. Suddenly, all of Hudson's injuries make sense.

"I help Wilde train. I don't compete."

"Not my fault you're scared."

Hudson snorts. "I competed once. Against Wilde. And even though he took it easy on me, he still kicked my ass. You want a turn? Have at it. You won't last more than a few seconds."

Darkness settles behind Hart's eyes, and he crosses his arms, slumping back in his chair and watching the matches like he's dying to get out there.

As far as fighting goes, I've never been a fan. But I can't deny there's something about the atmosphere and the crowd reactions that are pulling me into it. Match after match passes, and Ziggy snuggles into my side, like he's not that interested either. If he doesn't like fighting, I have no idea why he brought me here in the first place, but I'm sure I'll find out. Ziggy doesn't do things without a reason.

The match I'm watching ends, and as the crowd applauds, Wilde pushes to his feet.

"I'm challenging Foley," he shouts, and the crowd gets louder.

Hudson claps his hands together. "This is what we're here for."

But the name has caught my attention. "Foley ..." I repeat, and Ziggy's head lifts from my shoulder.

He nods.

"Wilde said he'd break something of Foley's, but ... Foley's a person?" My voice inches higher. "What's he breaking?"

Ziggy doesn't look half as concerned as I am. "My money is on a rib. He owes Foley at least five."

"A rib? He promised to break a bone? Why would Booker *want* that? He's a doctor."

The way Ziggy pats my knee is patronizing at best. "Because he's a doctor."

I don't want to know what he means by that.

But the match has my attention now, and not for good reasons. I'm unexpectedly concerned for some guy called Foley, who I've never met in my life.

It's not until the man takes his podium and I see the skeleton mouth tattooed over his own that I realize I have met him. Sort of. He drove through town once.

And fuck me. If it weren't for those tattoos, he'd be hot as hell. His black hair is slicked back, he's got the type of jawline that could cut glass, and his eyes look piercing even from here.

"I always forget how hot he is." Hudson buries his face in his hands.

"You see him every day," Hart says.

"Not Wilde. *Foley*. Look at the guy."

Hart tilts his head to the side. "He looks like a demon."

"Exactly."

"I didn't say that was a good thing."

The buzzer sounds, and Hudson's fists form in his lap. "Wilde's going to kick his ass."

And once they get started, I don't know how Hudson can be so confident.

This is madness.

CHAPTER
THIRTY-THREE

ZIGGY

should be watching the match. They move so quickly, but especially when it's Wilde and Foley fighting. These two are like lightning strikes colliding, and somehow, they take the hits and stay standing. They're fast and all strength. The type of fight that has you on the edge of your seat.

But my gaze is fixed on Kennedy. On his expressions. Trying to read how he really feels about Wilde's End.

He's been here months now, but all he knows is the isolation of Old End. The quiet of my mine. The labyrinth of the trees, and the casual warmth of the Cutty.

He doesn't know how deep Wilde's End goes. This is my world, my community, the people I've given a huge part of my life to. Like with my home, I want Kennedy to feel the same attachment I do. I want him to appreciate it for what it is.

Because Wilde's End isn't anything like the places we're from.

"Oh, shit." He winces at whatever just happened.

I don't understand the problem. They're both up there because they want to be, and they both know what they're risking. I've seen people walk away bleeding, broken, and even one guy who couldn't stop throwing up on himself. It's a brutal sport, and no one who competes is interested in taking it easy.

Kennedy groans and turns to me. "I'm not sure I can watch. I keep waiting for Wilde to break something."

"He might. He might not. They're as close to evenly matched as it gets. Foley might even be slightly better."

He flicks a look back toward where they're fighting. "Is it always like this?"

Yes.

"How do you keep up? They're moving too fast for me."

There's a special skill in surviving these matches but also making them watchable. And entertaining. Foley and Wilde have perfected how to do it all. It's why theirs always draw the biggest wagers. Wilde earns enough from one fight to get the town through the next month, and it's thanks to him that we never go without what we need.

Well, and Rooney, Lynx, and everyone else who chips in. But he lubricates that bridge between what the outside world has and what we need.

Kennedy flinches again.

"Don't like it?" I murmur, voice softer than before. I'm braced for him to tell me how much he hates it, but bewildered lines fill his forehead.

"It's interesting. I just … it's very violent."

It is, but it's an important part of our lives out here. "Living a life like we do out here isn't easy."

"Yeah, but they're purposely making it harder."

"I know you won't understand this, Kenny," Hart says from my other side, "but sometimes people just need to beat the shit out of something."

The buzzer sounds, and we all turn back to the ring in the center of the room. Wilde's standing on the top platform, panting hard and looking down at where Foley is lying on his back on the padded floor. When Foley lifts his arm above himself, the angle of it looks … wrong.

"Urg …" Kennedy says, cringing away. "Wilde actually did it."

"Not like it was on purpose," Hart replies, and he sounds disappointed.

Hudson slumps in his seat. "I've never been more turned on."

I'm still not comfortable enough to talk properly around them, so I don't correct Hart's assumption. I didn't see it, but it was definitely on purpose. A hit hard enough with Wilde's post could smash bone easily enough, and Wilde wouldn't have made a promise he didn't intend to follow through with.

They've both had more broken bones from this than I can count.

I watch as Foley pushes to his feet, arm cradled to his front as he cackles deeply. His normally smooth hair is the mess it always is once they finish fighting, and he stumbles immediately for Booker, his hangers-on following at a distance.

"Good thing you have a doctor here," Kennedy mutters.

It sounds like a coincidence, but I'm sure the only reason Booker settled here was thanks to Peril. Every month after the fights, he pulls an all-nighter tending to people, and he's in his element while he does it.

A few of the people around us stand and start moving down the row.

"Was that the last one?" Kennedy asks.

Looks like it.

We've been here for hours, but it passed quickly. It always does. I've stopped coming to Peril matches recently because it's a lot of people, and sitting alone while Wilde fights always makes me self-conscious.

I can't remember the last time I sat with a group of people.

"I can't believe it's over already," Hart says, following us from the row of seats. Hudson disappears, I'm assuming to find Wilde, and the twins follow me out of the building. Most people head to their cars, but a small line cuts off toward the chop shop. Booker's home is within view of the Lair, all the lights on giving it an illusion of warmth. Like an angler fish attracting prey.

My gaze moves from the line of people to the one lone form leaning against the side of the Lair.

Foley's watching the chop shop, arm held protectively against his torso, but he makes no move to join the others. In the shadows, his tattoos look more menacing than ever.

Kennedy's hand on my back steers me away.

"I don't like him," he murmurs by my ear.

He's not the only one. As the mayor of Dale, he's enemy number one in Wilde's End.

We reach my old truck, and I unlock the passenger-side door. Kennedy pulls it open, then pauses.

"Ah … so, is this … night over?"

I glance at where Hart was following us, but he's not there. "Your brother?"

Kennedy shrugs. "Said he was going to look at something and not to wait for him."

"Will he find his way back?"

I don't want to leave without Hart because I can tell how conflicted Kennedy is. One part of him wants to act like he doesn't care, the same way they do, but he's made of better stuff. He can't *not* worry about the people he loves.

"He's a grown man, and he said to go. So let's go."

I'm nervous as I kick at the dirt. "Will you stay the night?"

"With you? Always."

My eyes clash with his. There's nothing like spending the night wrapped around him, but I also remember what he asked for last time. He wants to fuck me. And remembering that has nerves flooding into my gut.

Very.

Happy.

Nerves.

"We need to go," he rasps.

My cock pumping full of blood agrees with him. I round the truck to climb in, and he's already inside waiting. Most of the cars have already left, heading for Wayward, where they gather after Peril matches, and I pull away without issue.

Kennedy mustn't be wearing his seat belt because the second we reach a narrow road, trees pressing tight on both sides, he slides across the bench seat and buries his face into my neck.

My gasp sounds louder in the quiet cab, and Kennedy presses a line of kisses up my throat to just below my ear. My skin is tingling, pulse chasing itself faster, and I arch to the side to give him more room.

With one eye on the road ahead, I sink into how Kennedy's making me feel.

"Ziggy," he breathes, voice gruff. "Need you. Fuck, I need you."

His hand rests on my thigh, and the way I almost immediately come is ridiculous. But his heavy, warm palm is only inches from where my cock is stuffed in my pants, and all I want is for him to touch it. To slide his hand higher and take me in his grip.

"Pull over," he tells me.

I almost run the truck off the road trying to find somewhere to stop. We're off the main route, so I don't think anyone will come this way, but I'm too horny to care.

"Turn the car off."

Right. That. I fumble the key in the ignition, but a moment later, the truck falls silent.

Kennedy reaches under my shirt, links his fingers over the waistband of my jeans, and then pulls me across the seat into the middle. He straddles my waist, head bowed over to stop from hitting the roof, and he takes my face in his hands as he brings his mouth to mine.

Like every other time, I'm Jell-O. Destined to bow to every whim, like trees ravaged by wind gusts in a storm. There's nothing calm and settling about the way he kisses me. Not when he grips my hair in fists or forces our mouths wider, his tongue deeper, teeth clashing together like coming up for air will ruin us.

Kennedy grinds down onto my lap, hard, thick shaft dragging along the length of mine, and my hands bunch his shirt in my tight grip as I try to stay anchored.

This giant, heavy, sweet man towering over me is too much.

My face is getting hot from the lack of air, my brain spotty from lust, and I scramble to push his open shirt from his shoulders before I shove his T-shirt up to his chest. I'm torn between leaving it there and breaking our kiss, but parting even for a second feels unbearable.

Kennedy doesn't give me a choice. He pulls away, dragging my T-shirt up over my head before he gets rid of his own. Then I have the mouthwatering view of his bare torso right in front of my face.

He takes my chin gently and angles it up so I meet his gaze.

"Yeah ..." he says in a rush. "I'm going to need you to ride me now."

CHAPTER
THIRTY-FOUR

KENNEDY

Ziggy has no idea what he does to me. Those large, sweet brown eyes. The way his small face fits perfectly in my hand. All that wild hair that feels so good in my grip. The way his piercings feel when we kiss.

If I weren't so horny, I'd spend all my time kissing him.

I reach down to rub him through his pants, and he rocks into my touch.

"Do … do you have … what we need?" he asks. His voice is breathy and low, so sexy it makes my balls ache.

"Sure do." I wasn't missing my chance. If he wants this, I'm going to be ready for him.

I've long stopped taking my wallet places out of habit, and stuffed the condom and travel lube into my pocket instead. With Ziggy being a virgin, I might have overdone it with how many lube packets I brought, but I want to make sure he enjoys this. I didn't like my first time bottoming, so I rarely do it, but with his piercing, I can't lie and say I'm not interested.

For tonight though, I need to get inside him.

"You still want to do this?" I check.

The slow, sexy smile that unfurls for me has nerves ripple through my gut. "I've been waiting for this my whole life."

Those words hit something beyond the physical. "Shit." I tug open my pants, and the truck feels a whole lot smaller as I roll off him and fight to get naked.

Being smaller than me, Ziggy has an easier time of it, and when I'm finally stripped and look over again, my breath catches in my chest.

He's stunning.

Long, pale frame. Narrow waist. Piercing through the head of his hard cock, like a jewel in a crown. He's stunning.

"How many piercings do you have?" I ask, wrapping my hand around my cock to make it behave.

"Sixteen."

My gaze hovers over those tight pink nipples. "Ever thought about getting these done?" I flick one, and he hisses.

"Briefly. But then I left home and haven't had one since." He reaches for my shoulders, and this time, he's the one who straddles me. My cock is trapped between us with nowhere to go, and it's torture. "What about you?" he asks.

"Me?"

Ziggy runs a thumb over my nipple, making me shiver. "Yeah. I've noticed how much you like them played with. Imagine a piercing here." He pinches my nipple and gives it a tug. "So much easier for me to tease them."

He doesn't need an easier time of it when each little tug sends a spark of pleasure through me. "Keep that up and I could come."

"Isn't that the point?"

"Not until I do it in your ass."

The hitched inhale from him makes me grin. He watches me as I lift my hand to my mouth and suck on my fingers until they're wet.

Since getting my tongue inside him, I haven't been able to stop thinking about Ziggy's hole. He turns me on so fucking much that I'm insatiable when it comes to him, and with me working so hard, I don't get to spend as much time naked with him as I'd like.

One day, we'll take a whole day off, just the two of us, in his bed, only leaving it when we need food and water.

Maybe not even then.

I slip my fingers between his cheeks, and Ziggy's grip on my shoulders tightens.

"Can you relax for me?" I tilt my head back so I can watch his face properly. He's only a few inches away, and I read the worry in his eyes easily.

He swallows deeply and nods.

"Good. That's the only thing I want you to focus on. I'll take care of the rest."

His exhale ghosts over my face, and then he reaches between us and wraps our cocks up in his grip. I sigh without meaning to, but I challenge anyone to be touched by Ziggy and not completely fall apart.

My fingers find his hole, brushing over the soft skin and remembering how hot it feels to be inside him. I'm all nervous anticipation as I rub his opening, trying to get him to relax enough for this to happen.

"I've got you," I murmur.

"I know." His hand slides from my shoulder, up to hold my neck, as his other strokes us slowly. He doesn't need to keep me on edge, but if it's keeping him horny, I'm going to bite my tongue and get through it. As good as it feels, I'm not coming until I'm inside him. And it feels really, really good.

I get the tip of my first finger past his tight ring and spend a few minutes dipping it in and out. Each time, I manage to get a little deeper, and I really have to fight against the way his body is trying to pull me in. He's hungry for it.

The thought makes my cock throb. I've never been overly

claimy and possessive, but there's something about knowing that no one else has ever experienced this. No one's gotten to enjoy him naked. No one else has kissed him or sunk into his body.

He's all mine.

I've so desperately wanted someone who was mine.

And Ziggy *feels* like it. Like I've been waiting for him. The way something in my chest has connected in a way that feels natural.

Nothing forced. No uncertainty.

My finger buries to the knuckle, and I smile softly at him. "You're doing so good."

His breathing has gotten louder, cock still rock hard, and his lips twitch like he wants to smile too. When I stroke my finger in and out, his eyes fall closed, and his forehead meets mine.

I close my eyes too, reveling in the feel of his soft hair tickling my face, in his hand on my dick, and his skin skimming mine. I bring my free hand up to rest on his back, and I love the way all that living, breathing warmth infects me.

When he's taking me easier, I tear the lube open with my teeth, coat my hand, and add a second finger. There's tension for a second, and I pause, letting him adjust, feeling him fight the way he naturally wants to resist and forces himself to relax instead.

"That's it …" I tell him. "Just like that."

"Keep going."

I test him out, slowly moving in and out. His cock has softened a little, but it doesn't take long for him to get it back as I work my fingers deeper.

The air in the cab has thickened with our heavy breathing, windows fogging and my hair sticking to my neck. Ziggy's panting has gotten heavier as he thrusts into his fist and back onto my fingers, the pain clearly gone. The more he enjoys himself, the more I can get into it as well. I stop overanalyzing and focus instead on the pressure around my fingers, how sexy he feels inside, and slowly work him open, knowing it'll be my cock's turn soon.

"You're perfect," I tell him, and the trueness of it grips my heart. There isn't a single goddamn thing I'd change about Ziggy, and I hope he feels the same. I hope I can be everything he needs me to be.

Because it's taken until this very moment for me to realize that I don't need a lot.

I just need to be loved.

I catch his lips in a kiss, and the way I know it's him even without being able to see is one of my favorite things. His piercings, his scent, the way he kisses me like he needs it.

I'd give Ziggy my life if he let me.

All of it.

I add another finger, but I'm barely aware of it, and when he keeps kissing, keeps stroking, it's like he hasn't noticed either. The need is ballooning around us, pressing down with this suffocating tension that has sweat prickling across skin. My lungs are tight from the heavy air, thighs slick from the friction between us, and when he moans, deep and longing, my balls pull tight.

"Ziggy ..." I mutter between kisses. "I need this. Need you so bad."

"Me too," he whispers, and that grip around my heart tightens. "What do I do?"

I pull my fingers out and search for the condom. In my need, I'm hardly paying attention to anything other than getting it open and rolling it down my shaft. Then I tear into the closest lube packet and squeeze it out over my cock. Before I can rub it in, Ziggy takes over.

His slick hand moves over me, feeling like a dream, and I have to catch his wrist to stop him.

"It's time for you to sit on my cock now."

A whimper starts and dies in the back of his throat. "How?"

There are too many positions I want to try with him that my brain short-circuits. We're limited in what we can do in the truck though, so my greediness will have to wait. "Ah ..." As much as

I'd love to see the exact moment I enter him for the first time, that won't work here. "Stay like this. That way, you can take me at your pace."

His eyes are hooded as he reaches down and positions my cock at his entrance. He looks almost as horny as I am, lips red and puffy, hair stuck to his face in damp clumps. "Like this?"

"Don't go too fast. Speaking from experience."

He holds my gaze as he presses down onto me, and there are a few seconds of resistance before he stretches open and sucks me in. The initial pressure around my cockhead is pure fucking bliss, and Ziggy pauses, squeezing impossibly tight before he relaxes again.

"You okay?"

It takes him a second. "Yeah." He lets go of my cock, both hands cupping my face, and his thumb swipes over my cheek. "How are you real?"

That whispered question shocks my brain silent. Ziggy's looking at me in a way I've never seen before. His guard is down, his openness is shining through, and all I feel is trust and warmth and something that's making my throat tight.

He sinks down onto me, and I don't regret not seeing it now.

Not when everything staring back at me is what I've been waiting for my whole life.

Someone who sees me. Who wants me. The kind of person as ready for this as I am.

And to get all of that from Ziggy, the one person who didn't hit me with an instatruck of love. He was a steady softness, a slow-burning addiction, the kind that crept into my soul before I knew what was happening and took me by surprise.

He's filled all the darkest corners that I didn't even know I had, and I'm scared and raw, but so, so ready for this.

I'm falling for him.

I never want to stop.

My hand tangles into his hair, and I tug his face to mine. Our mouths collide, and I funnel every last scrap of emotion into our kiss. Ziggy starts to move, rocking up and down on my cock, and the ripples he sends through my dick are enough to make my toes curl over.

We move together, a hungry, sweaty mess of limbs and want. I'm panting into his mouth, gripping his hip with one hand as I increase my thrusts. Ziggy's taking me easier now, and his precum is leaving sticky streaks over my skin.

It's incredible how much he turns me on. How I can want him, and it doesn't feel like I'm doing something wrong. I don't think there will ever be a time where I'm not scared I'll lose him, but while we're together, in moments like this, it's perfect.

Time with him settles something inside of me that has been hurting for a really long time.

He breaks our kiss to puff a labored breath over my lips. "I didn't know what I thought at first," he whispers. "But this is ..." His gasp hits me deep. "Kenny."

Fuck, I love hearing his voice. I love the scratchy way it clings to my name and fills it with more emotion than it's ever had before.

I'm tilting my hips in time with Ziggy riding me, and until right now, I'd almost forgotten how much I really love sex. Filling his body, feeling the way I'm making him tremble, how quickly he's losing control, the way his ass is gripping my cock, it's an explosion of good and only good—something I don't get a lot of in my life.

And it's only now, while I'm letting go, free of worry and high off this feeling, that it hits me how long it's been since I've had real sex. Desperate, needy, clingy sex is the usual. Sex where the pressure is on to make it good so they don't leave me has become the norm.

But Ziggy is still here. And better than that: he makes sure I know he's not going anywhere.

The freedom that comes with that is indescribable.

Ziggy moans, bouncing on my cock faster. I reach around to grip his shaking ass, wishing I could see it, even as I can't drag my gaze from his face. His eyes are glossy, so blissed-out, cheeks slapped red with pleasure as I tilt my hips to get as deep inside him as possible.

I'm achingly hard, and Ziggy has made a mess of my stomach as he grinds against it.

"You close?"

"Please," he struggles to get out. "T-touch me …"

I release one hand from his ass and wrap it around his needy dick. Ziggy gasps at the contact, and it almost makes me come. He feels almost too good. I'm trying to hold on for him, but I don't know how much longer I can make myself last.

Especially not when I remember that I'm the first person ever to have filled his hole.

And I'm going to make sure I'm the last.

I catch his mouth with mine, drawing him back into a kiss as I slam into him. I'm fucking him so fast that all I can hear is the way our bodies meet, mixed with his uncontrollable panting, and I can't take it anymore.

I'm burning up. The windows of the truck have completely fogged over, and the cab has gotten suffocating as our need thickens the air.

His sweaty body is flush against mine, and I've never been more turned on by anyone.

I have to keep him.

I have to.

He stiffens, ass clamping tight around me, and then his dick is throbbing in my hold. Cum floods from my fist onto my skin, and a tremor passes through me that pools in my balls until it gets to be too much.

I grunt as I come, rippling waves of my orgasm unbearable for a second before the high takes over. All that passes through my brain is his name and his lips and those eyes and the way I'm addicted to every single part of him.

He's panting hard, head on my shoulder, hands resting on my chest. I hold him. Just hold him. Letting myself sink into the moment and the knowledge that he's mine. I want to cuff him to me and never let him go.

Ziggy's lips meet my neck, and my eyes flutter against the softness.

"My sweet Ziggy."

He kisses me again. "My sunshine."

CHAPTER
THIRTY-FIVE

ZIGGY

Kennedy's up as the sun is barely starting to rise, and I blink through the darkness toward him.

"What are you doing?"

His attention snaps to me, and a smile fills his face. "Nothing. I just … think I might head off."

"I can drive you."

"No, get some sleep. I've got the hang of the walk now." Confusion itches at me as he leans in and presses his lips to mine. Before he can pull away though, I grab his arm, searching his eyes for any of that doubt he had before our picnic.

He knows exactly what I'm doing because he sighs. "Okay, okay. I'm being a scaredy-cat."

That's the last thing I'm expecting him to say.

His gaze flicks toward the darkness behind me. "Struggled to sleep. I kept hearing things all night."

My poor Kennedy. He's been trying really hard to get used to my place, but it isn't sticking. *I* know it's safe. I've lived here for eight years, and I've never had an incident.

I kiss him goodbye, wondering whether Rooney has sourced everything we need for a wall yet. The sooner I get it up and in place, the sooner he'll love my home as much as I do.

"It's so sweet you're doing all of this for Kennedy," Rooney says as we carry the supplies from my truck inside. I'm not a builder, but everyone in the End has picked things up along the way. Everything that exists out here, we've built with our bare hands, so when I asked for supplies for the wall, Rooney automatically assumed he'd be helping.

Apparently, so did Wilde and Lynx.

"I can't believe you're going to all this effort for one of those creatures," Lynx says through his teeth. "Let him be scared. I can even show up here in the dead of the night to make it happen."

"You don't need to wait for the dark," Rooney says, which is basically what we're all thinking.

Lynx's face crumples in confusion. "There's nothing scary about me."

"Except your giant knife," Rooney throws back, then points toward Bob, who's watching us. "And your attack dog."

Bob hisses.

"Don't call him a dog."

"Demon kitty, then."

Lynx pauses on his way back to the truck and eyes Bob. "Not sure I'd call him that either."

Rooney waves off his comment. "Whatever you want to call him, the point is that you're both terrifying. Wilde has the scars to prove it."

Wilde's hand immediately covers his neck, where the teeth marks are fading into his skin. "Just keep him over there."

"I don't *keep him* doing anything." Lynx storms back to the truck.

I know Lynx doesn't think he has any control over Bob, but there has to be a reason why the cat is sticking around.

"You been okay up here, Ziggy?" Wilde asks suddenly.

I eye him as I nod.

"There've been a few reports around town of things going missing now. Booker said some supplies have disappeared, Mase and Sonny are missing blankets they had drying, and Leo said he saw a man in the trees this morning."

"A man?" Rooney echoes. "Like a stranger?"

"I don't know how much to trust the word of a five-year-old, but it lines up with the weirdness, so I want us all to be alert."

"That makes sense," Rooney agrees. "Especially after the last time we had a stranger here."

It's rare that anything happens in Wilde's End. The town is so remote, with so few of us living here, that excitement is not a draw card. The last incident happened before I moved here, where a couple were hiding out in Hobby Straight with a group of stolen kids. Wilde and some others held them here until the police arrived, then lied and said they stumbled on the people while they were hiking.

There hasn't been anything since. That we know of.

And there isn't much that happens here without us knowing.

"I'm missing six carrots, two cucumbers, and a bush of blueberries has been stripped bare." Lynx dumps the wooden slats onto the tiled floor.

"Someone's hungry," Rooney says.

"Someone's *dead*," Lynx answers. "They also took my favorite knife. The second I find out who's stolen from me, I'll slice their skin from their body."

Rooney laughs. "And you say you're not creepy."

"I'm *not*." He says it like he takes personal offense to that. "I'm protective." His hand hovers over the handle of the machete strapped to his leg. "I have no issue disposing of the trash." He slants a look at me and Wilde. "No matter who they are."

I glare back. Lynx can think whatever he wants about the brothers, but I'm not going to let him threaten them. Any of them. If he hurt Kennedy, even a small amount, I wouldn't hesitate to do worse back. People can underestimate me all they like, but it will be their funeral.

No one will take him from me.

Lynx's razor-sharp eyes focus on my face. "What's this?" he asks softly, stalking closer. "Are you challenging me, little Ziggy?"

"Touch him and not even Bob will save you," Wilde warns.

"But I'm not the one making threats."

Wilde glances my way. "Whatever Ziggy's threatening, I agree with him."

"Me against the world yet again—" Bob's hiss cuts off Lynx's words. "And Bob. Sorry, Bob."

I huff and turn toward where I want the wall built. I point to it and roll my hands to show them we should get moving.

"So bossy …" Lynx taunts, getting everything set up. Then he leans in by my ear. "I slipped venison skewers into your fridge. I hope you both choke on them."

I pat the spot over my heart twice before Lynx looks away. Complain all he likes, he's still looking out for me. Kennedy, though … I wouldn't be surprised if he really does want him to choke. An attitude like that is going to come between me and Lynx, so he needs to figure out a way to bottle it. If the rest of us can adjust to the brothers and wait for the storm that's coming, he can too.

And while I'm sure there'll be a storm, Kennedy is the silver lining to it.

All I can do is let him shine on me and where we end up.

Sex last night was intense. The way he held me, cared for me, then how we came back here and talked until we fell asleep. I can't remember the last time I got to be with someone and not feel the crushing weight of anxiety on me. We had whole conversations, and it was easy. I barely froze up. I barely second-guessed myself.

I don't think I've ever felt that free. This morning, I'm back to being me again, and it fits like a second skin. The quiet, the awkwardness, those things still infect me. But with Kennedy, I get a break from it all. Like my stress and trauma is put on pause while I gather the energy to deal with it again.

The whole time we're building the wall, Rooney, Lynx, and Wilde talk about the thief. Foley is still in town after the fight last night, and Wilde keeps trying to link things back to him while Lynx shoots down every *what-if* scenario. Like the fact that Booker was setting his arm in a cast during the early hours of the morning, so there's no way Leo would have seen him.

While I don't like Foley, and he's definitely capable of theft and many other things, I also don't think he's behind it. The Dale has money, and they're random things for him to steal. Like, *six* carrots? I didn't even know Lynx paid that close attention, but I'm suddenly very grateful I've never tried to take food without asking.

All I know is that literally any of us better find this guy before Lynx does—given the way he's detailing all the many ways he has to torture the man.

"And if he laid so much as a finger on Leo, I'll pry every one of his fingernails from his hand before taking the digits bit by bit."

"If he touched any of the kids," Wilde tells Lynx, "I'll help you."

At least that's something we can all agree on. The kids growing up here have a whole community to protect them, and it's one of the ways I know that while Lynx might be … *different*, he's not evil. Because he adores the shit of the kids, and they all love him back.

I shuffle closer to him, away from Wilde and Rooney, and clear my throat.

He sighs. "What?"

"Do you know what love is?"

My question makes him pause and throw a disgusted look my way. "Love? It's fucking useless."

Useless?

"Yes. Useless. It makes you pathetic and weak. Like prey. The second you fall in love, you're done for."

"But … there are other types of love … aren't there?"

Some of the irritation leaves his face.

"Like … you love Leo."

His teeth clash together. "That little ankle-biter. He needs better self-preservation skills."

I give him a look to cut the shit.

"But he's a baby Wender, so he's *my* baby. And I'll slaughter anyone who comes near my cubs."

"Then … maybe love is … strength? As well?"

"Strength." He scoffs and drills the final piece of the wall into place. "Fun. Kindness. Protection. A reason to keep living."

Wilde and Rooney join us, and it takes Lynx a moment to notice them.

He glances over his shoulder at the three of us, and his whole face darkens into a leer. "It's also a reason to kill. You tell anyone I said all that, and you'll be sleeping with one eye open."

Done with the drill, he tosses it onto the floor and leaves. Bob joins him when he crosses the threshold of my place, and I watch them disappear into the trees.

"Ziggy," Rooney says from behind me. "Why are you asking about love?"

And it's times like these I'm grateful that they don't expect a response.

Because who would have thought Lynx would be the one to give me my answer?

Love is something different for all of us.

But Kennedy makes me stronger.

And like that, I think I understand it. Things are so much better with him because I *want* them to be better with him. He makes me feel *good* just by being him, and it makes me want to chase that feeling always. In everything.

Love doesn't have to be one thing, but if it exists, the possibilities are endless.

CHAPTER
THIRTY-SIX

"You did this for me?" I stare at the wall that's gone up in the hours since I left this morning.

"I had help … but yes."

"Wow, Ziggy." He's changed his home to make me feel better about being here. He didn't have to do that, and it's making my throat weirdly tight that he did.

I'm the one who does things for other people. It's not the other way around.

And while I definitely feel more at ease here, it doesn't change that creepiness lurking in the back of my mind, knowing all that the wall is hiding.

A creepiness Ziggy will never know about.

He's gone to all this trouble for me, so I'm going to work to be as comfortable here as he is. It'll take time, but I'll do it. The fact that I'm starting to think I might actually get that time with him is … almost too hard to believe. I don't have to rush any part of our relationship. It's almost impossible to believe.

"You like it?" His whispered words dare me to hear them.

But I'm grinning hard when I turn to where he's standing, his fingertips trailing over the timber. I catch him in a hug, and my face finds that groove between his shoulder and his neck as I squeeze the hell out of him. The familiar burst of lemony soap clouds me, and I'm not sure whether I want to laugh or cry, so I hold it all in. The important part is that Ziggy makes me feel anything other than sheer desperation.

That's there too, of course. But it's not the only thing, and I think that's progress?

It's too hard to know so early, but when I pull back and Ziggy's smiling at me in such an open way, I have hope that we're on the right path with this thing.

I mean, I know that *I* am, especially after last night, and as much as I want to say the L word, I won't.

It's hovering on my tongue whenever he's close enough to hear it, and I'm scared I'll end up screaming it at him to get it out. It's not the word itself that I'm scared of though—I've said it to basically everyone I've ever slept with at this point—it's that I want it to be right.

If I tell him I love him, I want him to be the last person ever to own that word from me.

The sound of a car approaching gives us the heads-up that we won't be alone for much longer. We leave the wall and everything that exists behind it and walk out the front to wait. There are low, dark storm clouds gathering overhead, and I assume we're in for another one of those afternoon storms that are so common here. It doesn't take long before Wilde's truck appears.

Hart puts down the passenger-side window. "Apparently, we're being summoned."

"What?"

He lifts his hands like he has no idea what's going on.

Hudson leans across him. "Town meeting. It's important."

I glance at Ziggy, who nods, and Wilde steers the truck back around to leave. I'm expecting that we'll walk wherever we're going, but Ziggy ducks back inside for his keys, moving faster than his usual relaxed pace. When he's back, he gives me a gentle shove toward his truck.

"Do you know what this is about?"

"Maybe."

I trail after him. "Maybe?"

He pauses by his door, looking at me over the truck's windshield. "I think there's a stranger in the End."

"Besides us, you mean?"

His lips kick up on one side. "You're not a stranger anymore." I follow him into the truck, and he gives me one of his sly looks, patting the seat between us. "We know each other *biblically*."

Heat rushes over me at the memory of last night. "Why don't we skip this meeting and fuck instead? I'd love a turn with that piercing inside me."

Ziggy's eyes flutter closed, and he presses down on his groin. "Nope, nope, no."

I open my mouth to suggest we let his dick decide when he turns on his truck and puts the radio on blast. It's a mix of singing and static, but he doesn't turn it down, just gives me a warning look and pulls the truck around.

It's not until there's nothing but harsh static coming through that I lean over and switch it off. "I'll behave. I promise."

That seems to satisfy him.

"So what's this meeting?"

"If you and your brothers are needed, I'm guessing it's for the whole town. I've only been to a handful of them, and they're always held when there's an emergency."

"This stranger is an emergency?"

"I guess we'll see."

I'm surprised when we pull up outside the town bar, but I guess other than the fighting arena, it's the only place large enough to fit everyone. There are only two other trucks outside, one of them Wilde's, and it's weird to think that most people out here don't own cars.

Inside is crowded, maybe twenty or thirty of us, and through the people staring my way, I pick out familiar faces. Wilde and Hudson down the other side, Hart holding up the wall by the door, Booker talking to a freckly guy I think I've seen before … and Lynx.

His bright red hair gives him away, and he's surrounded by a group of kids ranging from teens down to one teeny monster. He's entertaining them by stabbing a knife between his fingers, the *thunk-thunk-thunk* getting faster and faster with each pass.

If I had to pick anyone in this room to be a babysitter, it would not be him.

"I think that's everyone," Wilde says without so much as a hello. His face is serious, like it always is, but I grudgingly see why they made him leader. With his scars and the injuries from his fight last night, he looks like a badass. "I've been getting increasingly more reports of theft over the last week, until last night during Peril, Nox saw a man running from his property. Leo reported seeing the same man this morning before sunrise."

A ripple of conversation goes through the room.

"I think at this point, we start a full-scale search. This person needs to be found, and we know the End better than anyone." Even from the back of the room, I notice the way his jaw tightens. "And our *friends* from the Dale have decided to stick around and help us."

Foley stands from one of the front tables, wearing a dark red tank top, forearm in a cast, and a broad smile. "Wilde's End shares a border with the Dale, and I'd rather stop this pest on your territory than have it invade ours."

Wilde looks like he wishes he could give Foley an extra hit.

Honestly, seeing him clearer than last night, I get what Hudson means. The man could be a goddamn movie star with his looks—he's tall, Hollywood muscular, and inhumanly handsome—but those good looks are turned creepy with the tattoos across his face.

"Should we pair up?" Foley suggests.

"No," Wilde immediately cuts in. "We have sweep teams. We know what we're doing."

Foley eyes him like he wants to push back. "Fine. I'm joining Booker's."

The doctor lets out a long sigh but doesn't bother to fill the silence.

"Kids will be with me," Lynx says.

"They're not joining the search," a woman in her forties says. "I'll stay behind with them."

"Like hell you will." Lynx hands off his knife to the little one. "I have enough weapons to go around."

She huffs and crosses to take the knife away. I'd assume she's the kid's mom, but nothing about the way they're interacting supports that. "Weapons don't belong with children."

"They have to learn to hunt at some point, Viv."

"Not at five, they don't. And you're looking for a *person*, not a wild animal."

"We're in the presence of bad omens," he says, sending a chilling look back my way. "Anything can and will happen when two sides of the mirror meet."

"Enough superstition from you. The children will be fine here."

Lynx unstraps the machete from his side and taps it against the floor between his feet. Then, he gives a piercing whistle, and before I know what's happening, the kid has plucked the knife from Viv's hand and adopts a defensive pose. He pats the kid's head like he's patting a dog. "Down, boy."

I lean toward Ziggy. "Where the hell are that kid's parents?"

"Dead."

Oh. Well, okay. "Has Lynx adopted him?"

The look I get is pure confusion. He tugs me away from the

people closest to us and lowers his voice. "That's Nixon over there. He's the oldest brother, just turned twenty, but he's been here with the kids for three years now."

"Damn. How many kids?"

"Five younger siblings. Matt's about to turn eighteen as well, though."

"And they just … let their little brother hang around with Lynx?"

"You say that like Lynx gives people a choice in anything." Ziggy shrugs. "He's good with them. Nixon and Matt spent a lot of time with him as well."

This town keeps on getting weirder.

"Lynx, we need you in the search," Wilde says. "You can take Matt, Josie, and JJ, but the others will stay here with Viv."

"You think *she* can protect them?" He pushes to his feet and I wouldn't be at all surprised to see him start swinging that knife around again. It's not until Bob climbs out from under the table that I realize he's here as well.

"I think Leo's safer here than running around in the woods with a knife."

"But I'm a big boy!" Leo shouts.

Lynx pats his head again. "What Wilde says goes, little lion. I need you to protect Viv for me."

That calms him down, and without another word, Lynx leaves, three of the teens trailing after him.

"This is going to be a long day, isn't it?"

Ziggy smiles softly. "Once it's over, we can relax again. None of us are safe until we all are."

"It's kind of cool how you all look out for each other."

His fingers twist through mine, and he tugs me toward Wilde. "*We* look out for each other. You're one of us too now."

It surprises me how much I want that to be true.

CHAPTER
THIRTY-SEVEN

ZIGGY

The forest is gloomy. Foggy. The type of stillness that makes my head too quiet. Kennedy, Booker, and Foley are fanned out ahead of me as we cover the distance between Old End and the hillside I live on.

The last people who passed through here were dangerous. They had guns with them, and somehow, Wilde dealt with it, but he's always seemed superhuman to me.

If I'm confronted by someone with a gun … I don't know what I'll do. If *Kennedy* is? Yeah, I'll kill them.

We're all on high alert for any unusual sounds, and even Booker and Foley have set aside their antagonism to search. The forest is huge, but it's familiar, and if there's someone out here, we'll find them.

"I can't believe none of you brought a weapon," Foley says, lifting his Peril post a bit higher. It might not be one of Lynx's knives, but that thing aimed at the head would do real damage.

"We don't know that this person is dangerous," Kennedy points out.

"We don't know that they're not either," Foley throws back.

They both make a point, but a weapon was the furthest thing from my mind. Even if I did have one, there's no guarantee I would have used it.

"Now, now, boys," Booker says. "Wouldn't want you getting into a fight and getting injured, would we?"

Well, *he* would. Though I suppose after being up and at it all night that even he needs to rest. I know all the people in town, but Booker is one that I struggle to get a read on. Wilde likes to go to the swimming hole to relax, and Rooney likes to make soaps and candles and carve them into weird shapes. Lynx spends his free time cooking or with the kids. Booker though? I have no clue what he gets up to when no one is watching.

I'm not so sure that I want to know.

A loud crack comes from our left, and the four of us freeze. I'm peering through the trees, trying to make out any movement, but as the seconds stretch on without a sign, I relax.

No one there.

Kennedy turns to the rest of us. "We're never going to find this guy."

"We'll find him." Foley passes his stick to the other hand, and the small bit of sun we had disappears behind a heavy rain cloud. His piercing blue eyes turn toward the sky. "Let's keep moving."

Kennedy glances back at me. "You okay?"

I nod because out of the three of us, he's the one who doesn't know the forest well. If anything, I should be asking him that question.

"We need to get into the mind of our nighttime visitor," Booker says. "They're creeping in the dark and stealing food. Perhaps they're not here for nefarious reasons. Unfortunately."

"What's unfortunate about that?" The shock comes through in Kennedy's tone.

"I find the alternative much more fun."

Kennedy eyes him with the same wariness I normally do. "Chances are this guy is lost and needs help."

"Then why didn't he ask for it?" Foley pushes some long grass aside with his post. "I don't trust it."

"Also, I find that innocent people don't make off with very sharp, very large knives," Booker adds.

Kennedy stops walking. "He what?"

"Poor thing chose Lynx's favorite one too." Booker's smile spreads. "I'd hate to see what Lynx does to him once he's found."

"I almost hope the poor bastard isn't found," Kennedy croaks.

"If he's smart," Foley says, swiping more shrubs out of his way, "he'll be hidden somewhere off the main paths. With easy access. Shelter."

The storm clouds above rumble, making our creeping pointless.

"Definitely shelter," he repeats. "There aren't many places like that, right?"

"Hobby Straight was the first place we checked," Booker says. "Those creepy little cabins attract chaos."

"Surprised you don't live there." Kennedy flicks a look his way.

"Me?" Booker's voice turns overly dramatic and offended. "I exist for a quiet life. I'm a man of simple pleasures. A mere servant to my community."

"Fuck simple," Foley says. "The only pleasure you should be given is the kind that drives you out of your mind."

"Ah, but what if I'm already out of it?" Booker taps his temple, and I tune them out.

The few times I've seen the two of them together, it ends with Foley pissed off and storming away and Booker apathetic to whatever happened. They're starting to get loud, and if they keep it up, whoever we're looking for will hear us coming long before we see them.

At least between the thunder and the growing wind, it's drowning them out.

I glance behind me, that suspicious instinct growing. There really can't be many places to hide if I go off Foley's requirements, and since Hobby Straight is clear, it narrows the possibilities even more.

Leaves crunch under my feet, a thin fog clings at my ankles, and the deeper we walk into the forest, the more it feels pointless. There's no shelter this way. Only trees and trees and more trees.

We need to be smarter about this.

Off the main path. Easy access. Shelter. Access to food is probably high on the list too. So they'd have to be within walking distance of most of our homes.

That chilling feeling creeps up my spine again, and I glance back out of instinct.

Is this how Kennedy feels when he's at my place? If so, I don't blame him for being unsettled. I'd hate having to look over my shoulder and second-guess what's lurking.

For me, the darkness of my mine is comforting. The openness of the trees is the problem. It's never normally an issue, but knowing that someone is in our town, touching our things, potentially armed—it's a mystery that none of us wants.

So I can understand Kennedy's point of view when it comes to not knowing.

Maybe instead of the wall, I should have installed lights after all. Then he'd know exactly what was down there.

Nothing.

Or at least … it *should* be nothing.

Even though Kennedy felt like he was being watched. Even though he thought he heard something. My favorite shirt that wasn't where I left it.

My feet stall as a ridiculous idea burrows into my brain.

I think I know where the stranger is.

CHAPTER
THIRTY-EIGHT

KENNEDY

have no idea where I am. I'm following the others, just looking into more trees, like trying to find a needle in a haystack. The way they're all so confident they'll succeed is throwing me because there are miles to cover and not enough people to search. We've been set up for the impossible.

The smell of pine trees and wet air picks up on the breeze that twists through, and if we don't get this done soon, we're going to be caught out in this storm. It's already dark. The shadows are getting larger, and I'm just waiting for one of them to call this thing so I can get home. Or to Ziggy's. I don't know how his mine will go in a storm, but I assume he's made it through hundreds of them, so I'm interested in seeing how it works.

As long as it's him and me, preferably no clothes, I'll be fine.

The rumble overhead is threatening this time, and I glance at Foley and Booker to see if there's any reaction from them. Nothing. Because of course. All I know is that I'd hate to run into Foley in a dark alleyway.

I glance back at Ziggy, hoping he gets the message that I'm done with this—but he's not there.

My gaze moves from tree to tree, trying to find the one he's disappeared behind, and when he's not there, I push back the way we came. "Ziggy?"

"What are you doing?" Foley calls. "We have to keep going straight."

"Ziggy's gone." That doesn't get an answer. I'm trying to keep my voice level because he's probably fallen behind, but the further I go, the faster I move, the more I doubt that theory. Tree after tree passes, obscuring my line of sight, but when I yell louder and he doesn't answer, worry passes over me. Did he get lost? I dismiss the thought almost as soon as I have it. Ziggy knows Wilde's End, so that wouldn't make sense.

My breathing has gotten heavier by the time Foley and Booker catch up.

"He'll be fine," Foley says. "We have to stay on track."

"I'm not going anywhere until I know where he is."

"Disappeared into the shadows, did he?" Booker sounds like he's going to laugh at any moment. "Scared of the storm?"

"Ziggy's not scared of storms."

"Maybe he went back for something," Foley counters.

"Without telling us?"

"The guy doesn't *talk*."

"He does to me."

Foley lifts the giant stick he's carrying. It's thick and shiny, painted all black, and with it almost at eye level, I can make out the hand bones painted on the outside of his gloves. "We need to keep going."

I bat the stick away. "I told you, I'm not leaving without him."

"What exactly are you so worried about?"

"He was here one minute, and now he's gone. You don't think that's strange?"

"Ziggy knows his way around," Booker says, like he's talking to a child. "He's like a squirrel rummaging through the under-brush. He knows where we're going, and he'll catch back up."

None of that makes me feel any better. "He didn't get lost. And he's not scared of storms. And he didn't tell us he was leaving."

It clicks with Foley at the same moment why I'm so worried clicks with me.

"You think something happened to him."

"Or some*one*." My pulse is picking up as I even consider the possibility. There is no way in hell that I've finally found the one person who makes me feel like a relationship isn't torture and he's taken away from me. No goddamn way.

"If there was a struggle, we would have heard it."

Like Mother Nature is proving Foley wrong, thunder claps sharp and loud above us.

"We keep moving."

"I told you—"

"*If* by some chance you're right, hanging out here isn't going to help him. The faster we clear our area and get back to the meeting point, the faster we have the whole town looking for him. Now, stop holding us back and get moving."

I hate that he's making sense because all I want is to head to the meeting point now and demand that we forget about this stranger and find Ziggy. Unfortunately, I have no idea where I am, and without their help, I'm likely to be the one who goes missing next.

They're right that the likelihood of something happening is slim, but the way I feel about Ziggy won't let me *not* worry. Would he have gone off on his own? I really don't think so, but it's the only option that doesn't make me panic.

I follow close behind Foley and Booker, urging them on when-ever they slow down or start to bicker. Booker really, really doesn't like him, and I have no clue what the story is between them, but their lack of urgency is irritating the shit out of me.

It feels like forever before we clear the trees, and I make out a few people up ahead. I'm assuming this is the meeting point, and I leave Foley and Booker behind as I pick up the pace. Not even the sight of Lynx makes me slow down, and I walk right up to him and his Lord of the Flies troupe.

"Ziggy's missing."

Those unnerving eyes settle on me. "What did you say?"

"He was with us, and then I turned around, and he was gone."

Lynx bares his teeth, then lets out two short whistles, and the kids scatter. "Never should have trusted him with an outsider."

"How is this *my* fault?"

"Broken twins are like a broken mirror. Nothing but bad luck."

I frown, trying to work out what he's saying. "We're not broken."

His cackle is cut off by Foley and Booker joining us.

"Ziggy disappeared," Foley reports. "No sign of a struggle."

"A skilled hunter never leaves evidence behind." Lynx turns and follows the kids into the forest, leaving me more unsettled than ever.

"He's okay ... right?" I must be desperate if I'm looking for comfort from a man who willingly earned a broken arm and another who excitedly fixed it.

"Of course," Booker soothes, patting my chest and earning me a glare from Foley. "And if he's not ... I'm a doctor. I'll put him back in one piece."

CHAPTER
THIRTY-NINE

ZIGGY

've never run so hard in my life. I can't tell if it's sweat or rain running down my back, but I push harder, lungs burning, knowing I'm not meant for running, but I need to get home fast.

All I can hope is that my hunch is wrong, because the thought of someone being trapped alive?

My gut rolls over itself.

Maybe they're a murderer, for all I know, but being boxed in, surrounded by nothing but darkness?

Shit.

My thighs burn as I jump from one boulder to the next, taking the most direct route up the hill. What if they're injured? Or starving? Shit, even I'd be scared trapped like that.

The sight of my mine entrance brings relief and the motivation to move faster. I barrel inside, right up to the wall, and lungs struggling with my ragged breaths, I pound on the wood. No one answers.

"Hello?" My scratchy voice barely makes it past my lips. *"Hello?"*

Nothing. I hunch over my knees, forcing down oxygen and making my head spin. I'm wrong. I'm *probably* wrong.

I set my hand on the wall, trying to work out which way to go. Tear it all down and hope I find something? Or wait to see if anyone begs to be let out before I destroy our hard work?

I almost give a panicked laugh at myself because waiting? No fucking way.

There's no way I'll be able to break through without help, but my home is devoid of tools, so I grab my keys and head out to the storage carriages. The rain has started, and I'm half-drenched by the time I reach them. The new locks haven't been tampered with, and I let myself into the first one to grab an axe, then the next one for a flashlight and batteries.

Even in my rush, I lock up behind myself, then head back inside.

I really should have had Kennedy come with me. He'd make easy work of this wall, because while I'm good with my hands, I have the upper-body strength of a jellyfish.

Too late now. I pick up the axe and swing it as hard as I can. Stupid us building this stupid thing of hardwood. It's lucky the axe is sharp as fuck, otherwise I'd be making no progress. I swing and hack and hammer my way through the wall until there's a gap large enough to fit through.

I'm panting harder than I was when I got here, and I know I'll pay for all this exertion later, but for now, I toss the axe aside, pick up the flashlight, and slip through the hole.

It's cooler back here, the storm dulled slightly. My light bounces from wall to wall, revealing parts of my home I haven't seen in a long time.

"Hello?" I whisper.

What sounds like a stuttered breath comes from the right, and

I quickly turn in that direction. It only takes a second before my light finds a tear-streaked face.

Fuck.

I was right. Guilt hits hard, and I start forward, needing to check that he's okay, but as soon as I'm within a few feet, he jerks a huge knife up between us.

"Don't come any closer!"

I pause, keeping out of reach. The guy looks young, but there isn't a whole lot else I can make out about him. His hair is flattened to his head with dirt and what looks like blood, his face is filthy and covered in tears, and he's wearing what looks like my favorite T-shirt.

I watch him, and despite how scared he must be, his grip on the knife is steady.

"What do you want with me?" he demands.

For him to get out of my home would be a start. I slowly run the flashlight over him, trying to work out if there are any other injuries. It's impossible to tell, and after trying and failing, I slowly lower into a crouch and set the flashlight on the ground.

His eyes don't leave me as I lift my hands between us.

He pushes back tighter against the wall. "You want to kill me!"

I shake my head quickly.

"I heard you!"

Heard me? The memory of Lynx earlier today saying he'd kill whoever took his knife … Of course he would have witnessed that. Was he sitting here the whole time, watching us box him in and too scared to say anything?

"I want to help you," I force myself to say, but it comes out in a whisper.

"Don't lie to me!"

I shake my head again, frustrated that I can't explain. That I can't tell him we didn't know he was here and that Lynx would never harm him. That if he trusts me, I'll help him get out of here. "I want to help."

He stands suddenly, one hand flat to the wall behind him, while the other keeps the knife between us. "Get out of my way."

I stand slowly and step to the side.

He snatches up the flashlight, backing toward where I came in from.

But before he can get there, a low yawl echoes through the space, and when he turns, the flashlight lands on Lynx's grinning face.

"Well, well, well …" He leers, taking a careful step forward and making the man step back. "What do we have here? A rabbit caught in its den."

"Don't come any closer. I'll use this."

"Cleaver already knows the taste of my blood. We're very old friends."

"I don't care." The man's hold on the knife shakes for the first time. "Just let me pass."

"No." The smile slips from Lynx's face, and in the shadows of the mine, he looks demonic. "You took my things."

"I want to leave."

"I can't let that happen." And Lynx lifts up his machete. It's not as thick as the cleaver, but it's a lot longer, and I can't pick which one I'd want pointed at me.

All I know is that the look on Lynx's face confirms it would be whichever one he *isn't* holding. But if Lynx scares me and we're friends, I can't imagine how the man feels. He let us bury him alive so he wouldn't have to face Lynx.

It's on me to help him.

Palms clammy, I set my jaw and step between them both. "Enough." My voice shakes, and I want to crawl into a hole, but this is *my* goddamn home. "No one's getting hurt."

"The little mole man is making demands now, is he?"

"I'm serious." I have to clear the block in my throat. "You won't hurt him."

"But he owes me so much." Lynx's voice is a low, warning growl.

"Then he can work off payment like the rest of us do. This is *my* house, and you'll follow *my* rules."

The low *yowl* comes again, and when the flashlight dips slightly, it catches Bob's glowing eyes.

"What is that thing?" the man asks from behind me.

"That's Bob," Lynx says.

"B-Bob?"

"Yes. Bob. Bob the cat."

"Bob won't hurt him either," I say. Considering none of us has control over the animal, it's a bold demand, but I'm going to stand strong. This guy is terrified, and I can't blame him. Wilde's End isn't the easiest place to survive, and our years here have hardened us.

Lynx's eyes dip to meet mine. "I came to find you. Your pest is worried."

"Kennedy?"

"Go tell him you're safe. I'll take care of this one."

I hear the man move before I know what's happening. The light goes berserk, there's a thump, footsteps, a hiss, and then Lynx shrieks. Like his careful calm is exploding from him.

"He threw the fucking flashlight at me!"

A shadow crosses the hole I came in through, and I catch a glimpse of Lynx darting after it.

I have no idea what the hell I'm going to do, but I need to do something.

I chase the both of them, crawling through the hole, scrambling out of my place, and then running out into the rain. It takes me a moment to spot them, and when I do, I catch sight of Lynx gaining on the much smaller man. He pounces like a tiger, and they both slam into the ground.

I run, rain and wet hair trying to ruin my vision. No matter what, I can't let Lynx hurt him. I can't.

The cleaver is on the ground a few feet away, and Lynx is straddling the man's chest, knife at his throat and every muscle in his arm bulging.

I reach them quickly. "Get off him."

"Now is the time to be quiet," Lynx warns.

"I said get off him!"

Lynx's eyes flash, but he doesn't look away. "This is why I hate people. Even your favorite pets disappoint you."

I'm not sure whether to be surprised that I'm his favorite or offended that he called me his pet. He doesn't even call *Bob* his pet.

"*Please*, Lynx," I beg, hoping there's a scrap of humanity in there somewhere.

"It's my job to protect the town. To keep us *safe*." Lynx's eyes are wide, vein bulging in his forehead, arm shaking under the pressure of keeping himself steady.

"He's not a threat!" I shout, panic creeping in at the same time as the man loses it.

"Please let me go. I didn't mean to steal your stuff. I crashed here, and I'm lost and scared and—"

"*Shut the fuck up.*"

The man swallows his words.

"Lynx—"

"You too." The knife jerks closer to the guy's throat, and I don't know what else to do. My gaze darts to the cleaver. Surely Lynx wouldn't be able to stop me from getting to it in time. But even as I think that, Bob creeps into my line of sight, fur soaked, large ears pulled back and flat to his head, huge paws tense with every step.

Between the two of them, I wouldn't have a chance. Bob would die before he let something happen to Lynx.

"*Please.*"

Lynx's lips curl back. "The rules of the wild are absolute."

"Lynx—" I dart for the cleaver, safety be damned, when Bob moves.

I brace for him to pounce at me, but instead—

He throws himself over the man's head.

Lynx jolts in surprise, blade brushing Bob's fur, and the machete hits the ground.

"What …" He stares at the animal as all the fur on the back of its neck lifts.

I watch them both, eyes locked on each other for a long moment before Lynx leans in. "I could kill you," he hisses. "Gut you and use you for a rug."

Bob lets out his low warning noise that terrifies me, but Lynx only grabs the cat and drags him off the man. He doesn't pick the knife back up. Instead, he leans down, until his terror meets the man's panic, and while his first words are swallowed by the storm, I catch the rest.

"Welcome to Wilde's End, little rabbit. I've been outvoted, so it's time to face our fearless leader."

Lynx stands, dragging the man by the shirt after him. They're both drenched. Lynx's red hair is stuck to his face and neck on one side, the other shaved too close to see. The rain has washed a lot of dirt off the man, and even though his hair is damp, I think he might be blond. He's almost a whole head shorter than Lynx, and as the dirt leaves his face, it highlights how *pretty* he is.

"Be careful with him," I say, picking up the cleaver and then creeping closer to retrieve the machete as well.

Lynx doesn't stop me. "Keep those blades pointed at him, won't you? Wilde can decide what to do next."

CHAPTER
FORTY

'm not an impatient guy. I'm chill and relaxed and go with the flow—relationships excluded—but not knowing where Ziggy is or what's happened to him is eating me alive.

"They should be back," I say, pacing past Wilde and Hudson. The storm is over, leaving everything wet under the slivers of sun that peek out and disappear again. "They *should* be back by now, right?"

Wilde doesn't answer, muscle in his jaw tightening as Hudson sets his hand on his back. It's weird to see him lending anyone comfort, let alone Wilde, and I'd sort of like him to send some of that comfort my way instead.

I'm his brother.

And it's my boyfriend who up and disappeared.

"Ziggy's okay," Wilde finally grunts.

"You don't know that."

"I said he's okay, so he's okay."

My hands tighten at my sides. "It doesn't work like that! You don't get to say something is fine, and then it happens. Sometimes the world is fucked-up."

Wilde snaps. "You think I don't know that?" He gets in my face, the forced calm long gone. "I know what pain is. And if I say Ziggy is fine, then he's fine, right up until the second we learn otherwise."

It's then that it hits me Wilde isn't saying Ziggy's fine for my benefit. It's for his.

Hudson gets between us, hands on Wilde's chest, like he's holding him back, but Wilde is already deflating. It's so hard for me to acknowledge that Wilde actually cares about other people.

"Look at me," Hudson murmurs. "Ziggy's smart. He can handle himself. We both know he's fine, and if something happened, we'd know already. Okay?"

Slowly, Wilde nods. "Okay."

Then Hudson thumps his shoulder. "And yell at my brother like that again and we'll have real issues, got it?"

Wilde's stormy gaze moves slowly from Hudson to me. "Sorry."

"Uh, thank you?"

They huddle together, and if it weren't for my complete freak-out over Ziggy, that short interaction would actually give me hope for things with Hudson. But I can't hope for anything until I know Ziggy's okay.

"Five more minutes," I say, pacing again. "If he's not back in five minutes, I'm going looking." Not that I think I'll be able to do anything, but there's no way in hell I can keep waiting around. It feels like my damn chest is being torn out.

"If anything's happened to him—"

"Nothing's happened."

I send a glare Wilde's way. "I'll join Lynx in making a project for Booker."

"Wow, dark, bro," Hudson mutters, head on Wilde's shoulder.

It might be dark and not like me, but I think I mean it. I don't care if they think I'm being dramatic; even the possibility of Ziggy being hurt is making it hard to breathe. I talk about love and losing it all the time, but all my other relationships ending felt like failure. Like something to be embarrassed about. Something to beat myself up over.

Losing Ziggy feels like … nothing. Like being emptied of all the things that make me who I am and being left with a vacant existence.

I don't want to try again.

Because there is no *again*.

I said I wanted to fall in love for the last time.

And it feels a whole lot like falling in love for the first as well.

There's sound from the forest, and I look up to find Lynx manhandling a man into the opening with Ziggy right behind them.

Relief crashes into me.

The others barely register as I tear past them to get to Ziggy, and as soon as he's within reach, I haul him into a hug. It's like every cell in my body lets out a relieved breath, and I sink into the feel of him in my arms.

"Are you okay?" I ask, pulling back to check he's in one piece. "What happened?"

Ziggy's gaze strays over my shoulder to where the others are, and then he holds up the two enormous knives he's holding.

I look at them and back to the man in front of Ziggy. He's got waterlogged blond curls, big blue eyes, and I can't work out if he's wearing a huge T-shirt or a tiny dress. "That guy is who we were searching for?"

Ziggy nods. "Said his name is Sasha."

I watch as Wilde leads them up the short wooden steps and into the Cutty. "Did you want to go with them?"

"No."

Good. After the stress of the last hour or so, all I want is to crash, knowing that Ziggy is okay and everything is exactly the way it should be. "Did something happen, or did you just … leave?"

He's chewing on his tongue, and I can tell he's in that space where he really, really doesn't want to answer. I just hope he wins the fight because after all that stress, I want to be able to understand.

"I thought … I knew … where he was," he says, and his voice is a relief.

"It's okay," I tell him. "Take whatever time you need to."

"I don't want …" He pulls tight to himself. "You to be … mad at me."

Mad? At him?

It's then that I realize my body language. My expression. The way I'm holding his upper arms. How close I'm standing.

I release him so he has some space. "I'm not mad. I was worried because I kept picturing the worst, but …" And this part is hard for me to say. "I trust you. Whatever choice you made, I know you did it for the right reasons."

Ziggy reaches out and takes my hand, fingers slotting between mine. "Thank you."

The words *I love you* are on my tongue, but I hold them back. I always say them too early. I always drop them without meaning. This time, knowing exactly how much they really do mean, it's difficult to get them out. I don't want to scare Ziggy off.

I want him to get there in his own time.

"I knew where he was," Ziggy tries again. "Well, I had a hunch. And I was right. He took shelter in my home, and we trapped him in there. I knew he'd be scared, so I wanted to get to him as soon as possible."

"He was there the whole time?"

Ziggy nods, smile tilting upward. "You were right when you said you were hearing things."

"Fuck me. He has definitely seen us naked."

His chuckle is soft. "I really thought Lynx was going to kill him."

"What happened?"

"He chased him down, tackled him, had the knife … I yelled at him to stop, and when he didn't … I was going to take Lynx on."

"You were?" It's not that I don't think Ziggy is capable, but he's not a fighter. He's like me.

"I couldn't let him get hurt."

"Did Lynx touch you?" I might not be confrontational, but if he so much as scratched Ziggy—

"It didn't get to that. Bob stopped him instead."

"Wait. The *bobcat*? The one that's weirdly possessive of Lynx?"

"Yep."

"*Why?*"

Ziggy shrugs his narrow shoulders. "Anyone's guess. It was weird."

I'll say. The cat is the first to attack if it thinks Lynx is in danger, but then it stopped him from hurting a stranger?

With a sigh, I remind myself that I don't care. Lynx, Sasha, the cat, Wilde … none of them matter to me.

Not like Ziggy does.

And he's safe.

"You did the right thing," I assure him. "But next time, maybe you could give me the heads-up? So I don't feel like I'm about to puke and end up threatening everyone within earshot?"

His big eyes soften, and he squeezes my hand. "I'm sorry."

"I know. We're still learning at this thing, after all."

"I don't think I'll ever get used to having a boyfriend."

"It's okay." For the first time ever, it really is. "We've got time."

And we do. A lot of it. It's a whole new experience to not be in a rush to make him fall for me and to take the back seat in a relationship for once. Ziggy has the wheel. He's the one who'll get us to where we need to be.

And I trust him to do it.

"You threatened people?" he asks.

Not my finest moment. "I would have followed through on it too. For you." Ziggy is everything that's amazing in this world, and I want him to know it. "A few months ago, I never would have been able to stand up for myself. My default is to run from conflict." I cup his face, holding it exactly like my hands were made to do. "But if you can find your voice when it's needed, then so can I. You inspire me, Ziggy."

His eyes shine with all the words building inside him.

But he doesn't have to say one.

Because I know what Lynx means about Ziggy not needing words to communicate, and everything about him is proud of me.

The same way I'm proud of him.

CHAPTER
FORTY-ONE

Technically, it wasn't a date, but when we got to the rock by the river with the tree swing, I thought of it as the site of our first date. There was something about that moment—the relaxing afternoon, the crackling tension, Kennedy's bare, wet body—that cemented itself in my brain forever.

Today, I brought another picnic, and I set out a blanket with everything on it, wanting to be done before he gets here.

I only just manage it.

He's early, like he couldn't wait to see me, and considering I'm ear*lier*, that's saying something. Kennedy's smile is as big and warm as it always is, and I wonder if that will ever change. If there'll be a time that he doesn't look at me like he's excited just to be together.

He swamps me in a hug, mouth smacking a quick kiss to mine, before he steps back and strips off his shirt. He's already glistening with sweat, and I know he was up early working so he could take the afternoon off.

"Coming in with me?" he asks.

Like I could say no. I tug my shirt over my head, then push my shorts down too. I didn't bother with underwear since every time we're together, we end up having sex.

Kennedy groans, head dropping back. "You're too sexy not to touch."

I laugh and slap the hand that comes my way. He can touch all he likes, but he's washing off first so that I can do the same.

Without waiting for him, I step off the rock and into the water, continuing deeper until it reaches my hips. My half-hard cock bobs in front of me, but it's hard to pay it attention when Kennedy follows, all that tall, thick body making its way through the water.

"Now who's the tease?" I ask.

He wraps his hand around his semi and gives it a tug. "I really didn't know that I had so much cum in me. Maybe it's like a supply-and-demand thing. My balls know that I'm seeing you today, so they're going to be in high demand."

I'm almost certain it has nothing to do with that, and Kennedy is just a horny guy. It works for me. When it comes to him, I'm a horny guy too.

He reaches where I'm standing and wraps his arms around me. The feel of his skin on my skin is hotter than the sun shining down over us both.

"So. Another date," he says. "You're spoiling me."

"I'm trying." I reach up to play with his hair. "You deserve to have the actual romance you've always wanted. Actually, you deserve everything."

"You're too good for me."

"I don't think so. We work. And you make me happy. Considering how few people have bothered to do that in my life, I want you to know how much I appreciate it."

"You make me really happy too," he murmurs.

He leans in, mouth sealing over mine and strong tongue sweeping into my mouth. I'm surrounded by the scent of his sun-warmed skin and salt water, and I don't think there's ever been a time in my life when I've ever felt happier.

There are no secrets between us, no buried worries, no uncovered scars that we haven't bared for the other person. Everything about Kennedy and his life is held precious in my chest, and every day, I wake up blown away that I have him in my life.

A boyfriend.

A real-life man who's my friend and makes me see stars when I come. Who's patient and kind but fierce when he needs to be. Kennedy Bellamy is the entire package, and I hate that he was ever made to doubt that.

I'm still haunted by the voices that live in my head, but their words hold less weight. I'm happy. I know who I am. So their lies can live on, but I know they're lies.

I hope Kennedy can do the same with his demons.

His big hands reach down to palm my ass cheeks. It's something he does a lot, and the way he squeezes and kneads me there never fails to turn me on. It's possessive and sexy, and when he breaks our kiss to trail his lips down my neck, I could shiver into the sea.

While my blood heats, I reach up to play with one of his nipples. The immediate gasp that leaves him has me smirking through my arousal. It'll never get old how sensitive his nipples are, and the fact that I can play with them and have him rutting against me in seconds is incredible.

Kennedy drags his hard cock against mine under the water, and my eyes flutter back into my skull. How have I gone my entire life without sex? Being naked with him, enjoying ourselves, hearing his deep voice as he tells me exactly what he wants ... it brings me alive.

His large hands sweep up and down my back, making me feel so small under his touch. This man is consuming.

"Ziggy ..."

"Mmm?" I'm too worked up for any real answer.

"I want to feel that piercing inside me now."

Oh, fuck me. A weird little strangle sound comes from me.

"I'm taking that as a yes."

I nod to support his theory. It's a very, *very* strong yes.

"Your needy little face gets me every time. Come on."

Kennedy takes my hand and pulls me back the way he came. I expect him to climb out, but instead, he reaches for his pants, pulls out a packet of lube and a condom, then bends over the rock.

The water is up to our knees here, but the rock is a perfect height to put his ass where I need it, and when he reaches back to spread himself open …

Shit.

Fucking shit.

My cock throbs at the sight of his exposed hole, but Kennedy doesn't notice the way my head is about to explode because he tears open the lube and gets to it, rubbing his fingers over his entrance. I'm torn between wanting to do it myself and wanting to watch the show. But when his first finger sinks into his body and I haven't moved, it's impossible to take over. Kennedy prepping himself for my cock is the hottest thing I've ever seen.

Maybe one day, I'll wrap my head around the fact that I have a sexy, confident boyfriend, but I doubt it.

Sex has always been an abstract, unspoken thing.

Kennedy is making me see it in a very real way.

"Enjoying the view?" he calls back to me.

I run my gaze from his messy hair, down his broad back, over him stretching himself, and down his thick thighs to where they meet the water. I am *definitely* enjoying the view. Maybe too much.

I give my cock a quick tug as I watch him, and it's a struggle not to let myself have more. I'm rock hard, breathing deeply, wanting to touch him but not wanting to ruin a thing.

Two of his fingers press inside, and a whine gets trapped in my chest as I watch him spread around them.

I finally give in and stroke myself as I watch him work his

fingers deep. He's pressing them open, making sure he can take more, and it must feel good, judging by the way his back arches against the rock.

"Can't wait for this to be your cock," he says. "Normally, I hate bottoming, but the thought of you inside me … god, I want it. Want to feel you pushing in. Want your hands on my hips. Want you fucking me so hard and fast I can't think."

The water is loud as I move closer and snatch up the condom. I'm so ready for this, and I might not know what I'm doing, but it doesn't matter at this point. My only aim is for us both to feel good, and I'm goddamn going to make sure it happens.

Only I have no clue how to get the condom on. I've never had to before, and I have my piercing to work with, which makes it even more tricky.

Kennedy must notice me struggling because he straightens and turns, hands resting over mine.

"Let me."

I search his eyes for any disappointment.

"Never," he scoffs. "Any chance to touch your cock will always be hot as hell."

I can't disagree with him there. He's gentle as he rolls the latex down over my sensitive skin. Every brush of his fingers is a teasing promise, and by the time he has it on, I'm ready to go. I need to bury myself inside him.

"You ready?"

I nod, then remember to talk. It's important. "Are you?"

"Very." He presses a hard kiss to my lips. "Fuck my brains out, okay?"

I have no idea how to do that, but when Kennedy bends back over again, all I can focus on is the first step: entering him for the first time.

I move closer, legs slotting between his as I drag my cock along his crease. He's deliciously responsive, pressing back toward me and making my balls ache with what's to come.

"You good back there?"

In answer, I position myself at his opening and start to push inside. I'm not ready for the resistance, the pressure, and just when I'm worried that I won't fit, my top *pops* inside.

Fuuuuuuuuck.

I stop myself from going too deep, trying to mimic Kennedy's movements from our first time together, but I think my brain is leaking out through my ears. I'm very worried this is going to be a repeat of his blow job, but I'm already desperate to come.

Two inches deep, and I'm done for.

Shit.

I need to keep it together.

I take his hips like he said, tightening my grip on them to try and ground myself. This is fine. I can do it.

"I can take you all whenever you're ready," he assures me.

"Yeah, but I'm not so sure I can take it."

It takes him a second to catch on. "Ready to come?"

"A bit."

The bastard squeezes his hole around me. "That's the point, Ziggy. Fuck and come. Slow or fast, none of it matters to me so long as you're the one I'm doing this with."

The way his words are like a balm to my chest keeps me going. Fighting against the urge to let go, I slide further inside. Kennedy is tight, and it's not easy, but his ass is working with me to pull me in deeper. All my effort to stop myself from hurting him is wasted, because the deeper I go, the louder he groans, until I forget what I was worried about.

Keeping control is rapidly failing.

"You can do it, Ziggy," Kennedy says. "Let it all out."

I don't know if he says anything after that because I do exactly as he says.

The sun is hot at my back, the water is cool around my calves, and I thrust into Kennedy like it's my dying wish. His meaty ass slaps against my hips, reddening more and more every time we make contact. Every time we've had together has been so sweet and intimate that fucking him just to fuck him is like this foreign, powerful surge of adrenaline.

He feels incredible wrapped around my cock. I'm so consumed by him that I forget how close I was. Forget to stress about making this good. I give in to feeling and how turned on I am and let him overwhelm my senses.

His scent is swimming around me, his moans are driving me out of my mind, and our sun-warmed skin is prickling with sweat that makes every slap of our skin sound sinful.

He's pushing back onto my dick, and my balls are getting painfully tight. My arm muscles are locking up with how tightly I'm holding him, but I can't let go because it will throw off my rhythm, and I'm not ready to stop.

"Your piercing," he chokes out. "So, so good."

Satisfaction makes my limbs light. I've reached that happy, bubbly part where my brain doesn't know what's happening, and the pleasure building at the base of my spine is almost too much.

I'm close.

"Fuck," he grunts, and I'm abstractly aware of him jerking himself off. "Fuck, Zig. Fuck, fuck … *fuck* …"

Kennedy's ass clenches around me, and I'm unprepared for the pressure. I fuck him through it, rapidly losing the battle to keep going, and just when I think it couldn't possibly feel any better, my orgasm hits hard. I come with a body-racking shudder, bowing forward over Kennedy as I empty into the condom.

It goes on forever, and I turn to jelly, only standing by him holding me up. My lips meet the back of his neck, and I kiss him and kiss him and kiss him until my brain slowly trickles back online.

"Now, that's how you pound the life out of someone," he mutters, stretching beneath me.

I pull out, and somehow, we climb back out of the water.

We collapse onto the rock, needing another swim, but I've

never felt so amazing. I leave the condom for now and stretch out, feeling like a lazy lizard who just came his brains out.

"Was that good?" I ask because even though I know that he got off, it doesn't necessarily mean that he was okay with it all.

"Perfect." He smiles, eyes drifting closed. "Still not sure how much I want to bottom, but your piercing felt so good."

That fills me with satisfaction. "It's yours whenever you want it." I reach down to slot my hand into his. "And I'm good with bottoming. I also really, really like blowing you. We should do more of that."

He barks out a laugh. "You are full of good ideas."

I know I am. And speaking of good ideas …

I sit up, ditching the condom, then reach for the picnic basket and where I've hidden my gift. It's not like I can shower him in pretty things up here, but I hope this is enough. It was worth every cut and scrape and burn.

With a deep breath, I turn and hold it out to him.

Kennedy sits up, face immediately serious. "What's this?"

"I made it. For you."

He's staring at the little metal bird that I've assembled with wire, cogs, scraps of metal, and whatever spare parts I could find. It looks like a sparrow, and the only things not silver are the rust-colored wings.

"This is so cool. It's a bird."

Not just a bird. I wanted it to be special, and this was the hardest part to find. Rooney went out of his way to source it, and I'm going to owe him forever. I reach for the pin on the side and wind it up.

When I let go, music plays, and the little mouth moves up and down.

"*What?*" He holds it higher to watch it. "You *made* this? My boyfriend is a genius."

I warm at the "B" word. It's never going to get old. "Reminded me of you. You're always singing. Do you recognize the song?"

He listens for a moment. "Hold on … is that 'My, My, My'?"

I nod quickly. "Do you know why?"

"There's a reason?"

"Of course there's a reason."

It's obvious by his expression that he has no idea.

"It's the first song I heard you sing along to. Loudly. With dance moves and everything."

He tosses his head back with a laugh that reaches right into his chest. "How the hell did you remember that?"

"Because I remember everything about you."

That will never change. Kennedy deserves a man who'll worship him, and that's a job I'm happy to claim. I vow to never, ever let him feel unloved again.

CHAPTER
FORTY-TWO

Other than my times with Ziggy, I stick to myself. Normally, I'm the one running to fix things with my brothers, but if they're okay with this stiff relationship crusting over between us, then I will be too.

It's not on me to burst out of it.

As desperately as I want to.

The more I think about it, the more I'm convinced that our parents destroyed something precious in all of us. Hudson's self-worth. Hart's hope. And my ability to let go. I thought my past relationships were a prime example of that, but my brothers might take the cake.

The air between us is stale as we work. The conversation is dry. It's not as bad when other people are around, but just the three of us?

Painful.

I'm constantly biting my tongue.

"Hey, pass me that level," Hudson says.

It's basically between us, but there's no point in arguing. I pick it up, and his hand closes over it, but he doesn't take it.

"Kenny …"

My gaze lifts to his.

"I don't like this."

"Don't like what?"

Irritation crosses his features, but he stamps it down. "You're not happy."

"Can you blame me?"

"Guess not." He finally takes the tool, but we go on watching each other.

"Is there something you wanted to say?" I'm not going to get hopeful because my brothers have let me down too many times.

"I'm sorry I'm a shit brother."

I frown at the sudden rush of words. "You're not a shit brother."

"Considering last time we properly spoke, you told me to go and fuck myself, I think I'll disagree."

I was mad, and I had every right to be mad, but that's not what it was about at all. I turn and set my back against the wall. "I never said you were a shit brother. I said that I feel lonely and that we're supposed to be there for each other, but instead of that happening, we're always butting heads. I hate it."

"Me too." He runs his free hand roughly over his face. "I don't know how to fix it though. I'm so sick of feeling angry and like the smallest thing is one step away from disaster."

"Have you seen where we are?" Hart snarks.

I ignore him. If he wants to cling to whatever demons he has, that's on him. But if I have a chance to repair things, at least with one of them, I'm going to take it. "Do you feel like that around Wilde?"

Hudson doesn't answer at first, just taps the level in a steady beat against the timber floors. "He … keeps me in check. He knows my moods, and he knows when to ignore it and when to step in. Everything feels calmer around him. Which is huge, considering how everything started."

I'll never understand their relationship, but that's a whole lot more than Hudson's ever got out of his previous ones.

So I'll give a little and hope he meets me halfway.

"Okay. Then I will be civil."

"Toward Wilde?" The doubt in his voice comes through clearly.

"Yes." I huff, because I'm not the unreasonable one. "All I ever asked of him was to treat you right, and now that I know he's not using you as a punching bag and that it sounds like you might actually be communicating and maybe even good for each other …" I throw up my hands. "I can't complain about that."

"Right. Well, good."

"Good."

"And I'll apologize to Ziggy."

"What?"

Hudson screws up his face. "Don't make me say it again. But I'll do it, and I'll make sure he knows I'm serious."

Talking feelings in any capacity is something the both of them struggle with, and knowing Hudson will do that for me feels like the olive branch I've been waiting on.

"Thank you."

He smiles but can't meet my eyes. "Next time you feel alone, come to me. I might be an asshole sometimes, but I'll always be your big brother."

"Does that mean you'll tuck me in and give me forehead kisses too?" Hart asks, completely disinterested.

Hudson ignores him. "I'm serious."

"Thanks, but with Ziggy, I don't think I'll feel alone again."

"Yeah, but … you need someone outside of your relationship. That can't be everything. You know that, right?"

"I know. I've made friends with Rooney, and I've dropped in on that guy Sasha a few times."

"How is he?"

"No clue. I have a feeling something happened in Wayward, but he won't talk about it."

"Yeah, I got that impression."

Whatever it was, if I've learned anything, it's that running from a problem doesn't make it go away. Now that he's not scared for his life, he's a sweet guy, and he's actually serious about helping to pay off what he stole.

"Someone's here," Hartwell says, standing and dusting himself off.

I didn't hear anything, but the sound of a car door slamming comes a moment later. My brothers lead the way out, and while I don't think everything is magically fixed now, it's good to know that at least Hudson is committed to trying.

We step outside right as Wilde, Ziggy, and Rooney are tugging a hot water system off the back of the truck.

"What's this?" I ask as Hudson goes to help them.

"Ziggy's idea," Wilde grunts. "Apparently, he's not okay with you continuing to take cold showers."

Hudson lets go of the system suddenly. "Sounds like I picked the wrong wild man." He whacks Wilde on the shoulder. "Why don't you care about me?"

"Believe me, I've tried not to."

Rooney looks around at us all. "Isn't this nice? So much love in the air. Who would have thought we'd have so many blossoming romances to swoon over?"

I swear Wilde growls at him.

"After that reaction," I say, "I think it means Ziggy and I win. First, my songbird, and now hot water? My man spoils me."

"To be fair," Rooney jumps in, "this was a team effort. Ziggy's idea and execution, Wilde gave the okay for the money, and I went and sourced. The *three* of us are spoiling you."

"Why are you bothering though? You don't owe us anything."

"It's technically my job."

"Hey, maybe you could hook up with Hartwell and—"

"Say another word and die." Hart crosses his arms tightly, and it draws Rooney's attention.

"What's wrong, handsome? Not into men?"

Hart doesn't answer.

"Pity, because there's nothing I love more than a negative wet blanket who wouldn't know a scrap of happiness if it bit him in that delicious ass."

Hart glares harder, and I stare at Rooney, who keeps on smiling.

"Sorry that I'm not pretending to love this shithole," Hart grumbles.

"No, no, don't apologize. You continue on with this …" They set down the system, and Rooney waves a hand toward my twin. "Too-cool-to-care, growly, grumpy black cat attitude. The rest of us will enjoy our day."

My brother doesn't bother answering, just turns on his heel and heads back inside.

The others start talking about where to start, while I approach Ziggy.

"You did this for us?"

He turns an eye-shining smile on me.

Because of course he did this. Ziggy is the most considerate guy I know. He's never made me anxious or like I have to try to get his attention. He's never made me feel like I'm doing something wrong.

If I start fussing or getting too much, he gives me a calming look, and all the writhing anxiety of losing him fades away.

Ziggy knows exactly what my demons are, and I know his.

Things might not have started with a bang like I've always assumed romances do, but that was half of my problem. Trying to force something that didn't fit.

With him, I fit.

And he never lets me doubt it.

The way he squeezes my hand and looks at me gives me my answer.

Anything for you.

For the first time in my life, I believe it.

I trust Ziggy will never hurt me, and he trusts me to do the same.

EPILOGUE

THREE MONTHS LATER

ZIGGY

When Kennedy asked me to come with him to Wayward, I wasn't interested. First, people. No, thanks. Second, I really didn't want to run into Caroline again. He says she's backed off now, but I don't want to deal with the awkwardness of coming face-to-face with her.

I never thought we'd end up here.

"Hold tight," Kennedy says, grip crushing my hand. "We can get through this."

I don't know where this *we* business is coming from when he's the one in the chair. Trying to be sympathetic, I pat his hand, reminding him that I'm here. He's the one who decided to do this, not me, and I'm so curious to see if he'll go through with it.

If he does, I foresee a lot of fun in our future.

"You ready?" the woman asks, doing her best not to look amused.

He lets out a gust of air. "Ready."

Then she leans in, lines up with the dot on his nipple … and shoves the needle through.

A shriek echoes and dies in Kennedy's throat, my hand going numb from the pain. She sets the end on the barbell, him panting through it, and he turns wide eyes on me.

"How the fuck did you let them do that to your dick? Don't get me wrong, I'm reaping the benefits, but *fuck me*."

A laugh slips out. He's so dramatic. I ignore that he just announced to a complete stranger that I have my junk pierced and drop a kiss on his forehead. He's got this. The big baby.

"Still want the other one done?" his piercer asks, her amusement finally winning the battle.

"Yes. I think. Ah … yep. Yes. Do it."

This time, I peel my hand out of his and offer him the other one. Might as well even things up.

And this time when the piercing goes through, his shriek escapes and fills the small shop.

"Sorry, I didn't mean to … *fucking ouch!*"

"Yeah," the woman agrees. "It's painful. Getting your junk or your tongue done hurts more, I think, but nipples aren't pleasant."

"Why does anyone do this?" he asks, sounding faint.

"Body positivity." Her tone takes on a sly note. "And for a lot of people, it makes them more sensitive."

Kennedy's grumbling when he gets up out of the chair, and on a whim, I decide to support him in this. After all, it's weeks before we can have fun with them, so I might as well get this over and done with too.

I slip into his vacated chair.

They wear matching confused expressions.

Because I'm apparently not being obvious enough, I strip off my shirt.

"You want yours done too?" she asks.

I nod at Kennedy, letting him know he can talk for me.

"If you have time? He's obviously used to this process."

"Yeah, I think he's got more piercings than me," she says and goes to grab a consent form.

"You sure about this?" Kennedy asks.

"I considered a Jacob's ladder, but maybe we'll save that for our first-year anniversary."

He goes offline for a long moment. "Yes, please."

It's so cute the way my piercings turn him on. And just seeing the barbells glint through his nipples turns me on as well. I can't wait to drive him wild with them.

"Only one nipple," I tell him. "I need to give you a chance to catch up."

"That will never happen. I think we'll leave the piercings to you."

"Wait until those are healed, and then we'll see." I tug his earlobe. "You'd look hot as fuck with your ears done."

His lips twitch. "Noted."

"Is it still painful?" I drop my hand to run over his chest.

"Not like it was when she pierced them. It's more like a bruise feeling."

That's easy to handle.

"You sure you want to do this?" he checks. "You don't have to just because I did."

"I know. I want to do this together."

It's the right answer, judging by the way he gets all heart-eyed at me. He does that a lot. These small, sneaky moments when he can't believe he's found me, and it reminds me to be awed that I found him as well. I never would have thought that Kennedy would be more perfect than my dreams of him were.

My mouth feels dry as one word that's been surfacing a lot lately tries to take over. I've known it since the day I met him, but the longer we're together, the more it solidifies. It's there as we work silently side by side. It's there during our picnics, and our swimming, and when we have a whole conversation without opening our mouths. It's there when I hear him playing the song-bird, or he's singing along to the radio, and it's there in my mine, which is always so loud and full and busy when he's with me.

I can't hold it back anymore.

"I love you."

Kennedy blinks at me. Then blinks again. "Really?"

"Yeah." I swallow. "Always."

"Thank *fuck*. I've been wanting to say it for months now, and I was terrified I'd scare you off."

My grin is unbearable. "Say what?"

"How much I love you. You're so strong and special, and getting to be with you is still a pinch-me moment. I love brushing your hair back, and your cute little smiles, and the way you blush when I tell you what a pretty little hole you have. I love every-thing about you. And the best part of all of that is that you make it easy. I'm not scared to love you, and I finally know what it's like."

I tug him close because I need to kiss him and get some of this emotion out. Kennedy will never doubt, ever again, that he deserves the world. I'll prove it to him every day.

When the piercer comes back and does my piercing, I don't make a sound. It hurts, but there are worse things, and I sort of want to show off for him a little bit.

I want him to be as proud to be mine as I am to be his.

Because I finally know what love is.

Love is strength.

And sunshine.

Let's get ready for ...

LYNX AND
SASHA

BONUS SCENE

LYNX

cast a suspicious glare around the meeting, making sure all my cubs are accounted for. With the Cutty already full, it takes some time to pick them out from the crowds and it's not until I locate each and every one of them that I'm able to turn my attention to the intruder. He's got water-logged blond curls, big blue eyes, and I can't work out if he's wearing a T-shirt or a dress. At any rate, he's not what I thought I was hunting.

The prey finally finds its voice. "H-he tried to kill me."

Wilde's gaze snaps back to me. "Is that true?"

"He's still alive, isn't he?"

Bob interfering was not part of the plan, but I get the sense the ridiculous animal took pity on our prey as much as I did. He looks like the runt of the litter, rail thin and without an ounce of muscle to protect himself. If Ziggy had left him trapped behind the wall he would have been an easy meal for the rats.

"Wait ..." Nox says, glancing around. "*This* is who we were looking for?"

He has a point. I'd been picturing some dangerous, enormous man on the loose, and *this* guy …

"My name is Sasha," the prey snaps.

Wilde turns back to him. "Why are you in Wilde's End?"

Sasha's gaze goes from Wilde to me and back. "I crashed my car."

"Wait, it was your car we found?" Booker asks, running his eyes over the prey. "We assumed the person driving had hitch-hiked into town."

"How long ago was that?" I demand.

"Almost two weeks."

This guy's been living in town undetected for *that* long?

Wilde doesn't look happy either. "Where did you find him?"

I assume the question is for me. "Ziggy's place. He was hiding behind the wall we put up."

Wilde's eyebrows creep higher. "Fuck me."

"You trapped me there," Sasha says, sounding panicked.

He has no need for that emotion. "What are we going to do with him? He's stolen from us. That's against the rules."

"Technically that's not a rule," Wilde mutters.

"The alternative was that he starved," bleeding-heart Nox points out.

I shrug. "If he won't contribute, then yes."

"That's ridiculous. And never going to happen."

Wilde takes over. "The way we do things works for us. It keeps everything fair and makes sure we can provide for our town." He turns on Sasha. "If you want something, you work for it. You don't just take what you want. If you'd come to us for help, we would have told you that."

And even with the anger in Wilde's tone, Sasha scoffs. "You wanted me to confront the terrifying forest dwellers? I heard what you were saying when you trapped me in that mine. You wanted me dead."

"We wanted you gone."

Sasha jabs a finger at me. "*He* wanted me dead."

"He wants everyone dead, you're not special."

Common misconception. I don't want anyone dead. I want them away from me, with the means to defend themselves while they mind their own business.

"He was scared, we can all understand that," Nox pushes. "What's done is done, so how do we fix this?"

"He needs to get out of town." For once, I agree with Wilde. "Can you do that?"

"Not without my car. But I crashed it and couldn't get it to start."

"Little blue thing?" Wilde grunts. "With creepy animals in the back?"

"*Creepy?* They're cute plushies."

Ignoring Sasha, I turn to Wilde. "That sounds like a yes. Where's the car?"

"Towed it to Rooney's place."

"If it was towed, then I assume it's not working?"

He doesn't answer, but the twisted look he takes on makes it clear what the answer is. Without a working car, Sasha can't leave.

"I'll drop you in Wayward," Wilde finally says.

A scowl crosses Sasha's face. "I *left* there. I'm never going back."

"You'd prefer to hide out here and steal?" Nox asks.

"No, I'd prefer to have not drove off the fucking road so that I'd be literally anywhere other than a stupid small town by now."

The runt has teeth. Interesting.

"Well, you don't have that option, so Wayward it is." Wilde clenches his jaw. "You and your car can go back and try again later."

"I said I'm not doing that."

"And I'm not giving you a choice."

My eyes narrow, taking in the tension that pulls at his lanky frame. The way his jaw tightens even though he looks like he wants to cry.

Nox shuffles forward. "It doesn't sound like Wayward is an option. We need to come up with something else."

"There is nothing else."

"There's *always* something else."

Wilde turns his anger on Nox. "Oh, yeah? Like let him continue to steal and ruin our town?"

Before I can answer, Sasha makes a derisive sound. "Ruin? You've done enough of that on your own."

Me and Wilde turn identical glares on him.

"Now's the time to keep those thoughts to yourself," I warn him.

Nox cuts me off. "Can the car be fixed?"

"Probably."

"Okay. So why can't Sasha stay until it's done?"

"We don't have a mechanic here." Wilde's talking through his teeth, like admitting to a weakness in this town is painful. "It would take some time."

"I have one in Dale," Foley pipes up, but the casually helpful tone rings out like a warning to my ears. Apparently I'm not the only one.

"Oh really?" Wilde's eyes narrow. "And what limb would you want for that?"

Foley chuckles and holds up his broken arm. "Rich, coming from you. But no, no limb." Then he turns to Booker. "But I'm sure we could find a use for a doctor."

"How quickly I go from a prized possession to a bargaining chip," Booker sighs, wide grin across his face.

Wilde looks like he's chewing on his tongue. "I won't force you to do anything."

"Just some gentle coercion then?" But despite his words, Booker sounds delighted. "I suppose this whole plan rests on my shoulders."

There's a beat of silence while I wait for him to decide, but he goes on smiling at us all.

"So will you do it?" Nox prompts.

"Who can say?"

"You. You can say."

"Oh, I'm sure I could. These types of business transactions require deep thinking though, and I really need the time to consider things from all angles."

The look on Foley's face makes me think he expected that exact reply. "Take all the time you need." He stalks closer and leans down by Booker's ear. "I told you I'd wait forever if you made me."

I watch Booker's face and swear I detect the briefest flare of his nostrils. Fear, anger, or arousal? One of those things will call for me to step in, and I hope that it's either of the others because the only way I could take Foley down is by surprise. And he's not a man who'd be caught that easily.

Foley leaves without a backward glance, and I wonder how close he would let Booker get before he started dissecting his brain.

Booker goes on looking like nothing just happened.

Meanwhile, Nox scowls. "*Fine.* So until we find a mechanic, what do we do with Sasha?"

"*Don't* say Wayward," the prey warns and there's that spark again.

Wilde's teeth crunch together.

"The solution seems simple to me." Hudson, the city dweller, is using his *I'm the smartest person in the room* tone from where he's sitting behind Wilde. Always with his rabid animal between him and me. "Sasha took food, your rules here are that you work for what you take. So give him somewhere to live, he can work off whatever he stole plus the mechanic costs, and then once the car is fixed, he can fuck off to wherever he was going."

Wilde spreads his hands. "It's either that, or going back to Wayward. Your call."

"Is there a third option?"

"No."

Some of the fight leaves Sasha as he chews the inside of his cheek. "Will I be …" His gaze flicks toward me. "Safe?"

I stare the prey down, waiting for a flinch, a startle, a chink in his confidence. I grudgingly enjoy the way he holds my eyes. "As long as you don't steal so much as a crumb, or hurt anyone in this town, then yes." Of course I don't stop there. "But I'll be watching you."

"Would it kill you to go one conversation without being creepy?" Nox muses.

"It actually might."

I settle back against a table, Bob at my side, and watch them work out the details.

"That's decided then?" Nox glances between Wilde and Sasha, waiting to see who'll break first. Considering Wilde is a controlling dick, I expect him to argue the point, or agree to it first, but the prey beats him to it and holds out his hand.

Wilde stares at it for a moment, but doesn't shake it. "You can stay on Hobby Straight. The houses are small but have everything you need. Since you stole food, you can start there. We've got crops that need tending to."

"Manual labor?"

"Got a problem?"

The prey quickly shakes his head but before Wilde can storm off, Sasha sets a hand on his forearm. "Thank you for not making me go back there."

Wilde grunts and leaves, then Viv takes his place. She wraps an arm around Sasha's shoulders and steers him toward the bar area.

But I'm still stuck on those words.

Thank you for not making me go back there.

Spoken like the relief that comes after fear. What does this prickly little prey have to be fearful of though? I lick my lips slowly as I consider all the horrible things he might have faced before being buried alive, and the fact that whatever it was … he's still standing.

He's here.

Facing down Wilde.

And me.

And soon, he'll be helping me tend crops. Interesting.

I let out a sharp whistle, signaling to my cubs that I'm on the move. Then Bob follows me out the door, his soft fur under my fingertips pulling the dark memories away.

ACKNOWLEDGEMENTS

As with any book, this one took a hell of a lot of people to make happen.

The cover was created by the talented Rebecca at Story Styling Cover Designs with a gorgeous image by Michelle Lancaster, and edits were done by Sandra Dee at One Love Editing, with Lori Parks proofreading the bejeebus out of it.

Thanks to Emily Wittig for creating this amazing discreet cover.

Charity VanHuss you're the most amazing PA I could have ever dreamed up. Without you I'd be even more of a chaotic disaster and there isn't enough space to list the many hats you wear for me. Paige and Lara Janz, you round out my team in the most incredible way and I'm always excited to see what fun ideas you both have next.

Eden Finley, thank you for being there for all the doubt spirals and hand-holding. Whether you wanted to be or not.

My incredible author friends who beta read this book: you've made this so much better than I could have on my own.

Adam Gyllenhaal , you're a gem with his hilarious and thoughtful comments for both of the guys, and Kate Kauri your unhinged feral romance beta reading helped get this plot into something worth reading. Leo and Stephanie Tripp, thank you so much for sensitivity reading for Ziggy and helping me get our boy as accurate as possible.

For Gabe: thank you for lending the name Nox to this one (and future books in the series) and for being an amazing supporter of my Obsessed Patreon tier.

And of course, thanks to my fam bam. To my husband who constantly frees up time for me to write, and to my kids whose neediness reminds me the real word exists.

More **SAXON ...**

What do you do when you're a hit man ... who's terrible at his job?

At first, I thought it would be an easy payday. A few pew pews for bad people, a couple of suitcases of cash for me. People have done worse for an honest living. Probably.

The problem is that after a couple of jobs, I've never actually managed to unalive someone, and not for lack of trying. Apparently, a basic requirement of a hitman is being a good shot.

Despite my constant duck-ups—that my boss knows nothing about—I'm given another name, and I very nearly follow through. Only after obliterating this guy's ear and his fervent pleading to spare him, I've sent him into hiding and collected the cash anyway.

But wanted people are hard to hide, and bad guys don't like paying big money for loose ends.

Now that Van Gogh has shown his face again—sans ear—I've scammed my way into his security team, which is sort of ideal since I'm now highly wanted as well.

Unfortunately, we have some "trust issues" to "work through" from our meet-shoot, and with the gorgeous bastard's brother missing, he refuses to lay low until they're reunited.

I'm not sold on the plan, honestly, but this guy has me questioning my sexuality along with my career path, and I'm at the point where I'm determined to see a job through to the end. Or die trying.

But hey, at least then I'd finally deliver a body.

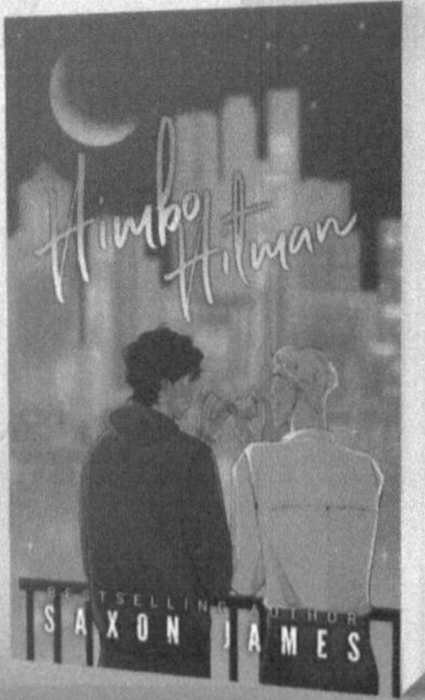

More SAXON ...

Christian

Being invited to my cousin's wedding really shouldn't be a big deal except, oh yeah, I haven't seen my family for a decade.
My parents turned their backs on me and I've done everything since to become successful and show them what they lost. Only, it's kinda hard to be a success when you're a walking trainwreck.
So I'm going to fake it. Hire a guy with an online presence so impressive they'll be desperate to welcome me back into the elitist fold, and roll into the wedding with the kind of confidence I've never felt a day in my life.
The plan's a knockout. Until my fake date cancels minutes before the ceremony.

Émile

One letter from my dearly departed grandfather, and suddenly I'm on a husband hunt. He's reworked his entire will so I'm set to inherit far more than I'm entitled to, and all because he's asked me to use that money for "good".
In order to get that inheritance, though, there's one stipulation: marriage. Even with his request, I'm tempted to stick to my original plan of getting as far from my wretched family as possible, and letting them fight it out. But then I run into a tall drink of scattered mess outside of a wedding who's in desperate need of a date, and the pieces click into place.
I help him, he helps me. Marriage, money, then go our separate ways.
Easy.
Now all I have to do is stop myself from falling for the guy.

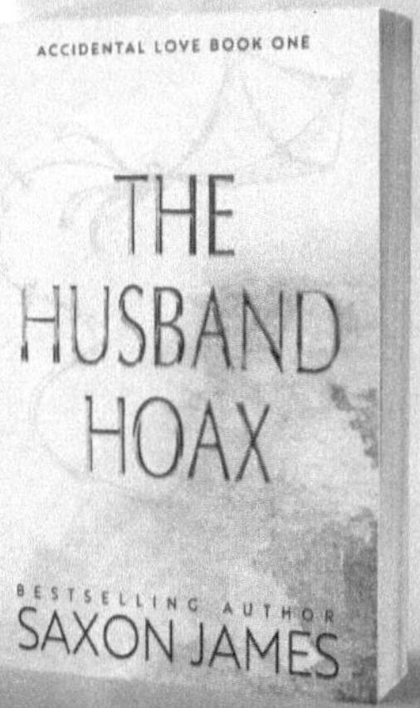

More SAXON ...

Payne

In search of: room to rent.
Must ignore the patheticness of a forty-year-old roommate.
Preferably dirt cheap as funds are tight (nonexistent).
There's nothing sadder than moving back to my hometown newly divorced,
homeless, and lost for what my next move is.
When my little brother's best friend offers me a place to stay in exchange for
menial duties, I swallow my pride and jump at the offer.
I need this.
I also need Beau to wear a shirt. And ditch the gray sweatpants. And not leave
his door ajar when he's in compromising positions ...

Beau

In search of: roommate.
Must be non smoker and non douchebag.
Room payment to be made in meal planning, repairs, and dumb jokes.
Since my career took off, I barely have time to breathe, let alone keep my life
in order. I'm naturally chaotic, make terrible decisions, and scare off potential
dates with my "weirdness".
So when Payne gets back into town and needs somewhere to stay, I offer him
my spare room with one condition: while he's staying with me, I need him to
help me become date-able.
And while he does that, I can focus on my other plan: ignoring that Payne is
the only man I've ever wanted to date.

More SAXON ...

We're basically Romeo and Juliet. But dudes. And without all the dying.

Chad

Being VP of Sigma Beta Psi is wild. I get all the benefits of being in charge with hardly any of the responsibility.
Parties, pranks, and frat politics—college life has never been sweeter.
Until I meet Bailey Prince.
He has the face of a goddamn angel. I don't know where he came from or why I'm so obsessed.
But I do know he's a Kappa. And our houses have a rivalry that's written into legend.

Bailey

At Rho Kappa Tau, I'm a legacy.
It's a lot of pressure, but I've always been responsible, never had that rebellious need to rock the boat, and I like it that way.
But after a party at Sigma—the jock frat—I meet Chad Doomsen, and for the first time in my life I want to step outside my square.
Our houses have always had a rivalry, but some of the guys seem to hate Chad specifically, and I don't know why.
He's surprisingly sweet and kind. At least to me.
I need to stay away. A relationship with Chad would be betraying the very legacy that brought me here. But I can't help myself. And it seems, neither can he.

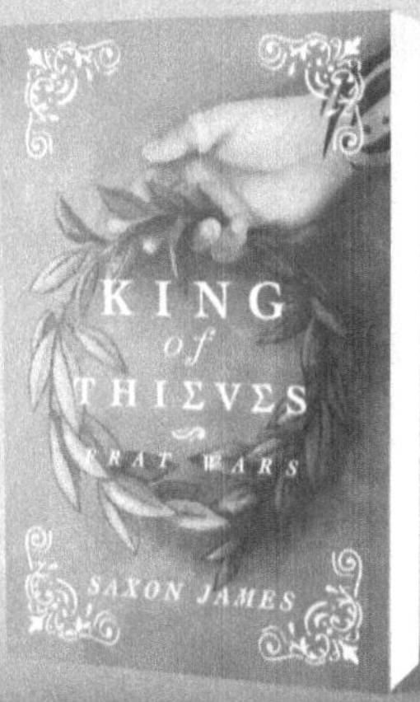

More **SAXON ...**

Austin

Dashwood Academy is a necessary evil. I learned that early on.
If I play their game and learn my role, when graduation comes around,
I'll be set for life. Exceeding all the dreams a guy like me ever had—even
if that means living a life that goes against everything I am.
But then Garrett Close enrolls at Dashwood and I can't stop thinking
about him. Wanting him. Watching him ...
And hating him for being the one person who can ruin everything.

Garrett

I don't know what it is about Austin du Pont but he acts like king of the
academy. Too good for the rest of us and not ready to spare me a
second glance.
Not that I should be worrying about a pretty boy with dead eyes.
Dashwood is my ticket to a degree from an internationally-revered
college. To the kind of high-profile life my parents never got to lead.
So why can't I stop thinking about Austin?
And why does he keep popping up in the most random places?
All I know is the closer Austin and I get, the more I start to doubt
Dashwood Academy is the simple college it pretends to be.

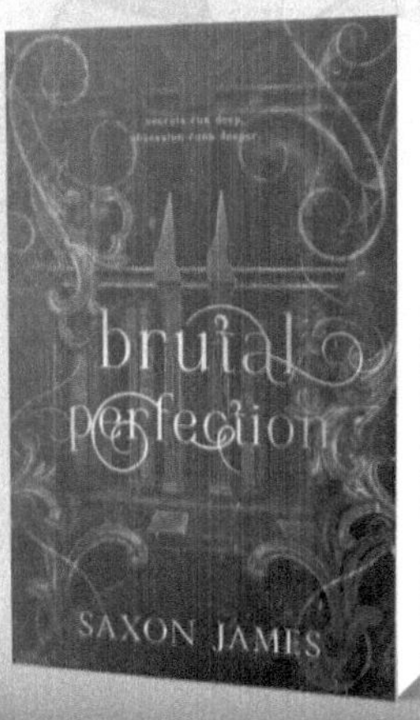

OTHER BOOKS BY SAXON JAMES

THE WILDE MEN SERIES:

Wilde's End

Ziggy's Voice

Lynx's Ruin

ACCIDENTAL LOVE SERIES:

The Husband Hoax

Not Dating Material

The Revenge Agenda

Just Romantically Invested

Not Catching Love

The Anti-Wingman (bonus prequel)

Friend for Hire (bonus novella)

FRAT WARS SERIES:

Frat Wars: King of Thieves

Frat Wars: Master of Mayhem

Frat Wars: Presidential Chaos

Royal Scoundrel (bonus novella)

DIVORCED MEN'S CLUB SERIES:

Roommate Arrangement

Platonic Rulebook

Budding Attraction

Employing Patience

System Overload

Forgotten Romance

Making Him Mine (bonus novella)

NEVER JUST FRIENDS SERIES:

Just Friends

Fake Friends

Getting Friendly

Friendly Fire

Bonus Short: Friends with Benefits

RECKLESS LOVE SERIES:

Denial

Risky

Tempting

STAND ALONES:

Himbo Hitman

Home Ice

CU HOCKEY SERIES WITH EDEN FINLEY:

Power Plays & Straight A's

Face Offs & Cheap Shots

Goal Lines & First Times

Line Mates & Study Dates

Puck Drills & Quick Thrills

See You in Boston (bonus novella)

PUCKBOYS SERIES WITH EDEN FINLEY:

Egotistical Puckboy

Irresponsible Puckboy

Shameless Puckboy

Foolish Puckboy

Clueless Puckboy

Bromantic Puckboy

Forbidden Puckboy

Possessive Puckboy

Stubborn Puckboy

Charming Puckboy

STAND ALONES WITH EDEN FINLEY:

Up in Flames

The Bastard and The Heir

Money Shot

FRANKLIN U SERIES (VARIOUS AUTHORS):

The Dating Disaster

A Stealthy Situation

And if you're after something a little sweeter, don't forget my YA
pen name

S. M. James.

These books are chock full of adorable, flawed characters with big hearts.

https://geni.us/smjames

WANT MORE FROM ME?

Follow Saxon James on any of the platforms below.
www.saxonjamesauthor.com
www.facebook.com / thesaxonjames /
www.amazon.com / Saxon-James / e / B082TP7BR7
www.bookbub.com / profile / saxon-james
www.instagram.com / saxonjameswrites /